Henry James

Henry James OM (15 April 1843 – 28 February 1916) was an American-British author regarded as a key transitional figure between literary realism and literary modernism, and is considered by many to be among the greatest novelists in the English language. He was the son of Henry James Sr. and the brother of renowned philosopher and psychologist William James and diarist Alice James.

He is best known for a number of novels dealing with the social and marital interplay between émigré Americans, English people, and continental Europeans. Examples of such novels include The Portrait of a Lady, The Ambassadors, and The Wings of the Dove. His later works were increasingly experimental. In describing the internal states of mind and social dynamics of his characters, James often made use of a style in which ambiguous or contradictory motives and impressions were overlaid or juxtaposed in the discussion of a character's psyche.(Source: Wikipedia)

Literary works:

Watch and Ward (1871)
Roderick Hudson (1875)
The American (1877)
The Europeans (1878)
Confidence (1879)
Washington Square (1880)
The Portrait of a Lady (1881)
The Bostonians (1886)
The Princess Casamassima (1886)
The Reverberator (1888)
The Tragic Muse (1890)
The Other House (1896)
The Spoils of Poynton (1897)
What Maisie Knew (1897)
The Awkward Age (1899)
The Sacred Fount (1901)

THE SELECTED WORKS

OF

HENRY JAMES

VOL. 12 (OF 36)

FOUR MEETINGS
EMBARRASSMENTS

PAPER
SKY
CLASSICS

An Imprint of Papersky Classics LLC

A Wholly Owned Subsidiary of Queenior LLC

A Melodragon Company

First Printing: 2020

ISBN 978-1-6627-1726-0 (Paperback)

ISBN 978-1-6627-1727-7 (Hardcover)

Published by Papersky Classics

www.paperskyclassics.com

Contents

THE SELECTED WORKS

OF

HENRY JAMES

VOL. 12 (OF 36)

FOUR MEETINGS

I saw her only four times, but I remember them vividly; she made an impression upon me. I thought her very pretty and very interesting,—a charming specimen of a type. I am very sorry to hear of her death; and yet, when I think of it, why should I be sorry? The last time I saw her she was certainly not—But I will describe all our meetings in order.

I.

The first one took place in the country, at a little tea-party, one snowy night. It must have been some seventeen years ago. My friend Latouche, going to spend Christmas with his mother, had persuaded me to go with him, and the good lady had given in our honor the entertainment of which I speak. To me it was really entertaining; I had never been in the depths of New England at that season. It had been snowing all day, and the drifts were knee-high. I wondered how the ladies had made their way to the house; but I perceived that at Grimwinter a conversazione offering the attraction of two gentlemen from New York was felt to be worth an effort.

Mrs. Latouche, in the course of the evening, asked me if I "did n't want to" show the photographs to some of the young ladies. The photographs were in a couple of great portfolios, and had been brought home by her son, who, like myself, was lately returned from Europe. I looked round and was struck with the fact that most of the young ladies were provided with an object of interest more absorbing than the most vivid sun-picture. But there was a person standing alone near the mantelshelf, and looking round the room with a small gentle smile which seemed at odds, somehow, with her isolation. I looked at her a moment, and then said, "I should like to show them to that young lady."

"Oh, yes," said Mrs. Latouche, "she is just the person. She doesn't care for flirting; I will speak to her."

I rejoined that if she did not care for flirting, she was, perhaps, not just the person; but Mrs. Latouche had already gone to propose the photographs to her.

"She's delighted," she said, coming back. "She is just the person, so quiet and so bright." And then she told me the young lady was, by name, Miss Caroline Spencer, and with this she introduced me.

Miss Caroline Spencer was not exactly a beauty, but she was a charming little figure. She must have been close upon thirty, but she was made almost like a little girl, and she had the complexion of a child. She had a very pretty head, and her hair was arranged as nearly as possible like the hair of a Greek bust, though indeed it was to be doubted if she had ever seen a Greek bust. She was "artistic," I suspected, so far as Grimwinter allowed such tendencies. She had a soft, surprised eye, and thin lips, with very pretty teeth. Round her neck she wore what ladies call, I believe, a "ruche," fastened with a very small pin in pink coral, and in her hand she carried a fan made of plaited straw and adorned with pink ribbon. She wore a scanty black silk dress. She spoke with a kind of soft precision, showing her white teeth between her narrow but tender-looking lips, and she seemed extremely pleased, even a little fluttered, at the prospect of my demonstrations. These went forward very smoothly, after I had moved the portfolios out of their corner and placed a couple of chairs near a lamp. The photographs were usually things I knew,—large views of Switzerland, Italy, and Spain, landscapes, copies of famous buildings, pictures, and statues. I said what I could about them, and my companion, looking at them as I held them up, sat perfectly still, with her straw fan raised to her underlip. Occasionally, as I laid one of the pictures down, she said very softly, "Have you seen that place?" I usually answered that I had seen it several times (I had been a great traveller), and then I felt that she looked at me askance for a moment with her pretty eyes. I had asked her at the outset whether she had been to Europe; to this she answered, "No, no, no," in a little quick, confidential whisper. But after that, though she never took her eyes off the pictures, she said so little that I was afraid she was bored. Accordingly, after we had finished one portfolio, I offered, if she desired it, to desist. I felt that she was not bored, but her reticence puzzled me, and I wished to make her speak. I turned round to look at her, and saw that there was a faint flush in each of her cheeks. She was waving her little fan to and fro. Instead of looking at me she fixed her eyes upon the other portfolio, which was leaning against the table.

"Won't you show me that?" she asked, with a little tremor in her voice. I could almost have believed she was agitated.

"With pleasure," I answered, "if you are not tired."

"No, I am not tired," she affirmed. "I like it—I love it."

And as I took up the other portfolio she laid her hand upon it, rubbing it softly.

"And have you been here too?" she asked.

On my opening the portfolio it appeared that I had been there. One of the first photographs was a large view of the Castle of Chillon, on the Lake of Geneva.

"Here," I said, "I have been many a time. Is it not beautiful?" And I pointed to the perfect reflection of the rugged rocks and pointed towers in the clear still water. She did not say, "Oh, enchanting!" and push it away to see the next picture. She looked awhile, and then she asked if it was not where Bonnivard, about whom Byron wrote, was confined. I assented, and tried to quote some of Byron's verses, but in this attempt I succeeded imperfectly.

She fanned herself a moment, and then repeated the lines correctly, in a soft, flat, and yet agreeable voice. By the time she had finished she was blushing. I complimented her and told her she was perfectly equipped for visiting Switzerland and Italy. She looked at me askance again, to see whether I was serious, and I added, that if she wished to recognize Byron's descriptions she must go abroad speedily; Europe was getting sadly dis-Byronized.

"How soon must I go?" she asked.

"Oh, I will give you ten years."

"I think I can go within ten years," she answered very soberly.

"Well," I said, "you will enjoy it immensely; you will find it very charming." And just then I came upon a photograph of some nook in a foreign city which I had been very fond of, and which recalled tender memories. I discoursed (as I suppose) with a certain eloquence; my companion sat listening, breathless.

"Have you been *very* long in foreign lands?" she asked, some time after I had ceased.

"Many years," I said.

"And have you travelled everywhere?"

"I have travelled a great deal. I am very fond of it; and, happily, I have been able."

Again she gave me her sidelong gaze. "And do you know the foreign languages?"

"After a fashion."

"Is it hard to speak them?"

"I don't believe you would find it hard," I gallantly responded.

"Oh, I shouldn't want to speak; I should only want to listen," she said. Then, after a pause, she added, "They say the French theatre is so beautiful."

"It is the best in the world."

"Did you go there very often?"

"When I was first in Paris I went every night."

"Every night!" And she opened her clear eyes very wide. "That to me is:—" and she hesitated a moment—"is very wonderful." A few minutes later she asked, "Which country do you prefer?"

"There is one country I prefer to all others. I think you would do the same."

She looked at me a moment, and then she said softly, "Italy?"

"Italy," I answered softly, too; and for a moment we looked at each other. She looked as pretty as if, instead of showing her photographs, I had been making love to her. To increase the analogy, she glanced away, blushing. There was a silence, which she broke at last by saying,—

"That is the place which, in particular, I thought of going to."

"Oh, that's the place, that's the place!" I said.

18

She looked at two or three photographs in silence. "They say it is not so dear."

"As some other countries? Yes, that is not the least of its charms."

"But it is all very dear, is it not?"

"Europe, you mean?"

"Going there and travelling. That has been the trouble. I have very little money. I give lessons," said Miss Spencer.

"Of course one must have money," I said, "but one can manage with a moderate amount."

"I think I should manage. I have laid something by, and I am always adding a little to it. It's all for that." She paused a moment, and then went on with a kind of suppressed eagerness, as if telling me the story were a rare, but a possibly impure satisfaction, "But it has not been only the money; it has been everything. Everything has been against it I have waited and waited. It has been a mere castle in the air. I am almost afraid to talk about it. Two or three times it has been a little nearer, and then I have talked about it and it has melted away. I have talked about it too much," she said hypocritically; for I saw that such talking was now a small tremulous ecstasy. "There is a lady who is a great friend of mine; she does n't want to go; I always talk to her about it. I tire her dreadfully. She told me once she did n't know what would become of me. I should go crazy if I did not go to Europe, and I should certainly go crazy if I did."

"Well," I said, "you have not gone yet, and nevertheless you are not crazy."

She looked at me a moment, and said, "I am not so sure. I don't think of anything else. I am always thinking of it. It prevents me from thinking of things that are nearer home, things that I ought to attend to. That is a kind of craziness."

"The cure for it is to go," I said.

"I have a faith that I shall go. I have a cousin in Europe!" she announced.

19

We turned over some more photographs, and I asked her if she had always lived at Grimwinter.

"Oh, no, sir," said Miss Spencer. "I have spent twenty-three months in Boston."

I answered, jocosely, that in that case foreign lands would probably prove a disappointment to her; but I quite failed to alarm her.

"I know more about them than you might think," she said, with her shy, neat little smile. "I mean by reading; I have read a great deal I have not only read Byron; I have read histories and guidebooks. I know I shall like it."

"I understand your case," I rejoined. "You have the native American passion,—the passion for the picturesque. With us, I think it is primordial,—antecedent to experience. Experience comes and only shows us something we have dreamt of."

"I think that is very true," said Caroline Spencer. "I have dreamt of everything; I shall know it all!"

"I am afraid you have wasted a great deal of time."

"Oh, yes, that has been my great wickedness."

The people about us had begun to scatter; they were taking their leave. She got up and put out her hand to me, timidly, but with a peculiar brightness in her eyes.

"I am going back there," I said, as I shook hands with her. "I shall look out for you."

"I will tell you," she answered, "if I am disappointed."

And she went away, looking delicately agitated, and moving her little straw fan.

II.

A few months after this I returned to Europe, and some three years elapsed. I had been living in Paris, and, toward the end of October, I went from that city to Havre, to meet my sister and her husband, who had written me that they were about to arrive there. On reaching Havre I found that the steamer was already in; I was nearly two hours late. I repaired directly to the hotel, where my relatives were already established. My sister had gone to bed, exhausted and disabled by her voyage; she was a sadly incompetent sailor, and her sufferings on this occasion had been extreme. She wished, for the moment, for undisturbed rest, and was unable to see me more than five minutes; so it was agreed that we should remain at Havre until the next day. My brother-in-law, who was anxious about his wife, was unwilling to leave her room; but she insisted upon his going out with me to take a walk and recover his landlegs. The early autumn day was warm and charming, and our stroll through the bright-colored, busy streets of the old French seaport was sufficiently entertaining. We walked along the sunny, noisy quays, and then turned into a wide, pleasant street, which lay half in sun and half in shade—a French provincial street, that looked like an old water-color drawing: tall, gray, steep-roofed, red-gabled, many-storied houses; green shutters on windows and old scroll-work above them; flower-pots in balconies, and white-capped women in doorways. We walked in the shade; all this stretched away on the sunny side of the street and made a picture. We looked at it as we passed along; then, suddenly, my brother-in-law stopped, pressing my arm and staring. I followed his gaze and saw that we had paused just before coming to a *café*, where, under an awning, several tables and chairs were disposed upon the pavement The windows were open behind; half a dozen plants in tubs were ranged beside the door; the pavement was besprinkled with clean bran. It was a nice little, quiet, old-fashioned *café*; inside, in the comparative dusk, I saw a stout, handsome woman, with pink ribbons in her cap, perched up with a mirror behind her back, smiling at some one who was out of sight. All this, however, I perceived afterwards; what I first observed was a lady sitting alone, outside, at one of the little marble-topped tables. My brother-in-law had stopped to look at her. There was something on the little table, but she was leaning back quietly, with her hands folded, looking down the street, away from us. I saw her only in something less than profile; nevertheless, I instantly felt that I had seen her before.

"The little lady of the steamer!" exclaimed my brother-in-law.

"Was she on your steamer?" I asked.

"From morning till night She was never sick. She used to sit perpetually at the side of the vessel with her hands crossed that way, looking at the eastward horizon."

"Are you going to speak to her?"

"I don't know her. I never made acquaintance with her. I was too seedy. But I used to watch her and—I don't know why—to be interested in her. She's a dear little Yankee woman. I have an idea she is a schoolmistress taking a holiday, for which her scholars have made up a purse."

She turned her face a little more into profile, looking at the steep gray house-fronts opposite to her. Then I said, "I shall speak to her myself."

"I would n't; she is very shy," said my brother-in-law.

"My dear fellow, I know her. I once showed her photographs at a tea-party."

And I went up to her. She turned and looked at me, and I saw she was in fact Miss Caroline Spencer. But she was not so quick to recognize me; she looked startled. I pushed a chair to the table and sat down.

"Well," I said, "I hope you are not disappointed!"

She stared, blushing a little; then she gave a small jump which betrayed recognition.

"It was you who showed me the photographs, at Grimwinter!"

"Yes, it was I. This happens very charmingly, for I feel as if it were for me to give you a formal reception here, an official welcome. I talked to you so much about Europe."

"You did n't say too much. I am so happy!" she softly exclaimed.

Very happy she looked. There was no sign of her being older; she was as gravely, decently, demurely pretty as before. If she had seemed before a thin-stemmed, mild-hued flower of Puritanism, it may be imagined whether in her present situation this delicate bloom was less apparent. Beside her an old gentleman was drinking absinthe; behind her the *dame de comptoir* in the pink ribbons was calling "Alcibiade! Alcibiade!" to the long-aproned waiter. I explained to Miss Spencer that my companion had lately been her shipmate, and my brother-in-law came up and was introduced to her. But she looked at him as if she had never seen him before, and I remembered that he had told me that her eyes were always fixed upon the eastward horizon. She had evidently not noticed him, and, still timidly smiling, she made no attempt whatever to pretend that she had. I stayed with her at the *café* door, and he went back to the hotel and to his wife. I said to Miss Spencer that this meeting of ours in the first hour of her landing was really very strange, but that I was delighted to be there and receive her first impressions.

"Oh, I can't tell you," she said; "I feel as if I were in a dream. I have been sitting here for an hour, and I don't want to move. Everything is so picturesque. I don't know whether the coffee has intoxicated me; it 's so delicious."

"Really," said I, "if you are so pleased with this poor prosaic Havre, you will have no admiration left for better things. Don't spend your admiration all the first day; remember it's your intellectual letter of credit. Remember all the beautiful places and things that are waiting for you; remember that lovely Italy!"

"I 'm not afraid of running short," she said gayly, still looking at the opposite houses. "I could sit here all day, saying to myself that here I am at last. It's so dark and old and different."

"By the way," I inquired, "how come you to be sitting here? Have you not gone to one of the inns?" For I was half amused, half alarmed, at the good conscience with which this delicately pretty woman had stationed herself in conspicuous isolation on the edge of the *trottoir*.

"My cousin brought me here," she answered. "You know I told you I had a cousin in Europe. He met me at the steamer this morning."

"It was hardly worth his while to meet you if he was to desert you so soon."

"Oh, he has only left me for half an hour," said Miss Spencer. "He has gone to get my money."

"Where is your money?"

She gave a little laugh. "It makes me feel very fine to tell you! It is in some circular notes."

"And where are your circular notes?"

"In my cousin's pocket."

This statement was very serenely uttered, but—I can hardly say why—it gave me a sensible chill At the moment I should have been utterly unable to give the reason of this sensation, for I knew nothing of Miss Spencer's cousin. Since he was her cousin, the presumption was in his favor. But I felt suddenly uncomfortable at the thought that, half an hour after her landing, her scanty funds should have passed into his hands.

"Is he to travel with you?" I asked.

"Only as far as Paris. He is an art-student, in Paris. I wrote to him that I was coming, but I never expected him to come off to the ship. I supposed he would only just meet me at the train in Paris. It is very kind of him. But he *is* very kind, and very bright."

I instantly became conscious of an extreme curiosity to see this bright cousin who was an art-student.

"He is gone to the banker's?" I asked.

"Yes, to the banker's. He took me to a hotel, such a queer, quaint, delicious little place, with a court in the middle, and a gallery all round, and a lovely landlady, in such a beautifully fluted cap, and such a perfectly fitting dress! After a while we came out to walk to the banker's, for I haven't got any French money. But I was very dizzy from the motion of the vessel, and I thought I had better sit down. He found this place for me here, and he went off to the banker's himself. I am to wait here till he comes back."

It may seem very fantastic, but it passed through my mind that he would never come back. I settled myself in my chair beside Miss Spencer and determined to await the event. She was extremely observant; there was something touching in it. She noticed everything that the movement of the street brought before us,—peculiarities of costume, the shapes of vehicles, the big Norman horses, the fat priests, the shaven poodles. We talked of these things, and there was something charming in her freshness of perception and the way her book-nourished fancy recognized and welcomed everything.

"And when your cousin comes back, what are you going to do?" I asked.

She hesitated a moment. "We don't quite know."

"When do you go to Paris? If you go by the four o'clock train, I may have the pleasure of making the journey with you."

"I don't think we shall do that. My cousin thinks I had better stay here a few days."

"Oh!" said I; and for five minutes said nothing more. I was wondering what her cousin was, in vulgar parlance, "up to." I looked up and down the street, but saw nothing that looked like a bright American art-student. At last I took the liberty of observing that Havre was hardly a place to choose as one of the æsthetic stations of a European tour. It was a place of convenience, nothing more; a place of transit, through which transit should be rapid. I recommended her to go to Paris by the afternoon train, and meanwhile to amuse herself by driving to the ancient fortress at the mouth of the harbor,— that picturesque circular structure which bore the name of Francis the First, and looked like a small castle of St. Angelo. (It has lately been demolished.)

She listened with much interest; then for a moment she looked grave.

"My cousin told me that when he returned he should have something particular to say to me, and that we could do nothing or decide nothing until I should have heard it. But I will make him tell me quickly, and then we will go to the ancient fortress. There is no hurry to get to Paris; there is plenty of time."

She smiled with her softly severe little lips as she spoke those last words. But I, looking at her with a purpose, saw just a tiny gleam of apprehension in her eye.

"Don't tell me," I said, "that this wretched man is going to give you bad news!"

"I suspect it is a little bad, but I don't believe it is very bad. At any rate, I must listen to it."

I looked at her again an instant. "You did n't come to Europe to listen," I said. "You came to see!" But now I was sure her cousin would come back; since he had something disagreeable to say to her, he certainly would turn up. We sat a while longer, and I asked her about her plans of travel She had them on her fingers' ends, and she told over the names with a kind of solemn distinctness: from Paris to Dijon and to Avignon, from Avignon to Marseilles and the Cornice road; thence to Genoa, to Spezia, to Pisa, to Florence, to Home. It apparently had never occurred to her that there could be the least incommodity in her travelling alone; and since she was unprovided with a companion I of course scrupulously abstained from disturbing her sense of security. At last her cousin came back. I saw him turn towards us out of a side street, and from the moment my eyes rested upon him I felt that this was the bright American art-student. He wore a slouch hat and a rusty black velvet jacket, such as I had often encountered in the Rue Bonaparte. His shirt-collar revealed the elongation of a throat which, at a distance, was not strikingly statuesque. He was tall and lean; he had red hair and freckles. So much I had time to observe while he approached the *café*, staring at me with natural surprise from under his umbrageous coiffure. When he came up to us I immediately introduced myself to him as an old acquaintance of Miss Spencer. He looked at me hard with a pair of little red eyes, then he made me a solemn bow in the French fashion, with his sombrero.

"You were not on the ship?" he said.

"No, I was not on the ship. I have been in Europe these three years."

He bowed once more, solemnly, and motioned me to be seated again. I sat down, but it was only for the purpose of observing him an instant; I saw it was time I should return to my sister. Miss Spencer's cousin was a queer fellow. Nature had not shaped him for a Raphaelesque or Byronic attire, and his velvet doublet and naked neck were not in harmony with his facial attributes. His hair was cropped close to his head; his ears were large and ill-adjusted to the same. He had a lackadaisical carriage and a sentimental droop which were peculiarly at variance with his keen, strange-colored eyes. Perhaps I was prejudiced, but I thought his eyes treacherous. He said nothing for some time; he leaned his hands on his cane and looked up and down the street Then at last, slowly lifting his cane and pointing with it, "That's a very nice bit," he remarked, softly. He had his head on one side, and his little eyes were half closed. I followed the direction of his stick; the object it indicated was a red cloth hung out of an old window. "Nice bit of color," he continued; and without moving his head he transferred his half-closed gaze to me. "Composes well," he pursued. "Make a nice thing." He spoke in a hard vulgar voice.

"I see you have a great deal of eye," I replied. "Your cousin tells me you are studying art." He looked at me in the same way without answering, and I went on with deliberate urbanity, "I suppose you are at the studio of one of those great men."

Still he looked at me, and then he said softly, "Gérôme."

"Do you like it?" I asked.

"Do you understand French?" he said.

"Some kinds," I answered.

He kept his little eyes on me; then he said, "J'adore la peinture!"

"Oh, I understand that kind!" I rejoined. Miss Spencer laid her hand upon her cousin's arm with a little pleased and fluttered movement; it was delightful to be among people who were on such easy terms with foreign tongues. I got up to take leave, and asked Miss Spencer where, in Paris, I might have the honor of waiting upon her. To what hotel would she go?

She turned to her cousin inquiringly, and he honored me again with his little languid leer. "Do you know the Hôtel des Princes?"

"I know where it is."

"I shall take her there."

"I congratulate you," I said to Caroline Spencer. "I believe it is the best inn in the world; and in case I should still have a moment to call upon you here, where are you lodged?"

"Oh, it's such a pretty name," said Miss Spencer gleefully. "À la Belle Normande."

As I left them her cousin gave me a great flourish with his picturesque hat.

III.

My sister, as it proved, was not sufficiently restored to leave Havre by the afternoon train; so that, as the autumn dusk began to fall, I found myself at liberty to call at the sign of the Fair Norman. I must confess that I had spent much of the interval in wondering what the disagreeable thing was that my charming friend's disagreeable cousin had been telling her. The "Belle Normande" was a modest inn in a shady bystreet, where it gave me satisfaction to think Miss Spencer must have encountered local color in abundance. There was a crooked little court, where much of the hospitality of the house was carried on; there was a staircase climbing to bedrooms on the outer side of the wall; there was a small trickling fountain with a stucco statuette in the midst of it; there was a little boy in a white cap and apron cleaning copper vessels at a conspicuous kitchen door; there was a chattering landlady, neatly laced, arranging apricots and grapes into an artistic pyramid upon a pink plate. I looked about, and on a green bench outside of an open door labelled *Salle à Manger*, I perceived Caroline Spencer. No sooner had I looked at her than I saw that something had happened since the morning. She was leaning back on her bench, her hands were clasped in her lap, and her eyes were fixed upon the landlady, at the other side of the court, manipulating her apricots.

But I saw she was not thinking of apricots. She was staring absently, thoughtfully; as I came near her I perceived that she had been crying. I sat down on the bench beside her before she saw me; then, when she had done so, she simply turned round, without surprise, and rested her sad eyes upon me. Something very bad indeed had happened; she was completely changed.

I immediately charged her with it. "Your cousin has been giving you bad news; you are in great distress."

For a moment she said nothing, and I supposed that she was afraid to speak, lest her tears should come back. But presently I perceived that in the short time that had elapsed since my leaving her in the morning she had shed them all, and that she was now softly stoical, intensely composed.

"My poor cousin is in distress," she said at last. "His news was bad." Then, after a brief hesitation, "He was in terrible want of money."

"In want of yours, you mean?"

"Of any that he could get—honestly. Mine was the only money."

"And he has taken yours?"

She hesitated again a moment, but her glance, meanwhile, was pleading. "I gave him what I had."

I have always remembered the accent of those words as the most angelic bit of human utterance I had ever listened to; but then, almost with a sense of personal outrage, I jumped up. "Good heavens!" I said, "do you call that getting, it honestly?"

I had gone too far; she blushed deeply. "We will not speak of it," she said.

"We *must* speak of it," I answered, sitting down again. "I am your friend; it seems to me you need one. What is the matter with your cousin?"

"He is in debt."

"No doubt! But what is the special fitness of your paying his debts?"

"He has told me all his story; I am very sorry for him."

"So am I! But I hope he will give you back your money."

"Certainly he will; as soon as he can."

"When will that be?"

"When he has finished his great picture."

"My dear young lady, confound his great picture! Where is this desperate cousin?"

She certainly hesitated now. Then,—"At his dinner," she answered.

I turned about and looked through the open door into the *salle à manger*. There, alone at the end of a long table, I perceived the object of Miss Spencer's compassion, the bright young art-student. He was dining too attentively to notice me at first; but in the act of setting down a well-emptied wineglass he caught sight of my observant attitude. He paused in his repast, and, with his head on one side and his meagre jaws slowly moving, fixedly returned my gaze. Then the landlady came lightly brushing by with her pyramid of apricots.

"And that nice little plate of fruit is for him?" I exclaimed.

Miss Spencer glanced at it tenderly. "They do that so prettily!" she murmured.

I felt helpless and irritated. "Come now, really," I said; "do you approve of that long strong fellow accepting your funds?" She looked away from me; I was evidently giving her pain. The case was hopeless; the long strong fellow had "interested" her.

"Excuse me if I speak of him so unceremoniously," I said. "But you are really too generous, and he is not quite delicate enough. He made his debts himself; he ought to pay them himself."

"He has been foolish," she answered; "I know that He has told me everything. We had a long talk this morning; the poor fellow threw himself upon my charity. He has signed notes to a large amount."

"The more fool he!"

"He is in extreme distress; and it is not only himself. It is his poor wife."

"Ah, he has a poor wife?"

"I didn't know it; but he confessed everything. He married two years since, secretly."

"Why secretly?"

Caroline Spencer glanced about her, as if she feared listeners. Then softly, in a little impressive tone,—"She was a countess!"

"Are you very sure of that?"

"She has written me a most beautiful letter."

"Asking you for money, eh?"

"Asking me for confidence and sympathy," said Miss Spencer. "She has been disinherited by her father. My cousin told me the story, and she tells it in her own way, in the letter. It is like an old romance. Her father opposed the marriage, and when he discovered that she had secretly disobeyed him he cruelly cast her off. It is really most romantic. They are the oldest family in Provence."

I looked and listened in wonder. It really seemed that the poor woman was enjoying the "romance" of having a discarded countess-cousin, out of Provence, so deeply as almost to lose the sense of what the forfeiture of her money meant for her.

"My dear young lady," I said, "you don't want to be ruined for picturesqueness' sake?"

"I shall not be ruined. I shall come back before long to stay with them. The Countess insists upon that."

"Come back! You are going home, then?"

She sat for a moment with her eyes lowered, then with an heroic suppression of a faint tremor of the voice,—"I have no money for travelling!" she answered.

"You gave it *all* up?"

"I have kept enough to take me home."

I gave an angry groan; and at this juncture Miss Spencer's cousin, the fortunate possessor of her sacred savings and of the hand of the Provençal countess, emerged from the little dining-room. He stood on the threshold for an instant, removing the stone from a plump apricot which he had brought away from the table; then he put the apricot into his mouth, and while he let it sojourn there, gratefully, stood looking at us, with his long legs apart and his hands dropped into the pockets of his velvet jacket. My companion got up, giving him a thin glance which I caught in its passage, and which expressed a strange commixture of resignation and fascination,—a sort of perverted exaltation. Ugly, vulgar, pretentious, dishonest, as I thought the creature, he had appealed successfully to her eager and tender imagination. I was deeply disgusted, but I had no warrant to interfere, and at any rate I felt that it would be vain.

The young man waved his hand with a pictorial gesture. "Nice old court," he observed. "Nice mellow old place. Good tone in that brick. Nice crooked old staircase."

Decidedly, I could n't stand it; without responding I gave my hand to Caroline Spencer. She looked at me an instant with her little white face and expanded eyes, and as she showed her pretty teeth I suppose she meant to smile.

"Don't be sorry for me," she said, "I am very sure I shall see something of this dear old Europe yet."

I told her that I would not bid her goodby; I should find a moment to come back the next morning. Her cousin, who had put on his sombrero again, flourished it off at me by way of a bow, upon which I took my departure.

The next morning I came back to the inn, where I met in the court the landlady, more loosely laced than in the evening. On my asking for Miss Spencer,—"*Partie*, monsieu," said the hostess. "She went away last night at ten o 'clock, with her—her—not her husband, eh?—in fine, her *monsieur*. They went down to the American ship." I turned away; the poor girl had been about thirteen hours in Europe.

IV.

I myself, more fortunate, was there some five years longer. During this period I lost my friend Latouche, who died of a malarious fever during a tour in the Levant. One of the first things I did on my return was to go up to Grimwinter to pay a consolatory visit to his poor mother. I found her in deep affliction, and I sat with her the whole of the morning that followed my arrival (I had come in late at night), listening to her tearful descant and singing the praises of my friend. We talked of nothing else, and our conversation terminated only with the arrival of a quick little woman who drove herself up to the door in a "carryall," and whom I saw toss the reins upon the horse's back with the briskness of a startled sleeper throwing back the bed-clothes. She jumped out of the carryall and she jumped into the room. She proved to be the minister's wife and the great town-gossip, and she had evidently, in the latter capacity, a choice morsel to communicate. I was as sure of this as I was that poor Mrs. Latouche was not absolutely too bereaved to listen to her. It seemed to me discreet to retire; I said I believed I would go and take a walk before dinner.

"And, by the way," I added, "if you will tell me where my old friend Miss Spencer lives, I will walk to her house."

The minister's wife immediately responded. Miss Spencer lived in the fourth house beyond the "Baptist church; the Baptist church was the one on the right, with that queer green thing over the door; they called it a portico, but it looked more like an old-fashioned bedstead.

"Yes, do go and see poor Caroline," said Mrs. Latouche. "It will refresh her to see a strange face."

"I should think she had had enough of strange faces!" cried the minister's wife.

"I mean, to see a visitor," said Mrs. Latouche, amending her phrase.

"I should think she had had enough of visitors!" her companion rejoined. "But *you* don't mean to stay ten years," she added, glancing at me.

"Has she a visitor of that sort?" I inquired, perplexed.

"You will see the sort!" said the minister's wife. "She's easily seen; she generally sits in the front yard. Only take care what you say to her, and be very sure you are polite."

"Ah, she is so sensitive?"

The minister's wife jumped up and dropped me a curtsey, a most ironical curtsey.

"That's what she is, if you please. She's a countess!"

And pronouncing this word with the most scathing accent, the little woman seemed fairly to laugh in the Countess's face. I stood a moment, staring, wondering, remembering.

"Oh, I shall be very polite!" I cried; and grasping my hat and stick, I went on my way.

I found Miss Spencer's residence without difficulty. The Baptist church was easily identified, and the small dwelling near it, of a rusty white, with a large central chimney-stack and a Virginia creeper, seemed naturally and properly the abode of a frugal old maid with a taste for the picturesque. As I approached I slackened my pace, for I had heard that some one was always sitting in the front yard, and I wished to reconnoitre. I looked cautiously over the low white fence which separated the small garden-space from the unpaved street; but I descried nothing in the shape of a countess. A small straight path led up to the crooked doorstep, and on either side of it was a little grass-plot, fringed with currant-bushes. In the middle of the grass, on either side, was a large quince-tree, full of antiquity and contortions, and beneath one of the quince-trees were placed a small table and a couple of chairs. On the table lay a piece of unfinished embroidery and two or three books in bright-colored paper covers. I went in at the gate and paused halfway along the path, scanning the place for some farther token of its occupant, before whom—I could hardly have said why—I hesitated abruptly to present myself. Then I saw that the poor little house was very shabby. I felt a sudden doubt of my right to intrude; for curiosity had been my motive, and curiosity here seemed singularly indelicate. While I hesitated, a figure appeared in the open doorway and stood there looking at me. I immediately recognized Caroline Spencer, but she looked at me as if she had never seen me before. Gently, but gravely and timidly, I advanced to the doorstep, and then I said, with an attempt at friendly badinage,—

"I waited for you over there to come back, but you never came."

"Waited where, sir?" she asked softly, and her light-colored eyes expanded more than before.

She was much older; she looked tired and wasted.

"Well," I said, "I waited at Havre."

She stared; then she recognized me. She smiled and blushed and clasped her two hands together. "I remember you now," she said. "I remember that day." But she stood there, neither coming out nor asking me to come in. She was embarrassed.

I, too, felt a little awkward. I poked my stick into the path. "I kept looking out for you, year after year," I said.

"You mean in Europe?" murmured Miss Spencer.

"In Europe, of course! Here, apparently, you are easy enough to find."

She leaned her hand against the unpainted doorpost, and her head fell a little to one side. She looked at me for a moment without speaking, and I thought I recognized the expression that one sees in women's eyes when tears are rising. Suddenly she stepped out upon the cracked slab of stone before the threshold and closed the door behind her. Then she began to smile intently, and I saw that her teeth were as pretty as ever. But there had been tears too.

"Have you been there ever since?" she asked, almost in a whisper.

"Until three weeks ago. And you—you never came back?"

Still looking at me with her fixed smile, she put her hand behind her and opened the door again. "I am not very polite," she said. "Won't you come in?"

"I am afraid I incommode you."

"Oh, no!" she answered, smiling more than ever. And she pushed back the door, with a sign that I should enter.

I went in, following her. She led the way to a small room on the left of the narrow hall, which I supposed to be her parlor, though it was at the back of the house, and we passed the closed door of another apartment which apparently enjoyed a view of the quince-trees. This one looked out upon a small woodshed and two clucking hens. But I thought it very pretty, until I saw that its elegance was of the most frugal kind; after which, presently, I thought it prettier still, for I had never seen faded chintz and old mezzotint engravings, framed in varnished autumn leaves, disposed in so graceful a fashion. Miss Spencer sat down on a very small portion of the sofa, with her hands tightly clasped in her lap. She looked ten years older, and it would have souuded very perverse now to speak of her as pretty. But I thought her so; or at least I thought her touching. She was peculiarly agitated. I tried to appear not to notice it; but suddenly, in the most inconsequent fashion,—it was an irresistible memory of our little friendship at Havre,—I said to her, "I do incommode you. You are distressed."

She raised her two hands to her face, and for a moment kept it buried in them. Then, taking them away,—"It's because you remind me—" she said.

"I remind you, you mean, of that miserable day at Havre?"

She shook her head. "It was not miserable. It was delightful."

"I never was so shocked as when, on going back to your inn the next morning, I found you had set sail again."

She was silent a moment; and then she said, "Please let us not speak of that."

"Did you come straight back here?" I asked.

"I was back here just thirty days after I had gone away."

"And here you have remained ever since?"

"Oh, yes!" she said gently.

"When are you going to Europe again?"

This question seemed brutal; but there was something that irritated me in the softness of her resignation, and I wished to extort from her some expression of impatience.

She fixed her eyes for a moment upon a small sunspot on the carpet; then she got up and lowered the window-blind a little, to obliterate it. Presently, in the same mild voice, answering my question, she said, "Never!"

"I hope your cousin repaid you your money."

"I don't care for it now," she said, looking away from me.

"You don't care for your money?"

"For going to Europe."

"Do you mean that you would not go if you could?"

"I can't—I can't," said Caroline Spencer. "It is all over; I never think of it."

"He never repaid you, then!" I exclaimed.

"Please—please," she began.

But she stopped; she was looking toward the door. There had been a rustling aud a sound of steps in the hall.

I also looked toward the door, which was open, and now admitted another person, a lady, who paused just within the threshold. Behind her came a young man. The lady looked at me with a good deal of fixedness, long enough for my glance to receive a vivid impression of herself. Then she turned to Caroline Spencer, and, with a smile and a strong foreign accent,—

"Excuse my interruption!" she said. "I knew not you had company, the gentleman came in so quietly."

With this she directed her eyes toward me again.

She was very strange; yet my first feeling was that I had seen her before. Then I perceived that I had only seen ladies who were very much like her. But I had seen them very far away from Grimwinter, and it was an odd sensation to be seeing her here. Whither was it the sight of her seemed to transport me? To some dusky landing before a shabby Parisian *quatrième*,—to an open door revealing a greasy antechamber, and to Madame leaning over the banisters, while she holds a faded dressing-gown together and bawls down to the portress to bring up her coffee. Miss Spencer's visitor was a very large woman, of middle age, with a plump, dead-white face, and hair drawn back *a la chinoise*. She had a small penetrating eye, and what is called in French an agreeable smile. She wore an old pink cashmere dressing-gown, covered with white embroideries, and, like the figure in my momentary vision, she was holding it together in front with a bare and rounded arm and a plump and deeply dimpled hand.

"It is only to spick about my *café*," she said to Miss Spencer, with her agreeable smile. "I should like it served in the garden under the leetle tree."

The young man behind her had now stepped into the room, and he also stood looking at me. He was a pretty-faced little fellow, with an air of provincial foppishness,—a tiny Adonis of Grimwinter. He had a small pointed nose, a small pointed chin, and, as I observed, the most diminutive feet. He looked at me foolishly, with his mouth open.

"You shall have your coffee," said Miss Spencer, who had a faint red spot in each of her cheeks.

"It is well!" said the lady in the dressing-gown. "Find your bouk," she added, turning to the young man.

He gazed vaguely round the room. "My grammar, d 'ye mean?" he asked, with a helpless intonation.

But the large lady was inspecting me, curiously, and gathering in her dressing-gown with her white arm.

"Find your bouk, my friend," she repeated.

"My poetry, d 'ye mean?" said the young man, also staring at me again.

"Never mind your bouk," said his companion. "To-day we will talk. We will make some conversation. But we must not interrupt. Come;" and she turned away. "Under the leetle tree," she added, for the benefit of Miss Spencer.

Then she gave me a sort of salutation, and a "Monsieur!" with which she swept away again, followed by the young man.

Caroline Spencer stood there with her eyes fixed upon the ground.

"Who is that?" I asked.

"The Countess, my cousin."

"And who is the young man?"

"Her pupil, Mr. Mixter."

This description of the relation between the two persons who had just left the room made me break into a little laugh. Miss Spencer looked at me gravely.

"She gives French lessons; she has lost her fortune."

"I see," I said. "She is determined to be a burden to no one. That is very proper."

Miss Spencer looked down on the ground again, "I must go and get the coffee," she said.

"Has the lady many pupils?" I asked.

"She has only Mr. Mixter. She gives all her time to him."

At this I could not laugh, though I smelt provocation; Miss Spencer was too grave. "He pays very well," she presently added, with simplicity. "He is very rich. He is very kind. He takes the Countess to drive." And she was turning away.

"You are going for the Countess's coffee?" I said.

"If you will excuse me a few moments."

"Is there no one else to do it?"

She looked at me with the softest serenity. "I keep no servants."

"Can she not wait upon herself?"

"She is not used to that."

"I see," said I, as gently as possible. "But before you go, tell me this: who is this lady?"

"I told you about her before—that day. She is the wife of my cousin, whom you saw."

"The lady who was disowned by her family in consequence of her marriage?"

"Yes; they have never seen her again. They have cast her off."

"And where is her husband?"

"He is dead."

"And where is your money?"

The poor girl flinched; there was something too consistent in my questions. "I don't know," she said wearily.

But I continued a moment. "On her husband's death this lady came over here?"

"Yes, she arrived one day."

"How long ago?"

"Two years."

"She has been here ever since?"

"Every moment."

"How does she like it?"

"Not at all."

"And how do *you* like it?"

Miss Spencer laid her face in her two hands an instant, as she had done ten minutes before.

Then, quickly, she went to get the Countess's coffee.

I remained alone in the little parlor; I wanted to see more, to learn more. At the end of five minutes the young man whom Miss Spencer had described as the Countess's pupil came in. He stood looking at me for a moment with parted lips. I saw he was a very rudimentary young man.

"She wants to know if you won't come out there," he observed at last.

"Who wants to know?"

"The Countess. That French lady."

"She has asked you to bring me?"

"Yes, sir," said the young man feebly, looking at my six feet of stature.

I went out with him, and we found the Countess sitting under one of the little quince-trees in front of the house. She was drawing a needle through the piece of embroidery which she had taken from the small table. She pointed graciously to the chair beside her, and I seated myself. Mr. Mixter glanced about him, and then sat down in the grass at her feet. He gazed upward, looking with parted lips from the Countess to me. "I am sure you speak French," said the Countess, fixing her brilliant little eyes upon me.

"I do, madam, after a fashion," I answered in the lady's own tongue.

"*Voilà!*" she cried most expressively. "I knew it so soon as I looked at you. You have been in my poor dear country."

"A long time."

"You know Paris?"

"Thoroughly, madam." And with a certain conscious purpose I let my eyes meet her own.

She presently, hereupon, moved her own and glanced down at Mr. Mixter "What are we talking about?" she demanded of her attentive pupil.

He pulled his knees up, plucked at the grass with his hand, stared, blushed a little. "You are talking French," said Mr. Mixter.

"*La belle découverte!*" said the Countess. "Here are ten months," she explained to me, "that I am giving him lessons. Don't put yourself out not to say he's an idiot; he won't understand you."

"I hope your other pupils are more gratifying," I remarked.

"I have no others. They don't know what French is in this place; they don't want to know. You may therefore imagine the pleasure it is to me to meet a person who speaks it like yourself." I replied that my own pleasure was not less; and she went on drawing her stitches through her embroidery, with her little finger curled out. Every few moments she put her eyes close to her work, nearsightedly. I thought her a very disagreeable person; she was coarse, affected, dishonest, and no more a countess than I was a caliph. "Talk to me of Paris," she went on. "The very name of it gives me an emotion! How long since you were there?"

"Two months ago."

"Happy man! Tell me something about it What were they doing? Oh, for an hour of the boulevard!"

"They were doing about what they are always doing,—amusing themselves a good deal."

"At the theatres, eh?" sighed the Countess. "At the *cafés-concerts*, at the little tables in front of the doors? *Quelle existence!* You know I am a Parisienne, monsieur," she added, "to my fingertips."

"Miss Spencer was mistaken, then," I ventured to rejoin, "in telling me that you are a Provençale."

She stared a moment, then she put her nose to her embroidery, which had a dingy, desultory aspect. "Ah, I am a Provençale by birth; but I am a Parisienne by—inclination."

"And by experience, I suppose?" I said.

She questioned me a moment with her hard little eyes. "Oh, experience! I could talk of experience if I wished. I never expected, for example, that experience had *this* in store for me." And she pointed with her bare elbow, and with a jerk of her head, at everything that surrounded her,—at the little white house, the quince-tree, the rickety paling, even at Mr. Mixter.

"You are in exile!" I said, smiling.

"You may imagine what it is! These two years that I have been here I have passed hours—hours! One gets used to things, and sometimes I think I have got used to this. But there are some things that are always beginning over again. For example, my coffee."

"Do you always have coffee at this hour?" I inquired.

She tossed back her head and measured me.

"At what hour would you prefer me to have it? I must have my little cup after breakfast."

"Ah, you breakfast at this hour?"

"At midday—*comme cela se fait*. Here they breakfast at a quarter past seven! That 'quarter past' is charming!"

"But you were telling me about your *coffee*? I observed sympathetically.

"My *cousine* can't believe in it; she can't understand it. She's an excellent girl; but that little cup of black coffee, with a drop of cognac, served at this hour,—they exceed her comprehension. So I have to break the ice every day, and it takes the coffee the time you see to arrive. And when it arrives, monsieur! If I don't offer you any of it you must not take it ill. It will be because I know you have drunk it on the boulevard."

I resented extremely this scornful treatment of poor Caroline Spencer's humble hospitality; but I said nothing, in order to say nothing uncivil. I only looked on Mr. Mixter, who had clasped his arms round his knees and was watching my companion's demonstrative graces in solemn fascination. She presently saw that I was observing him; she glanced at me with a little bold explanatory smile. "You know, he adores me," she murmured, putting her nose into her tapestry again. I expressed the promptest credence, and she went on. "He dreams of becoming my lover! Yes, it's his dream. He has read a French novel; it took him six months. But ever since that he has thought himself the hero, and me the heroine!"

Mr. Mixter had evidently not an idea that he was being talked about; he was too preoccupied with the ecstasy of contemplation. At this moment Caroline Spencer came out of the house, bearing a coffee-pot on a little tray. I noticed that on her way from the door to the table she gave me a single quick, vaguely appealing glance. I wondered what it signified; I felt that it signified a sort of half-frightened longing to know what, as a man of the world who had been in France, I thought of the Countess. It made me extremely uncomfortable. I could not tell her that the Countess was very possibly the runaway wife of a little hair-dresser. I tried suddenly, on the contrary, to show a high consideration for her. But I got up; I could n't stay longer. It vexed me to see Caroline Spencer standing there like a waiting-maid.

"You expect to remain some time at Grimwinter?" I said to the Countess.

She gave a terrible shrug.

"Who knows? Perhaps for years. When one is in misery!—*Chere belle*" she added, turning to Miss Spencer, "you have forgotten the cognac!"

I detained Caroline Spencer as, after looking a moment in silence at the little table, she was turning away to procure this missing delicacy. I silently gave her my hand in farewell. She looked very tired, but there was a strange hint of prospective patience in her severely mild little face. I thought she was rather glad I was going. Mr. Mixter had risen to his feet and was pouring out the Countess's coffee. As I went back past the Baptist church I reflected that poor Miss Spencer had been right in her presentiment that she should still see something of that dear old Europe.

EMBARRASSMENTS

THE FIGURE IN THE CARPET

I

I had done a few things and earned a few pence—I had perhaps even had time to begin to think I was finer than was perceived by the patronising; but when I take the little measure of my course (a fidgety habit, for it's none of the longest yet) I count my real start from the evening George Corvick, breathless and worried, came in to ask me a service. He had done more things than I, and earned more pence, though there were chances for cleverness I thought he sometimes missed. I could only however that evening declare to him that he never missed one for kindness. There was almost rapture in hearing it proposed to me to prepare for *The Middle_*, the organ of our lucubrations, so called from the position in the week of its day of appearance, an article for which he had made himself responsible and of which, tied up with a stout string, he laid on my table the subject. I pounced upon my opportunity—that is on the first volume of it—and paid scant attention to my friend's explanation of his appeal. What explanation could be more to the point than my obvious fitness for the task? I had written on Hugh Vereker, but never a word in *The Middle*, where my dealings were mainly with the ladies and the minor poets. This was his new novel, an advance copy, and whatever much or little it should do for his reputation I was clear on the spot as to what it should do for mine. Moreover, if I always read him as soon as I could get hold of him, I had a particular reason for wishing to read him now: I had accepted an invitation to Bridges for the following Sunday, and it had been mentioned in Lady Jane's note that Mr. Vereker was to be there. I was young enough to have an emotion about meeting a man of his renown, and innocent enough to believe the occasion would demand the display of an acquaintance with his "last."

Corvick, who had promised a review of it, had not even had time to read it; he had gone to pieces in consequence of news requiring—as on precipitate reflection he judged—that he should catch the night-mail to Paris. He had had a telegram from Gwendolen Erme in answer to his letter offering to fly to her aid. I knew already about Gwendolen Erme; I had never seen her, but I had my ideas, which were mainly to the effect that Corvick would marry her if her mother would only die. That lady seemed now in a fair way to oblige him; after some dreadful mistake about some climate or some waters, she had suddenly collapsed on the return from abroad. Her daughter, unsupported and alarmed, desiring to make a rush for home but hesitating at the risk, had accepted our friend's assistance, and it was my secret belief that at the sight of him Mrs. Erme would pull round. His own belief was scarcely to be called secret; it discernibly at any rate differed from mine. He had showed me Gwendolen's photograph with the remark that she wasn't pretty but was awfully interesting; she had published at the age of nineteen a novel in three volumes, "Deep Down," about which, in *The Middle*, he had been really splendid. He appreciated my present eagerness and undertook that the periodical in question should do no less; then at the last, with his hand on the door, he said to me: "Of course you'll be all right, you know." Seeing I was a trifle vague he added: "I mean you won't be silly."

"Silly—about Vereker! Why, what do I ever find him but awfully clever?"

"Well, what's that but silly? What on earth does 'awfully clever' mean? For God's sake try to get *at* him. Don't let him suffer by our arrangement. Speak of him, you know, if you can, as should have spoken of him."

I wondered an instant. "You mean as far and away the biggest of the lot—that sort of thing?"

Corvick almost groaned. "Oh, you know, I don't put them back to back that way; it's the infancy of art! But he gives me a pleasure so rare; the sense of "—he mused a little—"something or other."

I wondered again. "The sense, pray, of what?"

"My dear man, that's just what I want *you* to say!"

Even before Corvick had banged the door I had begun, book in hand, to prepare myself to say it. I sat up with Vereker half the night; Corvick couldn't have done more than that. He was awfully clever—I stuck to that, but he wasn't a bit the biggest of the lot. I didn't allude to the lot, however; I flattered myself that I emerged on this occasion from the infancy of art. "It's all right," they declared vividly at the office; and when the number appeared I felt there was a basis on which I could meet the great man; It gave me confidence for a day or two, and then that confidence dropped. I had fancied him reading it with relish, but if Corvick was not satisfied how could Vereker himself be? I reflected indeed that the heat of the admirer was sometimes grosser even than the appetite of the scribe. Corvick at all events wrote me from Paris a little ill-humouredly. Mrs. Erme was pulling round, and I hadn't at all said what Vereker gave him the sense of.

II

The effect of my visit to Bridges was to turn me out for more profundity. Hugh Vereker, as I saw him there, was of a contact so void of angles that I blushed for the poverty of imagination involved in my small precautions. If he was in spirits it was not because he had read my review; in fact on the Sunday morning I felt sure he hadn't read it, though *The Middle* had been out three days and bloomed, I assured myself, in the stiff garden of periodicals which gave one of the ormolu tables the air of a stand at a station. The impression he made on me personally was such that I wished him to read it, and I corrected to this end with a surreptitious hand what might be wanting in the careless conspicuity of the sheet. I am afraid I even watched the result of my manouvre, but up to luncheon I watched in vain.

When afterwards, in the course of our gregarious walk, I found myself for half an hour, not perhaps without another manoeuvre, at the great man's side, the result of his affability was a still livelier desire that he should not remain in ignorance of the peculiar justice I had done him. It was not that he seemed to thirst for justice; on the contrary I had not yet caught in his talk the faintest grunt of a grudge—a note for which my young experience had already given me an ear. Of late he had had more recognition, and it was pleasant, as we used to say in *The Middle*, to see that it drew him out. He wasn't of course popular, but I judged one of the sources of his good humour to be precisely that his success was independent of that. He had none the less become in a manner the fashion; the critics at least had put on a spurt and caught up with him. We had found out at last how clever he was, and he had had to make the best of the loss of his mystery. I was strongly tempted, as I walked beside him, to let him know how much of that unveiling was my act; and there was a moment when I probably should have done so had not one of the ladies of our party, snatching a place at his other elbow, just then appealed to him in a spirit comparatively selfish. It was very discouraging: I almost felt the liberty had been taken with myself.

I had had on my tongue's end, for my own part, a phrase or two about the right word at the right time; but later on I was glad not to have spoken, for when on our return we clustered at tea I perceived Lady Jane, who had not been out with us, brandishing *The Middle* with her longest arm. She had taken it up at her leisure; she was delighted with what she had found, and I saw that, as a mistake in a man may often be a felicity in a woman, she would practically do for me what I hadn't been able to do for myself. "Some sweet little truths that needed to be spoken," I heard her declare, thrusting the paper at rather a bewildered couple by the fireplace. She grabbed it away from them again on the reappearance of Hugh Vereker, who after our walk had been upstairs to change something. "I know you don't in general look at this kind of thing, but it's an occasion really for doing so. You *haven't* seen it? Then you must. The man has actually got *at* you, at what *I* always feel, you know." Lady Jane threw into her eyes a look evidently intended to give an idea of what she always felt; but she added that she couldn't have expressed it. The man in the paper expressed it in a striking manner. "Just see there, and there, where I've dashed it, how he brings it out." She had literally marked for him the brightest patches of my prose, and if I was a little amused Vereker himself may well have been. He showed how much he was when before us all Lady Jane wanted to read something aloud. I liked at any rate the way he defeated her purpose by jerking the paper affectionately out of her clutch. He would take it upstairs with him, would look at it on going to dress. He did this half an hour later—I saw it in his hand when he repaired to his room. That was the moment at which, thinking to give her pleasure, I mentioned to Lady Jane that I was the author of the review. I did give her pleasure, I judged, but perhaps not quite so much as I had expected. If the author was "only me" the thing didn't seem quite so remarkable. Hadn't I had the effect rather of diminishing the lustre of the article than of adding to my own? Her ladyship was subject to the most extraordinary drops. It didn't matter; the only effect I cared about was the one it would have on Vereker up there by his bedroom fire.

At dinner I watched for the signs of this impression, tried to fancy there was some happier light in his eyes; but to my disappointment Lady Jane gave me no chance to make sure. I had hoped she would call triumphantly down the table, publicly demand if she hadn't been right. The party was large—there were people from outside as well, but I had never seen a table long enough to deprive Lady Jane of a triumph. I was just reflecting in truth that this interminable board would deprive *me* of one, when the guest next me, dear woman—she was Miss Poyle, the vicar's sister, a robust, unmodulated person—had the happy inspiration and the unusual courage to address herself across it to Vereker, who was opposite, but not directly, so that when he replied they were both leaning forward. She inquired, artless body, what he thought of Lady Jane's "panegyric," which she had read—not connecting it however with her right-hand neighbour; and while I strained my ear for his reply I heard him, to my stupefaction, call back gaily, with his mouth full of bread: "Oh, it's all right—it's the usual twaddle!"

I had caught Vereker's glance as he spoke, but Miss Poyle's surprise was a fortunate cover for my own. "You mean he doesn't do you justice?" said the excellent woman.

Vereker laughed out, and I was happy to be able to do the same. "It's a charming article," he tossed us.

Miss Poyle thrust her chin half across the cloth.

"Oh you're so deep!" she drove home.

"As deep as the ocean! All I pretend is, the author doesn't see—"

A dish was at this point passed over his shoulder, and we had to wait while he helped himself.

"Doesn't see what?" my neighbour continued.

"Doesn't see anything."

"Dear me—how very stupid!"

"Not a bit," Vereker laughed again. "Nobody does."

The lady on his further side appealed to him, and Miss Poyle sank back to me. "Nobody sees anything!" she cheerfully announced; to which I replied that I had often thought so too, but had somehow taken the thought for a proof on my own part of a tremendous eye. I didn't tell her the article was mine; and I observed that Lady Jane, occupied at the end of the table, had not caught Vereker's words.

I rather avoided him after dinner, for I confess he struck me as cruelly conceited, and the revelation was a pain. "The usual twaddle"—my acute little study! That one's admiration should have had a reserve or two could gall him to that point? I had thought him placid, and he was placid enough; such a surface was the hard, polished glass that encased the bauble of his vanity. I was really ruffled, the only comfort was that if nobody saw anything George Corvick was quite as much out of it as I. This comfort however was not sufficient, after the ladies had dispersed, to carry me in the proper manner—I mean in a spotted jacket and humming an air—into the smoking-room. I took my way in some dejection to bed; but in the passage I encountered Mr. Vereker, who had been up once more to change, coming out of his room. *He* was humming an air and had on a spotted jacket, and as soon as he saw me his gaiety gave a start.

"My dear young man," he exclaimed, "I'm so glad to lay hands on you! I'm afraid I most unwittingly wounded you by those words of mine at dinner to Miss Poyle. I learned but half an hour ago from Lady Jane that you wrote the little notice in *The Middle*."

I protested that no bones were broken; but he moved with me to my own door, his hand on my shoulder, kindly feeling for a fracture; and on hearing that I had come up to bed he asked leave to cross my threshold and just tell me in three words what his qualification of my remarks had represented. It was plain he really feared I was hurt, and the sense of his solicitude suddenly made all the difference to me. My cheap review fluttered off into space, and the best things I had said in it became flat enough beside the brilliancy of his being there. I can see him there still, on my rug, in the firelight and his spotted jacket, his fine, clear face all bright with the desire to be tender to my youth. I don't know what he had at first meant to say, but I think the sight of my relief touched him, excited him, brought up words to his lips from far within. It was so these words presently conveyed to me something that, as I afterwards knew, he had never uttered to any one. I have always done justice to the generous impulse that made him speak; it was simply compunction for a snub unconsciously administered to a man of letters in a position inferior to his own, a man of letters moreover in the very act of praising him. To make the thing right he talked to me exactly as an equal and on the ground of what we both loved best. The hour, the place, the unexpectedness deepened the impression: he couldn't have done anything more exquisitely successful

III.

"I don't quite know how to explain it to you," he said, "but it was the very fact that your notice of my book had a spice of intelligence, it was just your exceptional sharpness that produced the feeling—a very old story with me, I beg you to believe—under the momentary influence of which I used in speaking to that good lady the words you so naturally resent. I don't read the things in the newspapers unless they're thrust upon me as that one was—it's always one's best friend that does it! But I used to read them sometimes—ten years ago. I daresay they were in general rather stupider then; at any rate it always seemed to me that they missed my little point with a perfection exactly as admirable when they patted me on the back as when they kicked me in the shins. Whenever since I've happened to have a glimpse of them they were still blazing away—still missing it, I mean, deliciously. *You* miss it, my dear fellow, with inimitable assurance; the fact of your being awfully clever and your article's being awfully nice doesn't make a hair's breadth of difference. It's quite with you rising young men," Vereker laughed, "that I feel most what a failure I am!"

I listened with intense interest; it grew intenser as he talked. "*You* a failure—heavens! What then may your 'little point' happen to be?"

"Have I got to *tell* you, after all these years and labours?" There was something in the friendly reproach of this—jocosely exaggerated—that made me, as an ardent young seeker for truth, blush to the roots of my hair. I'm as much in the dark as ever, though I've grown used in a sense to my obtuseness; at that moment, however, Vereker's happy accent made me appear to myself, and probably to him, a rare donkey. I was on the point of exclaiming, "Ah, yes, don't tell me: for my honour, for that of the craft, don't!" when he went on in a manner that showed he had read my thought and had his own idea of the probability of our some day redeeming ourselves. "By my little point I mean—what shall I call it?—the particular thing I've written my books most *for*. Isn't there for every writer a particular thing of that sort, the thing that most makes him apply himself, the thing without the effort to achieve which he wouldn't write at all, the very passion of his passion, the part of the business in which, for him, the flame of art burns most intensely? Well, it's *that!*"

I considered a moment. I was fascinated—easily, you'll say; but I wasn't going after all to be put off my guard. "Your description's certainly beautiful, but it doesn't make what you describe very distinct."

"I promise you it would be distinct if it should dawn on you at all." I saw that the charm of our topic overflowed for my companion into an emotion as lively as my own. "At any rate," he went on, "I can speak for myself: there's an idea in my work without which I wouldn't have given a straw for the whole job. It's the finest, fullest intention of the lot, and the application of it has been, I think, a triumph of patience, of ingenuity. I ought to leave that to somebody else to say; but that nobody does say it is precisely what we're talking about. It stretches, this little trick of mine, from book to book, and everything else, comparatively, plays over the surface of it. The order, the form, the texture of my books will perhaps some day constitute for the initiated a complete representation of it. So it's naturally the thing for the critic to look for. It strikes me," my visitor added, smiling, "even as the thing for the critic to find."

This seemed a responsibility indeed. "You call it a little trick?"

"That's only my little modesty. It's really an exquisite scheme."

"And you hold that you've carried the scheme out?"

"The way I've carried it out is the thing in life I think a bit well of myself for."

I was silent a moment. "Don't you think you ought—just a trifle—to assist the critic?"

"Assist him? What else have I done with every stroke of my pen? I've shouted my intention in his great blank face!" At this, laughing out again, Vereker laid his hand on my shoulder to show that the allusion was not to my personal appearance.

"But you talk about the initiated. There must therefore, you see, be initiation."

"What else in heaven's name is criticism supposed to be?" I'm afraid I coloured at this too; but I took refuge in repeating that his account of his silver lining was poor in something or other that a plain man knows things by. "That's only because you've never had a glimpse of it," he replied. "If you had had one the element in question would soon have become practically all you'd see. To me it's exactly as palpable as the marble of this chimney. Besides, the critic just *isn't* a plain man: if he were, pray, what would he be doing in his neighbour's garden? You're anything but a plain man yourself, and the very *raison d'être* of you all is that you're little demons of subtlety. If my great affair's a secret, that's only because it's a secret in spite of itself—the amazing event has made it one. I not only never took the smallest precaution to do so, but never dreamed of any such accident. If I had I shouldn't in advance have had the heart to go on. As it was I only became aware little by little, and meanwhile I had done my work."

"And now you quite like it?" I risked.

"My work?"

"Your secret. It's the same thing."

"Your guessing that," Vereker replied, "is a proof that you're as clever as I say!" I was encouraged by this to remark that he would clearly be pained to part with it, and he confessed that it was indeed with him now the great amusement of life. "I live almost to see if it will ever be detected." He looked at me for a jesting challenge; something at the back of his eyes seemed to peep out. "But I needn't worry—it won't!"

"You fire me as I've never been fired," I returned; "you make me determined to do or die." Then I asked: "Is it a kind of esoteric message?"

His countenance fell at this—he put out his hand as if to bid me goodnight. "Ah, my dear fellow, it can't be described in cheap journalese!"

I knew of course he would be awfully fastidious, but our talk had made me feel how much his nerves were exposed. I was unsatisfied—I kept hold of his hand. "I won't make use of the expression then," I said, "in the article in which I shall eventually announce my discovery, though I daresay I shall have hard work to do without it. But meanwhile, just to hasten that difficult birth, can't you give a fellow a clue?" I felt much more at my ease.

"My whole lucid effort gives him a clue—every page and line and letter. The thing's as concrete there as a bird in a cage, a bait on a hook, a piece of cheese in a mouse-trap. It's stuck into every volume as your foot is stuck into your shoe. It governs every line, it chooses every word, it dots every i, it places every comma."

I scratched my head. "Is it something in the style or something in the thought? An element of form or an element of feeling?"

He indulgently shook my hand again, and I felt my questions to be crude and my distinctions pitiful. "Good-night, my dear boy—don't bother about it. After all, you do like a fellow."

"And a little intelligence might spoil it?" I still detained him.

He hesitated. "Well, you've got a heart in your body. Is that an element of form or an element of feeling? What I contend that nobody has ever mentioned in my work is the organ of life."

"I see—it's some idea about life, some sort of philosophy. Unless it be," I added with the eagerness of a thought perhaps still happier, "some kind of game you're up to with your style, something you're after in the language. Perhaps it's a preference for the letter P!" I ventured profanely to break out. "Papa, potatoes, prunes—that sort of thing?" He was suitably indulgent: he only said I hadn't got the right letter. But his amusement was over; I could see he was bored. There was nevertheless something else I had absolutely to learn. "Should you be able, pen in hand, to state it clearly yourself—to name it, phrase it, formulate it?"

"Oh," he almost passionately sighed, "if I were only, pen in hand, one of *you* chaps!"

"That would be a great chance for you of course. But why should you despise us chaps for not doing what you can't do yourself?"

"Can't do?" He opened his eyes. "Haven't I done it in twenty volumes? I do it in my way," he continued. "You don't do it in yours."

"Ours is so devilish difficult," I weakly observed.

"So is mine. We each choose our own. There's no compulsion. You won't come down and smoke?"

"No. I want to think this thing out."

"You'll tell me then in the morning that you've laid me bare?"

"I'll see what I can do; I'll sleep on it. But just one word more," I added. We had left the room—I walked again with him a few steps along the passage.

"This extraordinary 'general intention,' as you call it—for that's the most vivid description I can induce you to make of it—is then generally a sort of buried treasure?"

His face lighted. "Yes, call it that, though it's perhaps not for me to do so."

"Nonsense!" I laughed. "You know you're hugely proud of it."

"Well, I didn't propose to tell you so; but it *is* the joy of my soul!"

"You mean it's a beauty so rare, so great?"

He hesitated a moment. "The loveliest thing in the world!" We had stopped, and on these words he left me; but at the end of the corridor, while I looked after him rather yearningly, he turned and caught sight of my puzzled face. It made him earnestly, indeed I thought quite anxiously, shake his head and wave his finger. "Give it up—give it up!"

This wasn't a challenge—it was fatherly advice. If I had had one of his books at hand I would have repeated my recent act of faith—I would have spent half the night with him. At three o'clock in the morning, not sleeping, remembering moreover how indispensable he was to Lady Jane, I stole down to the library with a candle. There wasn't, so far as I could discover, a line of his writing in the house.

IV

Returning to town I feverishly collected them all; I picked out each in its order and held it up to the light. This gave me a maddening month, in the course of which several things took place. One of these, the last, I may as well immediately mention, was that I acted on Vereker's advice: I renounced my ridiculous attempt. I could really make nothing of the business; it proved a dead loss. After all, before, as he had himself observed, I liked him; and what now occurred was simply that my new intelligence and vain preoccupation damaged my liking. I not only failed to find his general intention—I found myself missing the subordinate intentions I had formerly found. His books didn't even remain the charming things they had been for me; the exasperation of my search put me out of conceit of them. Instead of being a pleasure the more they became a resource the less; for from the moment I was unable to follow up the author's hint I of course felt it a point of honour not to make use professionally of my knowledge of them. I *had* no knowledge—nobody had any. It was humiliating, but I could bear it—they only annoyed me now. At last they even bored me, and I accounted for my confusion—perversely, I confess—by the idea that Vereker had made a fool of me. The buried treasure was a bad joke, the general intention a monstrous *pose*.

The great incident of the time however was that I told George Corvick all about the matter and that my information had an immense effect upon him. He had at last come back, but so, unfortunately, had Mrs. Erme, and there was as yet, I could see, no question of his nuptials. He was immensely stirred up by the anecdote I had brought from Bridges; it fell in so completely with the sense he had had from the first that there was more in Vereker than met the eye. When I remarked that the eye seemed what the printed page had been expressly invented to meet he immediately accused me of being spiteful because I had been foiled. Our commerce had always that pleasant latitude. The thing Vereker had mentioned to me was exactly the thing he, Corvick, had wanted me to speak of in my review. On my suggesting at last that with the assistance I had now given him he would doubtless be prepared to speak of it himself he admitted freely that before doing this there was more he must understand. What he would have said, had he reviewed the new book, was that there was evidently in the writer's inmost art something to *be* understood. I hadn't so much as hinted at that: no wonder the writer hadn't been flattered! I asked Corvick what he really considered he meant by his own supersubtlety, and, unmistakably kindled, he replied: "It isn't for the vulgar—it isn't for the vulgar!" He had hold of the tail of something; he would pull hard, pull it right out. He pumped me dry on Vereker's strange confidence and, pronouncing me the luckiest of mortals, mentioned half a dozen questions he wished to goodness I had had the gumption to put. Yet on the other hand he didn't want to be told too much—it would spoil the fun of seeing what would come. The failure of my fun was at the moment of our meeting not complete, but I saw it ahead, and Corvick saw that I saw it. I, on my side, saw likewise that one of the first things he would do would be to rush off with my story to Gwendolen.

On the very day after my talk with him I was surprised by the receipt of a note from Hugh Vereker, to whom our encounter at Bridges had been recalled, as he mentioned, by his falling, in a magazine, on some article to which my signature was appended. "I read it with great pleasure," he wrote, "and remembered under its influence our lively conversation by your bedroom fire. The consequence of this has been that I begin to measure the temerity of my having saddled you with a knowledge that you may find something of a burden. Now that the fit's over I can't imagine how I came to be moved so much beyond my wont. I had never before related, no matter in what expansion, the history of my little secret, and I shall never speak of the business again. I was accidentally so much more explicit with you than it had ever entered into my game to be, that I find this game—I mean the pleasure of playing it—suffers considerably. In short, if you can understand it, I've spoiled a part of my fun. I really don't want to give anybody what I believe you clever young men call the tip. That's of course a selfish solicitude, and I name it to you for what it may be worth to you. If you're disposed to humour me, don't repeat my revelation. Think me demented—it's your right; but don't tell anybody why."

The sequel to this communication was that as early on the morrow as I dared I drove straight to Mr. Vereker's door. He occupied in those years one of the honest old houses in Kensington-square. He received me immediately, and as soon as I came in I saw I had not lost my power to minister to his mirth. He laughed out at the sight of my face, which doubtless expressed my perturbation. I had been indiscreet—my compunction was great. "I *have* told somebody," I panted, "and I'm sure that, person will by this time have told somebody else! It's a woman, into the bargain."

"The person you've told?"

"No, the other person. I'm quite sure he must have told her."

"For all the good it will do her—or do *me!* A woman will never find out."

"No, but she'll talk all over the place: she'll do just what you don't want."

Vereker thought a moment, but he was not so disconcerted as I had feared: he felt that if the harm was done it only served him right. "It doesn't matter—don't worry."

"I'll do my best, I promise you, that your talk with me shall go no further."

"Very good; do what you can."

"In the meantime," I pursued, "George Corvick's possession of the tip may, on his part, really lead to something."

"That will be a brave day."

I told him about Corvick's cleverness, his admiration, the intensity of his interest in my anecdote; and without making too much of the divergence of our respective estimates mentioned that my friend was already of opinion that he saw much further into a certain affair than most people. He was quite as fired as I had been at Bridges. He was moreover in love with the young lady: perhaps the two together would puzzle something out.

Vereker seemed struck with this. "Do you mean they're to be married?"

"I daresay that's what it will come to."

"That may help them," he conceded, "but we must give them time!"

I spoke of my own renewed assault and confessed my difficulties; whereupon he repeated his former advice: "Give it up, give it up!" He evidently didn't think me intellectually equipped for the adventure. I stayed half an hour, and he was most good-natured, but I couldn't help pronouncing him a man of shifting moods. He had been free with me in a mood, he had repented in a mood, and now in a mood he had turned indifferent. This general levity helped me to believe that, so far as the subject of the tip went, there wasn't much in it. I contrived however to make him answer a few more questions about it, though he did so with visible impatience. For himself, beyond doubt, the thing we were all so blank about was vividly there. It was something, I guessed, in the primal plan, something like a complex figure in a Persian carpet. He highly approved of this image when I used it, and he used another himself. "It's the very string," he said, "that my pearls are strung on!" The reason of his note to me had been that he really didn't want to give us a grain of succour—our destiny was a thing too perfect in its way to touch. He had formed the habit of depending upon it, and if the spell was to break it must break by some force of its own. He comes back to me from that last occasion—for I was never to speak to him again—as a man with some safe secret for enjoyment. I wondered as I walked away where he had got *his* tip.

V

When I spoke to George Corvick of the caution I had received he made me feel that any doubt of his delicacy would be almost an insult. He had instantly told Gwendolen, but Gwendolen's ardent response was in itself a pledge of discretion. The question would now absorb them, and they would enjoy their fun too much to wish to share it with the crowd. They appeared to have caught instinctively Vereker's peculiar notion of fun. Their intellectual pride, however, was not such as to make them indifferent to any further light I might throw on the affair they had in hand. They were indeed of the "artistic temperament," and I was freshly struck with my colleague's power to excite himself over a question of art. He called it letters, he called it life—it was all one thing. In what he said I now seemed to understand that he spoke equally for Gwendolen, to whom, as soon as Mrs. Erme was sufficiently better to allow her a little leisure, he made a point of introducing me. I remember our calling together one Sunday in August at a huddled house in Chelsea, and my renewed envy of Corvick's possession of a friend who had some light to mingle with his own. He could say things to her that I could never say to him. She had indeed no sense of humour and, with her pretty way of holding her head on one side, was one of those persons whom you want, as the phrase is, to shake, but who have learnt Hungarian by themselves. She conversed perhaps in Hungarian with Corvick; she had remarkably little English for his friend. Corvick afterwards told me that I had chilled her by my apparent indisposition to oblige her with the detail of what Vereker had said to me. I admitted that I felt I had given thought enough to this exposure: hadn't I even made up my mind that it was hollow, wouldn't stand the test? The importance they attached to it was irritating—it rather envenomed my dissent.

That statement looks unamiable, and what probably happened was that I felt humiliated at seeing other persons derive a daily joy from an experiment which had brought me only chagrin. I was out in the cold while, by the evening fire, under the lamp, they followed the chase for which I myself had sounded the horn. They did as I had done, only more deliberately and sociably—they went over their author from the beginning. There was no hurry, Corvick said—the future was before them and the fascination could only grow; they would take him page by page, as they would take one of the classics, inhale him in slow draughts and let him sink deep in. I doubt whether they would have got so wound up if they had not been in love: poor Vereker's secret gave them endless occasion to put their young heads together. None the less it represented the kind of problem for which Corvick had a special aptitude, drew out the particular pointed patience of which, had he lived, he would have given more striking and, it is to be hoped, more fruitful examples. He at least was, in Vereker's words, a little demon of subtlety. We had begun by disputing, but I soon saw that without my stirring a finger his infatuation would have its bad hours. He would bound off on false scents as I had done—he would clap his hands over new lights and see them blown out by the wind of the turned page. He was like nothing, I told him, but the maniacs who embrace some bedlamitical theory of the cryptic character of Shakespeare. To this he replied that if we had had Shakespeare's own word for his being cryptic he would immediately have accepted it. The case there was altogether different—we had nothing but the word of Mr. Snooks. I rejoined that I was stupefied to see him attach such importance even to the word of Mr. Vereker. He inquired thereupon whether I treated Mr. Vereker's word as a lie. I wasn't perhaps prepared, in my unhappy rebound, to go as far as that, but I insisted that till the contrary was proved I should view it as too fond an imagination. I didn't, I confess, say—I didn't at that time quite know—all I felt. Deep down, as Miss Erme would have said, I was uneasy, I was expectant. At the core of my personal confusion—for my curiosity lived in its ashes—was the sharpness of a sense that Corvick would at last probably come out somewhere. He made, in defence of his credulity, a great point of the fact that from of old, in his study of this genius, he had caught whiffs and hints of he didn't know what, faint wandering notes of a hidden music. That was just the rarity, that was the charm: it fitted so perfectly into what I reported.

If I returned on several occasions to the little house in Chelsea I daresay it was as much for news of Vereker as for news of Miss Erme's mamma. The hours spent there by Corvick were present to my fancy as those of a chessplayer bent with a silent scowl, all the lamplit winter, over his board and his moves. As my imagination filled it out the picture held me fast. On the other side of the table was a ghostlier form, the faint figure of an antagonist good-humouredly but a little wearily secure—an antagonist who leaned back in his chair with his hands in his pockets and a smile on his fine clear face. Close to Corvick, behind him, was a girl who had begun to strike me as pale and wasted and even, on more familiar view, as rather handsome, and who rested on his shoulder and hung upon his moves. He would take up a chessman and hold it poised a while over one of the little squares, and then he would put it back in its place with a long sigh of disappointment. The young lady, at this, would slightly but uneasily shift her position and look across, very hard, very long, very strangely, at their dim participant. I had asked them at an early stage of the business if it mightn't contribute to their success to have some closer communication with him. The special circumstances would surely be held to have given me a right to introduce them. Corvick immediately replied that he had no wish to approach the altar before he had prepared the sacrifice. He quite agreed with our friend both as to the sport and as to the honour—he would bring down the animal with his own rifle. When I asked him if Miss Erme were as keen a shot he said after an hesitation: "No; I'm ashamed to say she wants to set a trap. She'd give anything to see him; she says she requires another tip. She's really quite morbid about it. But she must play fair—she *shan't* see him!" he emphatically added. I had a suspicion that they had even quarrelled a little on the subject—a suspicion not corrected by the way he more than once exclaimed to me: "She's quite incredibly literary, you know—quite fantastically!" I remember his saying of her that she felt in italics and thought in capitals. "Oh, when I've run him to earth," he also said, "then, you know, I shall knock at his door. Rather—I beg you to believe. I'll have it from his own lips: 'Right you are, my boy; you've done it this time!' He shall crown me victor—with the critical laurel."

Meanwhile he really avoided the chances London life might have given him of meeting the distinguished novelist; a danger however that disappeared with Vereker's leaving England for an indefinite absence, as the newspapers announced—going to the south for motives connected with the health of his wife, which had long kept her in retirement. A year—more than a year—had elapsed since the incident at Bridges, but I had not encountered him again. I think at bottom I was rather ashamed—I hated to remind him that though I had irremediably missed his point a reputation for acuteness was rapidly overtaking me. This scruple led me a dance; kept me out of Lady Jane's house, made me even decline, when in spite of my bad manners she was a second time so good as to make me a sign, an invitation to her beautiful seat. I once saw her with Vereker at a concert and was sure I was seen by them, but I slipped out without being caught. I felt, as on that occasion I splashed along in the rain, that I couldn't have done anything else; and yet I remember saying to myself that it was hard, was even cruel. Not only had I lost the books, but I had lost the man himself: they and their author had been alike spoiled for me. I knew too which was the loss I most regretted. I had liked the man still better than I had liked the books.

VI

Six months after Vereker had left England George Corvick, who made his living by his pen, contracted for a piece of work which imposed on him an absence of some length and a journey of some difficulty, and his undertaking of which was much of a surprise to me. His brother-in-law had become editor of a great provincial paper, and the great provincial paper, in a fine flight of fancy, had conceived the idea of sending a "special commissioner" to India. Special commissioners had begun, in the "metropolitan press," to be the fashion, and the journal in question felt that it had passed too long for a mere country cousin. Corvick had no hand, I knew, for the big brush of the correspondent, but that was his brother-in-law's affair, and the fact that a particular task was not in his line was apt to be with himself exactly a reason for accepting it. He was prepared to out-Herod the metropolitan press; he took solemn precautions against priggishness, he exquisitely outraged taste. Nobody ever knew it—the taste was all his own. In addition to his expenses he was to be conveniently paid, and I found myself able to help him, for the usual fat book, to a plausible arrangement with the usual fat publisher. I naturally inferred that his obvious desire to make a little money was not unconnected with the prospect of a union with Gwendolen Erme. I was aware that her mother's opposition was largely addressed to his want of means and of lucrative abilities, but it so happened that, on my saying the last time I saw him something that bore on the question of his separation from our young lady, he exclaimed with an emphasis that startled me: "Ah, I'm not a bit engaged to her, you know!"

"Not overtly," I answered, "because her mother doesn't like you. But I've always taken for granted a private understanding."

"Well, there *was* one. But there isn't now." That was all he said, except something about Mrs. Erme's having got on her feet again in the most extraordinary way—a remark from which I gathered he wished me to think he meant that private understandings were of little use when the doctor didn't share them. What I took the liberty of really thinking was that the girl might in some way have estranged him. Well, if he had taken the turn of jealousy for instance it could scarcely be jealousy of me. In that case (besides the absurdity of it) he wouldn't have gone away to leave us together. For some time before his departure we had indulged in no allusion to the buried treasure, and from his silence, of which mine was the consequence, I had drawn a sharp conclusion. His courage had dropped, his ardour had gone the way of mine—this inference at least he left me to enjoy. More than that he couldn't do; he couldn't face the triumph with which I might have greeted an explicit admission. He needn't have been afraid, poor dear, for I had by this time lost all need to triumph. In fact I considered that I showed magnanimity in not reproaching him with his collapse, for the sense of his having thrown up the game made me feel more than ever how much I at last depended on him. If Corvick had broken down I should never know; no one would be of any use if *he* wasn't. It wasn't a bit true that I had ceased to care for knowledge; little by little my curiosity had not only begun to ache again, but had become the familiar torment of my consciousness. There are doubtless people to whom torments of such an order appear hardly more natural than the contortions of disease; but I don't know after all why I should in this connection so much as mention them. For the few persons, at any rate, abnormal or not, with whom my anecdote is concerned, literature was a game of skill, and skill meant courage, and courage meant honour, and honour meant passion, meant life. The stake on the table was of a different substance, and our roulette was the revolving mind, but we sat round the green board as intently as the grim gamblers at Monte Carlo. Gwendolen Erme, for that matter, with her white face and her fixed eyes, was of the very type of the lean ladies one had met in the temples of chance. I recognised in Corvick's absence that she made this analogy vivid. It was extravagant, I admit, the way she lived for the art of the pen. Her passion visibly preyed upon her, and in her presence I felt almost tepid. I got hold of "Deep Down" again: it was a desert in which she had lost herself, but in which too she had dug a wonderful hole in the sand—a cavity out of which Corvick had still more remarkably pulled her.

Early in March I had a telegram from her, in consequence of which I repaired immediately to Chelsea, where the first thing she said to me was: "He has got it, he has got it!"

She was moved, as I could see, to such depths that she must mean the great thing. "Vereker's idea?"

"His general intention. George has cabled from Bombay."

She had the missive open there; it was emphatic, but it was brief. "Eureka. Immense." That was all—he had saved the money of the signature. I shared her emotion, but I was disappointed. "He doesn't say what it is."

"How could he—in a telegram? He'll write it."

"But how does he know?"

"Know it's the real thing? Oh, I'm sure when you see it you do know. *Vera incessu patuit dea!*"

"It's you, Miss Erme, who are a dear for bringing me such news!"—I went all lengths in my high spirits. "But fancy finding our goddess in the temple of Vishnu! How strange of George to have been able to go into the thing again in the midst of such different and such powerful solicitations!"

"He hasn't gone into it, I know; it's the thing itself, let severely alone for six months, that has simply sprung out at him like a tigress out of the jungle. He didn't take a book with him—on purpose; indeed he wouldn't have needed to—he knows every page, as I do, by heart. They all worked in him together, and some day somewhere, when he wasn't thinking, they fell, in all their superb intricacy, into the one right combination. The figure in the carpet came out. That's the way he knew it would come and the real reason— you didn't in the least understand, but I suppose I may tell you now—why he went and why I consented to his going. We knew the change would do it, the difference of thought, of scene, would give the needed touch, the magic shake. We had perfectly, we had admirably calculated. The elements were all in his mind, and in the *secousse* of a new and intense experience they just struck light." She positively struck light herself—she was literally, facially luminous. I stammered something about unconscious cerebration, and she continued: "He'll come right home—this will bring him."

"To see Vereker, you mean?"

"To see Vereker—and to see *me*. Think what he'll have to tell me!"

I hesitated. "About India?"

"About fiddlesticks! About Vereker—about the figure in the carpet."

"But, as you say, we shall surely have that in a letter."

She thought like one inspired, and I remembered how Corvick had told me long before that her face was interesting. "Perhaps it won't go in a letter if it's 'immense.'"

"Perhaps not if it's immense bosh. If he has got something that won't go in a letter he hasn't got *the* thing. Vereker's own statement to me was exactly that the 'figure' *would* go in a letter."

"Well, I cabled to George an hour ago—two words," said Gwendolen.

"Is it indiscreet of me to inquire what they were?"

She hung fire, but at last she brought them out. "'Angel, write.'"

"Good!" I exclaimed. "I'll make it sure—I'll send him the same."

VII

My words however were not absolutely the same—I put something instead of "angel"; and in the sequel my epithet seemed the more apt, for when eventually we heard from Corvick it was merely, it was thoroughly to be tantalised. He was magnificent in his triumph, he described his discovery as stupendous; but his ecstasy only obscured it—there were to be no particulars till he should have submitted his conception to the supreme authority. He had thrown up his commission, he had thrown up his book, he had thrown up everything but the instant need to hurry to Rapallo, on the Genoese shore, where Vereker was making a stay. I wrote him a letter which was to await him at Aden—I besought him to relieve my suspense. That he found my letter was indicated by a telegram which, reaching me after weary days and without my having received an answer to my laconic dispatch at Bombay, was evidently intended as a reply to both communications. Those few words were in familiar French, the French of the day, which Corvick often made use of to show he wasn't a prig. It had for some persons the opposite effect, but his message may fairly be paraphrased. "Have patience; I want to see, as it breaks on you, the face you'll make!" "*Tellement envie de voir ta tête!*"—that was what I had to sit down with. I can certainly not be said to have sat down, for I seem to remember myself at this time as rushing constantly between the little house in Chelsea and my own. Our impatience, Gwendolen's and mine, was equal, but I kept hoping her light would be greater. We all spent during this episode, for people of our means, a great deal of money in telegrams, and I counted on the receipt of news from Rapallo immediately after the junction of the discoverer with the discovered. The interval seemed an age, but late one day I heard a hansom rattle up to my door with a crash engendered by a hint of liberality. I lived with my heart in my mouth and I bounded to the window—a movement which gave me a view of a young lady erect on the footboard of the vehicle and eagerly looking up at my house. At sight of me she flourished a paper with a movement that brought me straight down, the movement with which, in melodramas, handkerchiefs and reprieves are flourished at the foot of the scaffold.

"Just seen Vereker—not a note wrong. Pressed me to bosom—keeps me a month." So much I read on her paper while the cabby dropped a grin from his perch. In my excitement I paid him profusely and in hers she suffered it; then as he drove away we started to walk about and talk. We had talked, heaven knows, enough before, but this was a wondrous lift. We pictured the whole scene at Rapallo, where he would have written, mentioning my name, for permission to call; that is *I* pictured it, having more material than my companion, whom I felt hang on my lips as we stopped on purpose before shop-windows we didn't look into. About one thing we were clear: if he was staying on for fuller communication we should at least have a letter from him that would help us through the dregs of delay. We understood his staying on, and yet each of us saw, I think, that the other hated it. The letter we were clear about arrived; it was for Gwendolen, and I called upon her in time to save her the trouble of bringing it to me. She didn't read it out, as was natural enough; but she repeated to me what it chiefly embodied. This consisted of the remarkable statement that he would tell her when they were married exactly what she wanted to know.

"Only when we're married—not before," she explained. "It's tantamount to saying—isn't it?—that I must marry him straight off!" She smiled at me while I flushed with disappointment, a vision of fresh delay that made me at first unconscious of my surprise. It seemed more than a hint that on me as well he would impose some tiresome condition. Suddenly, while she reported several more things from his letter, I remembered what he had told me before going away. He found Mr. Vereker deliriously interesting and his own possession of the secret a kind of intoxication. The buried treasure was all gold and gems. Now that it was there it seemed to grow and grow before him; it was in all time, in all tongues, one of the most wonderful flowers of art. Nothing, above all, when once one was face to face with it, had been more consummately done. When once it came out it came out, was there with a splendour that made you ashamed; and there had not been, save in the bottomless vulgarity of the age, with every one tasteless and tainted, every sense stopped, the smallest reason why it should have been overlooked. It was immense, but it was simple—it was simple, but it was immense, and the final knowledge of it was an experience quite apart. He intimated that the charm of such an experience, the desire to drain it, in its freshness, to the last drop, was what kept him there close to the source. Gwendolen, frankly radiant as she tossed me these fragments, showed the elation of a prospect more assured than my own. That brought me back to the question of her marriage, prompted me to ask her if what she meant by what she had just surprised me with was that she was under an engagement.

"Of course I am!" she answered. "Didn't you know it?" She appeared astonished; but I was still more so, for Corvick had told me the exact contrary. I didn't mention this, however; I only reminded her that I had not been to that degree in her confidence, or even in Corvick's, and that moreover I was not in ignorance of her mother's interdict. At bottom I was troubled by the disparity of the two assertions; but after a moment I felt that Corvick's was the one I least doubted. This simply reduced me to asking myself if the girl had on the spot improvised an engagement—vamped up an old one or dashed off a new—in order to arrive at the satisfaction she desired. I reflected that she had resources of which I was destitute; but she made her case slightly more intelligible by rejoining presently: "What the state of things has been is that we felt of course bound to do nothing in mamma's lifetime."

"But now you think you'll just dispense with your mother's consent?"

"Ah, it may not come to that!" I wondered what it might come to, and she went on: "Poor dear, she may swallow the dose. In fact, you know," she added with a laugh, "she really *must!*"—a proposition of which, on behalf of every one concerned, I fully acknowledged the force.

VIII

Nothing more annoying had ever happened to me than to become aware before Corvick's arrival in England that I should not be there to put him through. I found myself abruptly called to Germany by the alarming illness of my younger brother, who, against my advice, had gone to Munich to study, at the feet indeed of a great master, the art of portraiture in oils. The near relative who made him an allowance had threatened to withdraw it if he should, under specious pretexts, turn for superior truth to Paris—Paris being somehow, for a Cheltenham aunt, the school of evil, the abyss. I deplored this prejudice at the time, and the deep injury of it was now visible—first in the fact that it had not saved the poor boy, who was clever, frail and foolish, from congestion of the lungs, and second in the greater remoteness from London to which the event condemned me. I am afraid that what was uppermost in my mind during several anxious weeks was the sense that if we had only been in Paris I might have run over to see Corvick. This was actually out of the question from every point of view: my brother, whose recovery gave us both plenty to do, was ill for three months, during which I never left him and at the end of which we had to face the absolute prohibition of a return to England. The consideration of climate imposed itself, and he was in no state to meet it alone. I took him to Meran and there spent the summer with him, trying to show him by example how to get back to work and nursing a rage of another sort that I tried not to show him.

The whole business proved the first of a series of phenomena so strangely combined that, taken together (which was how I had to take them) they form as good an illustration as I can recall of the manner in which, for the good of his soul doubtless, fate sometimes deals with a man's avidity. These incidents certainly had larger bearings than the comparatively meagre consequence we are here concerned with—though I feel that consequence also to be a thing to speak of with some respect. It's mainly in such a light, I confess, at any rate, that at this hour the ugly fruit of my exile is present to me. Even at first indeed the spirit in which my avidity, as I have called it, made me regard this term owed no element of ease to the fact that before coming back from Rapallo George Corvick addressed me in a way I didn't like. His letter had none of the sedative action that I must to-day profess myself sure he had wished to give it, and the march of occurrences was not so ordered as to make up for what it lacked. He had begun on the spot, for one of the quarterlies, a great last word on Vereker's writings, and this exhaustive study, the only one that would have counted, have existed, was to turn on the new light, to utter—oh, so quietly!—the unimagined truth. It was in other words to trace the figure in the carpet through every convolution, to reproduce it in every tint. The result, said Corvick, was to be the greatest literary portrait ever painted, and what he asked of me was just to be so good as not to trouble him with questions till he should hang up his masterpiece before me. He did me the honour to declare that, putting aside the great sitter himself, all aloft in his indifference, I was individually the connoisseur he was most working for. I was therefore to be a good boy and not try to peep under the curtain before the show-was ready: I should enjoy it all the more if I sat very still.

I did my best to sit very still, but I couldn't help giving a jump on seeing in *The Times* after I had been a week or two in Munich and before, as I knew, Corvick had reached London, the announcement of the sudden death of poor Mrs. Erme. I instantly wrote to Gwendolen for particulars, and she replied that her mother had succumbed to long-threatened failure of the heart. She didn't say, but I took the liberty of reading into her words, that from the point of view of her marriage and also of her eagerness, which was quite a match for mine, this was a solution more prompt than could have been expected and more radical than waiting for the old lady to swallow the dose. I candidly admit indeed that at the time—for I heard from her repeatedly—I read some singular things into Gwendolen's words and some still more extraordinary ones into her silences. Pen in hand, this way, I live the time over, and it brings back the oddest sense of my having been for months and in spite of myself a kind of coerced spectator. All my life had taken refuge in my eyes, which the procession of events appeared to have committed itself to keep astare. There were days when I thought of writing to Hugh Vereker and simply throwing myself on his charity. But I felt more deeply that I hadn't fallen quite so low, besides which, quite properly, he would send me about my business. Mrs.

Erme's death brought Corvick straight home, and within the month he was united "very quietly"—as quietly I suppose as he meant in his article to bring out his *trouvaille*—to the young lady he had loved and quitted. I use this last term, I may parenthetically say, because I subsequently grew sure that at the time he went to India, at the time of his great news from Bombay, there was no engagement whatever. There was none at the moment she affirmed the opposite. On the other hand he certainly became engaged the day he returned. The happy pair went down to Torquay for their honeymoon, and there, in a reckless hour, it occurred to poor Corvick to take his young bride a drive. He had no command of that business: this had been brought home to me of old in a little tour we had once made together in a dogcart. In a dogcart he perched his companion for a rattle over Devonshire hills, on one of the likeliest of which he brought his horse, who, it was true, had bolted, down with such violence that the occupants of the cart were hurled forward and that he fell horribly on his head. He was killed on the spot; Gwendolen escaped unhurt.

I pass rapidly over the question of this unmitigated tragedy, of what the loss of my best friend meant for me, and I complete my little history of my patience and my pain by the frank statement of my having, in a postscript to my very first letter to her after the receipt of the hideous news, asked Mrs. Corvick whether her husband had not at least finished the great article on Vereker. Her answer was as prompt as my inquiry: the article, which had been barely begun, was a mere heartbreaking scrap. She explained that Corvick had just settled down to it when he was interrupted by her mother's death; then, on his return, he had been kept from work by the engrossments into which that calamity plunged them. The opening pages were all that existed; they were striking, they were promising, but they didn't unveil the idol. That great intellectual feat was obviously to have formed his climax. She said nothing more, nothing to enlighten me as to the state of her own knowledge—the knowledge for the acquisition of which I had conceived her doing prodigious things. This was above all what I wanted to know: had *she* seen the idol unveiled? Had there been a private ceremony for a palpitating audience of one? For what else but that ceremony had the previous ceremony been enacted? I didn't like as yet to press her, though when I thought of what had passed between us on the subject in Corvick's absence her reticence surprised me. It was therefore not till much later, from Meran, that I risked another appeal, risked it in some trepidation, for she continued to tell me nothing. "Did you hear in those few days of your blighted bliss," I wrote, "what we desired so to hear?" I said "we" as a little hint; and she showed me she could take a little hint. "I heard everything," she replied, "and I mean to keep it to myself!"

IX

It was impossible not to be moved with the strongest sympathy for her, and on my return to England I showed her every kindness in my power. Her mother's death had made her means sufficient, and she had gone to live in a more convenient quarter. But her loss had been great and her visitation cruel; it never would have occurred to me moreover to suppose she could come to regard the enjoyment of a technical tip, of a piece of literary experience, as a counterpoise to her grief. Strange to say, none the less, I couldn't help fancying after I had seen her a few times that I caught a glimpse of some such oddity. I hasten to add that there had been other things I couldn't help fancying; and as I never felt I was really clear about these, so, as to the point I here touch on, I give her memory the benefit of every doubt. Stricken and solitary, highly accomplished and now, in her deep mourning, her maturer grace, and her uncomplaining sorrow incontestably handsome, she presented herself as leading a life of singular dignity and beauty. I had at first found a way to believe that I should soon get the better of the reserve formulated the week after the catastrophe in her reply to an appeal as to which I was not unconscious that it might strike her as mistimed. Certainly that reserve was something of a shock to me—certainly it puzzled me the more I thought of it, though I tried to explain it, with moments of success, by the supposition of exalted sentiments, of superstitious scruples, of a refinement of loyalty. Certainly it added at the same time hugely to the price of Vereker's secret, precious as that mystery already appeared. I may as well confess abjectly that Mrs. Corvick's unexpected attitude was the final tap on the nail that was to fix, as they say, my luckless idea, convert it into the obsession of which I am for ever conscious. But this only helped me the more to be artful, to be adroit, to allow time to elapse before renewing my suit. There were plenty of speculations for the interval, and one of them was deeply absorbing. Corvick had kept his information from his young friend till after the removal of the last barriers to their intimacy; then he had let the cat out of the bag. Was it Gwendolen's idea, taking a hint from him, to liberate this animal only on the basis of the renewal of such a relation? Was the figure in the carpet traceable or describable only for husbands and wives—for lovers supremely united? It came back to me in a mystifying manner that in Kensington-square, when I told him that Corvick would have told the girl he loved, some word had dropped from Vereker that gave colour to this possibility. There might be little in it, but there was enough to make me wonder if I should have to marry Mrs. Corvick to get what I wanted. Was I prepared to offer her this price for the blessing of her knowledge? Ah! that way madness lay—so I said to myself at least in bewildered hours. I could see meanwhile the torch she refused to pass on flame away in her chamber of memory—pour through her eyes a light that made a glow in her lonely house. At the end of six months I was fully sure of what this warm presence made up to her for. We had talked again and again of the man who had brought us together, of his talent, his character, his personal charm, his certain career, his dreadful doom, and even of his clear purpose in that great study which was to have been a supreme literary portrait, a kind of critical Vandyke or Velasquez. She had conveyed to me in abundance that she was tongue-tied by her perversity, by her piety, that she would never break the silence it had not been given to the "right person," as she said, to break. The hour however finally arrived. One evening when I had been sitting with her longer than usual I laid my hand firmly on her arm.

"Now, at last, what *is* it?"

She had been expecting me; she was ready. She gave a long, slow, soundless headshake, merciful only in being inarticulate. This mercy didn't prevent its hurling at me the largest, finest, coldest "Never!" I had yet, in the course of a life that had known denials, had to take full in the face. I took it and was aware that with the hard blow the tears had come into my eyes. So for a while we sat and looked at each other; after which I slowly rose. I was wondering if some day she would accept me; but this was not what I brought out. I said as I smoothed down my hat: "I know what to think then; it's nothing!"

A remote, disdainful pity for me shone out of her dim smile; then she exclaimed in a voice that I hear at this moment: "It's my *life!*" As I stood at the door she added: "You've insulted him!"

"Do you mean Vereker?"

"I mean—the Dead!"

I recognised when I reached the street the justice of her charge. Yes, it was her life—I recognised that too; but her life none the less made room with the lapse of time for another interest. A year and a half after Corvick's death she published in a single volume her second novel, "Overmastered," which I pounced on in the hope of finding in it some tell-tale echo or some peeping face. All I found was a much better book than her younger performance, showing I thought the better company she had kept. As a tissue tolerably intricate it was a carpet with a figure of its own; but the figure was not the figure I was looking for. On sending a review of it to *The Middle* I was surprised to learn from the office that a notice was already in type. When the paper came out I had no hesitation in attributing this article, which I thought rather vulgarly overdone, to Drayton Deane, who in the old days had been something of a friend of Corvick's, yet had only within a few weeks made the acquaintance of his widow. I had had an early copy of the book, but Deane had evidently had an earlier. He lacked all the same the light hand with which Corvick had gilded the gingerbread—he laid on the tinsel in splotches.

X

Six months later appeared "The Right of Way," the last chance, though we didn't know it, that we were to have to redeem ourselves. Written wholly during Vereker's absence, the book had been heralded, in a hundred paragraphs, by the usual ineptitudes. I carried it, as early a copy as any, I this time flattered myself, straightway to Mrs. Corvick. This was the only use I had for it; I left the inevitable tribute of *The Middle* to some more ingenious mind and some less irritated temper. "But I already have it," Gwendolen said. "Drayton Deane was so good as to bring it to me yesterday, and I've just finished it."

"Yesterday? How did he get it so soon?"

"He gets everything soon. He's to review it in *The Middle*."

"He—Drayton Deane—review Vereker?" I couldn't believe my ears.

"Why not? One fine ignorance is as good as another."

I winced, but I presently said: "You ought to review him yourself!"

"I don't 'review,'" she laughed. "I'm reviewed!"

Just then the door was thrown open. "Ah yes, here's your reviewer!" Drayton Deane was there with his long legs and his tall forehead: he had come to see what she thought of "The Right of Way," and to bring news which was singularly relevant. The evening papers were just out with a telegram on the author of that work, who, in Rome, had been ill for some days with an attack of malarial fever. It had at first not been thought grave, but had taken in consequence of complications a turn that might give rise to anxiety. Anxiety had indeed at the latest hour begun to be felt.

I was struck in the presence of these tidings with the fundamental detachment that Mrs. Corvick's public regret quite failed to conceal: it gave me the measure of her consummate independence. That independence rested on her knowledge, the knowledge which nothing now could destroy and which nothing could make different. The figure in the carpet might take on another twist or two, but the sentence had virtually been written. The writer might go down to his grave: she was the person in the world to whom—as if she had been his favoured heir—his continued existence was least of a need. This reminded me how I had observed at a particular moment—after Corvick's death—the drop of her desire to see him face to face. She had got what she wanted without that. I had been sure that if she hadn't got it she wouldn't have been restrained from the endeavour to sound him personally by those superior reflections, more conceivable on a man's part than on a woman's, which in my case had served as a deterrent. It wasn't however, I hasten to add, that my case, in spite of this invidious comparison, wasn't ambiguous enough. At the thought that Vereker was perhaps at that moment dying there rolled over me a wave of anguish—a poignant sense of how inconsistently I still depended on him. A delicacy that it was my one compensation to suffer to rule me had left the Alps and the Apennines between us, but the vision of the waning opportunity made me feel as if I might in my despair at last have gone to him. Of course I would really have done nothing of the sort. I remained five minutes, while my companions talked of the new book, and when Drayton Deane appealed to me for my opinion of it I replied, getting up, that I detested Hugh Vereker—simply couldn't read him. I went away with the moral certainty that as the door closed behind me Deane would remark that I was awfully superficial. His hostess wouldn't contradict him.

I continue to trace with a briefer touch our intensely odd concatenation. Three weeks after this came Vereker's death, and before the year was out the death of his wife. That poor lady I had never seen, but I had had a futile theory that, should she survive him long enough to be decorously accessible, I might approach her with the feeble flicker of my petition. Did she know and if she knew would she speak? It was much to be presumed that for more reasons than one she would have nothing to say; but when she passed out of all reach I felt that renouncement was indeed my appointed lot. I was shut up in my obsession for ever—my gaolers had gone off with the key. I find myself quite as vague as a captive in a dungeon about the time that further elapsed before Mrs. Corvick became the wife of Drayton Deane. I had foreseen, through my bars, this end of the business, though there was no indecent haste and our friendship had rather fallen off. They were both so "awfully intellectual" that it struck people as a suitable match, but I knew better than any one the wealth of understanding the bride would contribute to the partnership. Never, for a marriage in literary circles—so the newspapers described the alliance—had a bride been so handsomely dowered. I began with due promptness to look for the fruit of their union—that fruit, I mean, of which the premonitory symptoms would be peculiarly visible in the husband. Taking for granted the splendour of the lady's nuptial gift, I expected to see him make a show commensurate with his increase of means. I knew what his means had been— his article on "The Right of Way" had distinctly given one the figure. As he was now exactly in the position in which still more exactly I was not I watched from month to month, in the likely periodicals, for the heavy message poor Corvick had been unable to deliver and the responsibility of which would have fallen on his successor. The widow and wife would have broken by the rekindled hearth the silence that only a widow and wife might break, and Deane would be as aflame with the knowledge as Corvick in his own hour, as Gwendolen in hers had been. Well, he was aflame doubtless, but the fire was apparently not to become a public blaze. I scanned the periodicals in vain: Drayton Deane filled them with exuberant pages, but he withheld the page I most feverishly sought. He wrote on a thousand subjects, but never on the subject of Vereker. His special line was to tell truths that other people either "funked," as he said, or overlooked, but he never told the only truth that seemed to me in these days to signify. I met the couple in those literary circles referred to in the papers: I have sufficiently intimated that it was only in such circles we were all constructed to revolve. Gwendolen was more than ever committed to them by the publication of her third novel, and I myself definitely classed by holding the opinion that this work was inferior to its immediate predecessor. Was it worse because she had been keeping worse company? If her secret was, as she had told me, her life—a fact discernible in her increasing bloom, an air of conscious privilege that, cleverly corrected by pretty charities, gave distinction to her appearance—it had yet not a direct influence on her work. That only made—everything only made—one yearn the more for it, rounded it off with a mystery finer and subtler.

XI

It was therefore from her husband I could never remove my eyes: I hovered about him in a manner that might have made him uneasy. I went even so far as to engage him in conversation. *Didn't* he know, hadn't he come into it as a matter of course?—that question hummed in my brain. Of course he knew; otherwise he wouldn't return my stare so queerly. His wife had told him what I wanted, and he was amiably amused at my impotence. He didn't laugh—he was not a laugher: his system was to present to my irritation, so that I should crudely expose myself, a conversational blank as vast as his big bare brow. It always happened that I turned away with a settled conviction from these unpeopled expanses, which seemed to complete each other geographically and to symbolise together Drayton Deane's want of voice, want of form. He simply hadn't the art to use what he knew; he literally was incompetent to take up the duty where Corvick had left it. I went still further—it was the only glimpse of happiness I had. I made up my mind that the duty didn't appeal to him. He wasn't interested, he didn't care. Yes, it quite comforted me to believe him too stupid to have joy of the thing I lacked. He was as stupid after as before, and that deepened for me the golden glory in which the mystery was wrapped. I had of course however to recollect that his wife might have imposed her conditions and exactions. I had above all to recollect that with Vereker's death the major incentive dropped. He was still there to be honoured by what might be done—he was no longer there to give it his sanction. Who, alas, but he had the authority?

Two children were born to the pair, but the second cost the mother her life. After this calamity I seemed to see another ghost of a chance. I jumped at it in thought, but I waited a certain time for manners, and at last my opportunity arrived in a remunerative way. His wife had been dead a year when I met Drayton Deane in the smoking-room of a small club of which we both were members, but where for months—perhaps because I rarely entered it—I had not seen him. The room was empty and the occasion propitious. I deliberately offered him, to have done with the matter for ever, that advantage for which I felt he had long been looking.

"As an older acquaintance of your late wife's than even you were," I began, "you must let me say to you something I have on my mind. I shall be glad to make any terms with you that you see fit to name for the information she had from George Corvick—the information, you know, that he, poor fellow, in one of the happiest hours of his life, had straight from Hugh Vereker."

He looked at me like a dim phrenological bust. "The information———?"

"Vereker's secret, my dear man—the general intention of his books: the string the pearls were strung on, the buried treasure, the figure in the carpet."

He began to flush—the numbers on his bumps to come out. "Vereker's books had a general intention?"

I stared in my turn. "You don't mean to say you don't know it?" I thought for a moment he was playing with me. "Mrs. Deane knew it; she had it, as I say, straight from Corvick, who had, after infinite search and to Vereker's own delight, found the very mouth of the cave. Where *is* the mouth? He told after their marriage—and told alone—the person who, when the circumstances were reproduced, must have told you. Have I been wrong in taking for granted that she admitted you, as one of the highest privileges of the relation in which you stood to her, to the knowledge of which she was after Corvick's death the sole depositary? All *I* know is that that knowledge is infinitely precious, and what I want you to understand is that if you will in your turn admit *me* to it you will do me a kindness for which I shall be everlastingly grateful."

He had turned at last very red; I daresay he had begun by thinking I had lost my wits. Little by little he followed me; on my own side I stared with a livelier surprise. "I don't know what you're talking about," he said.

He wasn't acting—it was the absurd truth. "She *didn't* tell you———"

"Nothing about Hugh Vereker."

I was stupefied; the room went round. It had been too good even for that! "Upon your honour?"

"Upon my honour. What the devil's the matter with you?" he demanded.

"I'm astounded—I'm disappointed. I wanted to get it out of you."

"It isn't *in* me!" he awkwardly laughed. "And even if it were———"

"If it were you'd let me have it—oh yes, in common humanity. But I believe you. I see—I see!" I went on, conscious, with the full turn of the wheel, of my great delusion, my false view of the poor man's attitude. What I saw, though I couldn't say it, was that his wife hadn't thought him worth enlightening. This struck me as strange for a woman who had thought him worth marrying. At last I explained it by the reflection that she couldn't possibly have married him for his understanding. She had married him for something else. He was to some extent enlightened now, but he was even more astonished, more disconcerted: he took a moment to compare my story with his quickened memories. The result of his meditation was his presently saying with a good deal of rather feeble form:

"This is the first I hear of what you allude to. I think you must be mistaken as to Mrs. Drayton Deane's having had any unmentioned, and still less any unmentionable, knowledge about Hugh Vereker. She would certainly have wished it—if it bore on his literary character—to be used."

"It *was* used. She used it herself. She told me with her own lips that she 'lived' on it."

I had no sooner spoken than I repented of my words; he grew so pale that I felt as if I had struck him. "Ah, 'lived'—!" he murmured, turning short away from me.

My compunction was real; I laid my hand on his shoulder. "I beg you to forgive me—I've made a mistake. You *don't* know what I thought you knew. You could, if I had been right, have rendered me a service; and I had my reasons for assuming that you would be in a position to meet me."

"Your reasons?" he asked. "What were your reasons?"

I looked at him well; I hesitated; I considered. "Come and sit down with me here, and I'll tell you." I drew him to a sofa, I lighted another cigarette and, beginning with the anecdote of Vereker's one descent from the clouds, I gave him an account of the extraordinary chain of accidents that had in spite of it kept me till that hour in the dark. I told him in a word just what I've written out here. He listened with deepening attention, and I became aware, to my surprise, by his ejaculations, by his questions, that he would have been after all not unworthy to have been trusted by his wife. So abrupt an experience of her want of trust had an agitating effect on him, but I saw that immediate shock throb away little by little and then gather again into waves of wonder and curiosity—waves that promised, I could perfectly judge, to break in the end with the fury of my own highest tides. I may say that to-day as victims of unappeased desire there isn't a pin to choose between us. The poor man's state is almost my consolation; there are indeed moments when I feel it to be almost my revenge.

GLASSES

I

Yes indeed, I say to myself, pen in hand, I can keep hold of the thread and let it lead me back to the first impression. The little story is all there, I can touch it from point to point; for the thread, as I call it, is a row of coloured beads on a string. None of the beads are missing—at least I think they're not: that's exactly what I shall amuse myself with finding out.

I had been all summer working hard in town and then had gone down to Folkestone for a blow. Art was long, I felt, and my holiday short; my mother was settled at Folkestone, and I paid her a visit when I could. I remember how on this occasion, after weeks, in my stuffy studio, with my nose on my palette, I sniffed up the clean salt air and cooled my eyes with the purple sea. The place was full of lodgings, and the lodgings were at that season full of people, people who had nothing to do but to stare at one another on the great flat down. There were thousands of little chairs and almost as many little Jews; and there was music in an open rotunda, over which the little Jews wagged their big noses. We all strolled to and fro and took pennyworths of rest; the long, level cliff-top, edged in places with its iron rail, might have been the deck of a huge crowded ship. There were old folks in Bath chairs, and there was one dear chair, creeping to its last full stop, by the side of which I always walked. There was in fine weather the coast of France to look at, and there were the usual things to say about it; there was also in every state of the atmosphere our friend Mrs. Meldrum, a subject of remark not less inveterate. The widow of an officer in the Engineers, she had settled, like many members of the martial miscellany, well within sight of the hereditary enemy, who however had left her leisure to form in spite of the difference of their years a close alliance with my mother. She was the heartiest, the keenest, the ugliest of women, the least apologetic, the least morbid in her misfortune. She carried it high aloft, with loud sounds and free gestures, made it flutter in the breeze as if it had been the flag of her country. It consisted mainly of a big red face, indescribably out of drawing, from which she glared at you through gold-rimmed aids to vision, optic circles of such diameter and so frequently displaced that some one had vividly spoken of her as flattening her nose against the glass of her spectacles. She was extraordinarily near-sighted, and whatever they did to other objects they magnified immensely the kind eyes behind them. Blessed conveniences they were, in their hideous, honest strength—they showed the good lady everything in the world but her own queerness. This element was enhanced by wild braveries of dress, reckless charges of colour and stubborn resistances of cut, wonderous encounters in which the art of the toilet seemed to lay down its life. She had the tread of a grenadier and the voice of an angel.

In the course of a walk with her the day after my arrival I found myself grabbing her arm with sudden and undue familiarity. I had been struck by the beauty of a face that approached us and I was still more affected when I saw the face, at the sight of my companion, open like a window thrown wide. A smile fluttered out of it as brightly as a drapery dropped from a sill—a drapery shaken there in the sun by a young lady flanked with two young men, a wonderful young lady who, as we drew nearer, rushed up to Mrs. Meldrum with arms flourished for an embrace. My immediate impression of her had been that she was dressed in mourning, but during the few moments she stood talking with our friend I made more discoveries. The figure from the neck down was meagre, the stature insignificant, but the desire to please towered high, as well as the air of infallibly knowing how and of never, never missing it. This was a little person whom I would have made a high bid for a good chance to paint. The head, the features, the colour, the whole facial oval and radiance had a wonderful purity; the deep grey eyes—the most agreeable, I thought, that I had ever seen—brushed with a kind of winglike grace every object they encountered. Their possessor was just back from Boulogne, where she had spent a week with dear Mrs. Floyd-Taylor: this accounted for the effusiveness of her reunion with dear Mrs. Meldrum. Her black garments were of the freshest and daintiest; she suggested a pink-and-white wreath at a showy funeral. She confounded us for three minutes with her presence; she was a beauty of the great conscious, public, responsible order. The young men, her companions, gazed at her and grinned: I could see there were very few moments of the day at which young men, these or others, would not be so occupied. The people who approached took leave of their manners; every one seemed to linger and gape. When she brought her face close to Mrs. Meldrum's—and she appeared to be always bringing it close to somebody's— it was a marvel that objects so dissimilar should express the same general identity, the unmistakable character of the English gentlewoman. Mrs. Meldrum sustained the comparison with her usual courage, but I wondered why she didn't introduce me: I should have had no objection to the bringing of such a face close to mine. However, when the young lady moved on with her escort she herself bequeathed me a sense that some such *rapprochement* might still occur. Was this by reason of the general frequency of encounters at Folkestone, or by reason of a subtle acknowledgment that she contrived to make of the rights, on the part of others, that such beauty as hers created? I was in a position to answer that question after Mrs. Meldrum had answered a few of mine.

II

Flora Saunt, the only daughter of an old soldier, had lost both her parents, her mother within a few months. Mrs. Meldrum had known them, disapproved of them, considerably avoided them: she had watched the girl, off and on, from her early childhood. Flora, just twenty, was extraordinarily alone in the world—so alone that she had no natural chaperon, no one to stay with but a mercenary stranger, Mrs. Hammond Synge, the sister-in-law of one of the young men I had just seen. She had lots of friends, but none of them nice: she kept picking up impossible people. The Floyd-Taylors, with whom she had been at Boulogne, were simply horrid. The Hammond Synges were perhaps not so vulgar, but they had no conscience in their dealings with her.

"She knows what I think of them," said Mrs. Meldrum, "and indeed she knows what I think of most things."

"She shares that privilege with most of your friends!" I replied laughing.

"No doubt; but possibly to some of my friends it makes a little difference. That girl doesn't care a button. She knows best of all what I think of Flora Saunt."

"And what may your opinion be?"

"Why, that she's not worth talking about—an idiot too abysmal."

"Doesn't she care for that?"

"Just enough, as you saw, to hug me till I cry out. She's too pleased with herself for anything else to matter."

"Surely, my dear friend," I rejoined, "she has a good deal to be pleased with!"

"So every one tells her, and so you would have told her if I had given you a chance. However, that doesn't signify either, for her vanity is beyond all making or mending. She believes in herself, and she's welcome, after all, poor dear, having only herself to look to. I've seldom met a young woman more completely at liberty to be silly. She has a clear course—she'll make a showy finish."

"Well," I replied, "as she probably will reduce many persons to the same degraded state, her partaking of it won't stand out so much."

"If you mean that the world's full of twaddlers I quite agree with you!" cried Mrs. Meldrum, trumpeting her laugh half across the Channel.

I had after this to consider a little what she would call my mother's son, but I didn't let it prevent me from insisting on her making me acquainted with Flora Saunt; indeed I took the bull by the horns, urging that she had drawn the portrait of a nature which common charity now demanded that she should put into relation with a character really fine. Such a frail creature was just an object of pity. This contention on my part had at first of course been jocular; but strange to say it was quite the ground I found myself taking with regard to our young lady after I had begun to know her. I couldn't have said what I felt about her except that she was undefended; from the first of my sitting with her there after dinner, under the stars—that was a week at Folkestone of balmy nights and muffled tides and crowded chairs—I became aware both that protection was wholly absent from her life and that she was wholly indifferent to its absence.

The odd thing was that she was not appealing: she was abjectly, divinely conceited, absurdly, fantastically happy. Her beauty was as yet all the world to her, a world she had plenty to do to live in. Mrs. Meldrum told me more about her, and there was nothing that, as the centre of a group of giggling, nudging spectators, she was not ready to tell about herself. She held her little court in the crowd, upon the grass, playing her light over Jews and Gentiles, completely at ease in all promiscuities. It was an effect of these things that from the very first, with every one listening, I could mention that my main business with her would be just to have a go at her head and to arrange in that view for an early sitting. It would have been as impossible, I think, to be impertinent to her as it would have been to throw a stone at a plate-glass window; so any talk that went forward on the basis of her loveliness was the most natural thing in the world and immediately became the most general and sociable. It was when I saw all this that I judged how, though it was the last thing she asked for, what one would ever most have at her service was a curious compassion. That sentiment was coloured by the vision of the dire exposure of a being whom vanity had put so off her guard. Hers was the only vanity I have ever known that made its possessor superlatively soft. Mrs. Meldrum's further information contributed moreover to these indulgences—her account of the girl's neglected childhood and queer continental relegations, with straying, squabbling, Monte-Carlo-haunting parents; the more invidious picture, above all, of her pecuniary arrangement, still in force, with the Hammond Synges, who really, though they never took her out—practically she went out alone—had their hands half the time in her pocket. She had to pay for everything, down to her share of the wine-bills and the horses' fodder, down to Bertie Hammond Synge's fare in the "Underground" when he went to the City for her. She had been left with just money enough to turn her head; and it hadn't even been put in trust, nothing prudent or proper had been done with it. She could spend her capital, and at the rate she was going, expensive, extravagant and with a swarm of parasites to help, it certainly wouldn't last very long.

"Couldn't *you* perhaps take her, independent, unencumbered as you are?" I asked of Mrs. Meldrum. "You're probably, with one exception, the sanest person she knows, and you at least wouldn't scandalously fleece her."

"How do you know what I wouldn't do?" my humorous friend demanded. "Of course I've thought how I can help her—it has kept me awake at night. But I can't help her at all; she'll take nothing from me. You know what she does—she hugs me and runs away. She has an instinct about me, she feels that I've one about her. And then she dislikes me for another reason that I'm not quite clear about, but that I'm well aware of and that I shall find out some day. So far as her settling with me goes it would be impossible moreover here: she wants naturally enough a much wider field. She must live in London—her game is there. So she takes the line of adoring me, of saying she can never forget that I was devoted to her mother—which I wouldn't for the world have been—and of giving me a wide berth. I think she positively dislikes to look at me. It's all right; there's no obligation; though people in general can't take their eyes off me."

"I see that at this moment," I replied. "But what does it matter where or how, for the present, she lives? She'll marry infallibly, marry early, and everything then will change."

"Whom will she marry?" my companion gloomily asked.

"Any one she likes. She's so abnormally pretty she can do anything. She'll fascinate some nabob or some prince."

"She'll fascinate him first and bore him afterwards. Moreover she's not so pretty as you make her out; she has a scrappy little figure."

"No doubt; but one doesn't in the least notice it."

"Not now," said Mrs. Meldrum, "but one will when she's older."

"When she's older she'll be a princess, so it won't matter."

"She has other drawbacks," my companion went on. "Those wonderful eyes are good for nothing but to roll about like sugar-balls—which they greatly resemble—in a child's mouth. She can't use them."

"Use them? Why, she does nothing else."

"To make fools of young men, but not to read or write, not to do any sort of work. She never opens a book, and her maid writes her notes. You'll say that those who live in glass houses shouldn't throw stones. Of course I know that if I didn't wear my goggles I shouldn't be good for much."

"Do you mean that Miss Saunt ought to sport such things?" I exclaimed with more horror than I meant to show.

"I don't prescribe for her; I don't know that they're what she requires."

"What's the matter with her eyes?" I asked after a moment.

"I don't exactly know; but I heard from her mother years ago that even as a child they had had for a while to put her into spectacles and that, though she hated them and had been in a fury of disgust, she would always have to be extremely careful. I'm sure I hope she is!"

I echoed the hope, but I remember well the impression this made upon me—my immediate pang of resentment, a disgust almost equal to Flora's own. I felt as if a great rare sapphire had split in my hand.

III

This conversation occurred the night before I went back to town. I settled on the morrow to take a late train, so that I had still my morning to spend at Folkestone, where during the greater part of it I was out with my mother. Every one in the place was as usual out with some one else, and even had I been free to go and take leave of her I should have been sure that Flora Saunt would not be at home. Just where she was I presently discovered: she was at the far end of the cliff, the point at which it overhangs the pretty view of Sandgate and Hythe. Her back however was turned to this attraction; it rested with the aid of her elbows, thrust slightly behind her so that her scanty little shoulders were raised toward her ears, on the high rail that inclosed the down. Two gentlemen stood before her whose faces we couldn't see but who even as observed from the rear were visibly absorbed in the charming figure-piece submitted to them. I was freshly struck with the fact that this meagre and defective little person, with the cock of her hat and the flutter of her crape, with her eternal idleness, her eternal happiness, her absence of moods and mysteries and the pretty presentation of her feet, which especially now in the supported slope of her posture occupied with their imperceptibility so much of the foreground—I was reminded anew, I say, how our young lady dazzled by some art that the enumeration of her merits didn't explain and that the mention of her lapses didn't affect. Where she was amiss nothing counted, and where she was right everything did. I say she was wanting in mystery, but that after all was her secret. This happened to be my first chance of introducing her to my mother, who had not much left in life but the quiet look from under the hood of her chair at the things which, when she should have quitted those she loved, she could still trust to make the world good for them. I wondered an instant how much she might be moved to trust Flora Saunt, and then while the chair stood still and she waited I went over and asked the girl to come and speak to her. In this way I saw that if one of Flora's attendants was the inevitable young Hammond Synge, master of ceremonies of her regular court, always offering the use of a telescope and accepting that of a cigar, the other was a personage I had not yet encountered, a small pale youth in showy knickerbockers, whose eyebrows and nose and the glued points of whose little moustache were extraordinarily uplifted and sustained. I remember taking him at first for a foreigner and for something of a pretender: I scarcely know why, unless because of the motive I felt in the stare he fixed on me when I asked Miss Saunt to come away. He struck me a little as a young man practising the social art of "impertinence"; but it didn't matter, for Flora came away with alacrity, bringing all her prettiness and pleasure and gliding over the grass in that rustle of delicate mourning which made the endless variety of her garments, as a painter could take heed, strike one always as the same obscure elegance. She seated herself on the floor of my mother's chair, a little too much on her right instep as I afterwards gathered, caressing her stiff hand, smiling up into her cold face, commending and approving her without a reserve and without a doubt. She told her immediately, as if it were something for her to hold on by, that she was soon to sit to me for a "likeness," and these words gave me a chance to inquire if it would be the fate of the picture, should I finish it, to be presented to the young man in the knickerbockers. Her lips, at this, parted in a stare; her eyes darkened to the purple of one of the shadow-patches on the sea. She showed for the passing instant the face of some splendid tragic mask, and I remembered for the inconsequence of it what Mrs. Meldrum had said about her sight. I had derived from this lady a worrying impulse to catechise her, but that didn't seem exactly kind; so I substituted another question, inquired who the pretty young man in knickerbockers might happen to be.

"Oh, a gentleman I met at Boulogne. He has come over to see me." After a moment she added: "He's Lord Iffield."

I had never heard of Lord Iffield, but her mention of his having been at Boulogne helped me to give him a niche. Mrs. Meldrum had incidentally thrown a certain light on the manners of Mrs. Floyd-Taylor, Flora's recent hostess in that charming town, a lady who, it appeared, had a special vocation for helping rich young men to find a use for their leisure. She had always one or other in hand and she had apparently on this occasion pointed her lesson at the rare creature on the opposite coast. I had a vague idea that Boulogne was not a resort of the aristocracy; at the same time there might very well have been a strong attraction there even for one of the darlings of fortune. I could perfectly understand in any case that such a darling should be drawn to Folkestone by Flora Saunt. But it was not in truth of these things I was thinking; what was uppermost in my mind was a matter which, though it had no sort of keeping, insisted just then on coming out.

"Is it true, Miss Saunt," I suddenly demanded, "that you're so unfortunate as to have had some warning about your beautiful eyes?"

I was startled by the effect of my words; the girl threw back her head, changing colour from brow to chin. "True? Who in the world says so?" I repented of my question in a flash; the way she met it made it seem cruel, and I saw that my mother looked at me in some surprise. I took care, in answer to Flora's challenge, not to incriminate Mrs. Meldrum. I answered that the rumour had reached me only in the vaguest form and that if I had been moved to put it to the test my very real interest in her must be held responsible. Her blush died away, but a pair of still prettier tears glistened in its track. "If you ever hear such a thing said again you can say it's a horrid lie!" I had brought on a commotion deeper than any I was prepared for; but it was explained in some degree by the next words she uttered: "I'm happy to say there's nothing the matter with any part of my body; not the least little thing!" She spoke with her habitual complacency, with triumphant assurance; she smiled again, and I could see that she was already sorry she had shown herself too disconcerted. She turned it off with a laugh. "I've good eyes, good teeth, a good digestion and a good temper. I'm sound of wind and limb!" Nothing could have been more characteristic than her blush and her tears, nothing less acceptable to her than to be thought not perfect in every particular. She couldn't submit to the imputation of a flaw. I expressed my delight in what she told me, assuring her I should always do battle for her; and as if to rejoin her companions she got up from her place on my mother's toes. The young men presented their backs to us; they were leaning on the rail of the cliff. Our incident had produced a certain awkwardness, and while I was thinking of what next to say she exclaimed irrelevantly: "Don't you know? He'll be Lord Considine." At that moment the youth marked for this high destiny turned round, and she went on, to my mother: "I'll introduce him to you—he's awfully nice." She beckoned and invited him with her parasol; the movement struck me as taking everything for granted. I had heard of Lord Considine and if I had not been able to place Lord Iffield it was because I didn't know the name of his eldest son. The young man took no notice of Miss Saunt's appeal; he only stared a moment and then on her repeating it quietly turned his back. She was an odd creature: she didn't blush at this; she only said to my mother apologetically, but with the frankest, sweetest amusement: "You don't mind, do you? He's a monster of shyness!" It was as if she were sorry for every one—for Lord Iffield, the victim of a complaint so painful, and for my mother, the object of a trifling incivility. "I'm sure I don't want him!" said my mother; but Flora added some remark about the rebuke she would give him for slighting us. She would clearly never explain anything by any failure of her own power. There rolled over me while she took leave of us and floated back to her friends a wave of tenderness superstitious and silly. I seemed somehow to see her go forth to her fate; and yet what should fill out this orb of a high destiny if not such beauty and such joy? I had a dim idea that Lord Considine was a great proprietor, and though there mingled with it a faint impression that I shouldn't like his son the result of the two images was a whimsical prayer that the girl mightn't miss her possible fortune.

IV

One day in the course of the following June there was ushered into my studio a gentleman whom I had not yet seen but with whom I had been very briefly in correspondence. A letter from him had expressed to me some days before his regret on learning that my "splendid portrait" of Titras Flora Louisa Saunt, whose full name figured by her own wish in the catalogue of the exhibition of the Academy, had found a purchaser before the close of the private view. He took the liberty of inquiring whether I might have at his service some other memorial of the same lovely head, some preliminary sketch, some study for the picture. I had replied that I had indeed painted Miss Saunt more than once and that if he were interested in my work I should be happy to show him what I had done. Mr. Geoffrey Dawling, the person thus introduced to me, stumbled into my room with awkward movements and equivocal sounds—a long, lean, confused, confusing young man, with a bad complexion and large, protrusive teeth. He bore in its most indelible pressure the postmark, as it were, of Oxford, and as soon as he opened his mouth I perceived, in addition to a remarkable revelation of gums, that the text of the queer communication matched the registered envelope. He was full of refinements and angles, of dreary and distinguished knowledge. Of his unconscious drollery his dress freely partook; it seemed, from the gold ring into which his red necktie was passed to the square toe-caps of his boots, to conform with a high sense of modernness to the fashion before the last. There were moments when his overdone urbanity, all suggestive stammers and interrogative quavers, made him scarcely intelligible; but I felt him to be a gentleman and I liked the honesty of his errand and the expression of his good green eyes.

As a worshipper at the shrine of beauty however he needed explaining, especially when I found he had no acquaintance with my brilliant model; had on the mere evidence of my picture taken, as he said, a tremendous fancy to her face. I ought doubtless to have been humiliated by the simplicity of his judgment of it, a judgment for which the rendering was lost in the subject, quite leaving out the element of art. He was like the innocent reader for whom the story is "really true" and the author a negligible quantity. He had come to me only because he wanted to purchase, and I remember being so amused at his attitude, which I had never seen equally marked in a person of education, that I asked him why, for the sort of enjoyment he desired, it wouldn't be more to the point to deal directly with the lady. He stared and blushed at this: it was plain the idea frightened him. He was an extraordinary case—personally so modest that I could see it had never occurred to him. He had fallen in love with a painted sign and seemed content just to dream of what it stood for. He was the young prince in the legend or the comedy who loses his heart to the miniature of the outland princess. Until I knew him better this puzzled me much—the link was so missing between his sensibility and his type. He was of course bewildered by my sketches, which implied in the beholder some sense of intention and quality; but for one of them, a comparative failure, he ended by conceiving a preference so arbitrary and so lively that, taking no second look at the others, he expressed the wish to possess it and fell into the extremity of confusion over the question of the price. I simplified that problem, and he went off without having asked me a direct question about Miss Saunt, yet with his acquisition under his arm. His delicacy was such that he evidently considered his rights to be limited; he had acquired none at all in regard to the original of the picture. There were others—for I was curious about him—that I wanted him to feel I conceded: I should have been glad of his carrying away a sense of ground acquired for coming back. To insure this I had probably only to invite him, and I perfectly recall the impulse that made me forbear. It operated suddenly from within while he hung about the door and in spite of the diffident appeal that blinked in his gentle grin. If he was smitten with Flora's ghost what mightn't be the direct force of the luminary that could cast such a shadow? This source of radiance, flooding my poor place, might very well happen to be present the next time he should turn up. The idea was sharp within me that there were complications it was no mission of mine to bring about. If they were to occur they might occur by a logic of their own.

Let me say at once that they did occur and that I perhaps after all had something to do with it. If Mr. Dawling had departed without a fresh appointment he was to reappear six months later under protection no less adequate than that of our young lady herself. I had seen her repeatedly for months: she had grown to regard my studio as the tabernacle of her face. This prodigy was frankly there the sole object of interest; in other places there were occasionally other objects. The freedom of her manners continued to be stupefying; there was nothing so extraordinary save the absence in connection with it of any catastrophe. She was kept innocent by her egotism, but she was helped also, though she had now put off her mourning, by the attitude of the lone orphan who had to be a law unto herself. It was as a lone orphan that she came and went, as a lone orphan that she was the centre of a crush. The neglect of the Hammond Synges gave relief to this character, and she paid them handsomely to be, as every one said, shocking. Lord Iffield had gone to India to shoot tigers, but he returned in time for the private view: it was he who had snapped up, as Flora called it, the gem of the exhibition.

My hope for the girl's future had slipped ignominiously off his back, but after his purchase of the portrait I tried to cultivate a new faith. The girl's own faith was wonderful. It couldn't however be contagious: too great was the limit of her sense of what painters call values. Her colours were laid on like blankets on a cold night. How indeed could a person speak the truth who was always posturing and bragging? She was after all vulgar enough, and by the time I had mastered her profile and could almost with my eyes shut do it in a single line I was decidedly tired of her perfection. There grew to be something silly in its eternal smoothness. One moved with her moreover among phenomena mismated and unrelated; nothing in her talk ever matched with anything out of it. Lord Iffield was dying of love for her, but his family was leading him a life. His mother, horrid woman, had told some one that she would rather he should be swallowed by a tiger than marry a girl not absolutely one of themselves. He had given his young friend unmistakable signs, but he was lying low, gaining time: it was in his father's power to be, both in personal and in pecuniary ways, excessively nasty to him. His father wouldn't last for ever— quite the contrary; and he knew how thoroughly, in spite of her youth, her beauty and the swarm of her admirers, some of them positively threatening in their passion, he could trust her to hold out. There were richer, cleverer men, there were greater personages too, but she liked her "little viscount" just as he was, and liked to think that, bullied and persecuted, he had her there so luxuriously to rest upon. She came back to me with tale upon tale, and it all might be or mightn't. I never met my pretty model in the world—she moved, it appeared, in exalted circles—and could only admire, in her wealth of illustration, the grandeur of her life and the freedom of her hand.

I had on the first opportunity spoken to her of Geoffrey Dawling, and she had listened to my story so far as she had the art of such patience, asking me indeed more questions about him than I could answer; then she had capped my anecdote with others much more striking, revelations of effects produced in the most extraordinary quarters: on people who had followed her into railway-carriages; guards and porters even who had literally stuck there; others who had spoken to her in shops and hung about her house-door; cabmen, upon her honour, in London, who, to gaze their fill at her, had found excuses to thrust their petrifaction through the very glasses of four-wheelers. She lost herself in these reminiscences, the moral of which was that poor Mr. Dawling was only one of a million. When therefore the next autumn she flourished into my studio with her odd companion at her heels her first care was to make clear to me that if he was now in servitude it wasn't because she had run after him. Dawling hilariously explained that when one wished very much to get anything one usually ended by doing so—a proposition which led me wholly to dissent and our young lady to asseverate that she hadn't in the least wished to get Mr. Dawling. She mightn't have wished to get him, but she wished to show him, and I seemed to read that if she could treat him as a trophy her affairs were rather at the ebb. True there always hung from her belt a promiscuous fringe of scalps. Much at any rate would have come and gone since our separation in July. She had spent four months abroad, where, on Swiss and Italian lakes, in German cities, in Paris, many accidents might have happened.

V

I had been again with my mother, but except Mrs. Meldrum and the gleam of France had not found at Folkestone my old resources and pastimes. Mrs. Meldrum, much edified by my report of the performances, as she called them, in my studio, had told me that to her knowledge Flora would soon be on the straw: she had cut from her capital such fine fat slices that there was almost nothing more left to swallow. Perched on her breezy cliff the good lady dazzled me as usual by her universal light: she knew so much more about everything and everybody than I could ever squeeze out of my colour-tubes. She knew that Flora was acting on system and absolutely declined to be interfered with: her precious reasoning was that her money would last as long as she should need it, that a magnificent marriage would crown her charms before she should be really pinched. She had a sum put by for a liberal outfit; meanwhile the proper use of the rest was to decorate her for the approaches to the altar, keep her afloat in the society in which she would most naturally meet her match. Lord Iffield had been seen with her at Lucerne, at Cadenabbia; but it was Mrs. Meldrum's conviction that nothing was to be expected of him but the most futile flirtation. The girl had a certain hold of him, but with a great deal of swagger he hadn't the spirit of a sheep: he was in fear of his father and would never commit himself in Lord Considine's lifetime. The most Flora might achieve would be that he wouldn't marry some one else. Geoffrey Dawling, to Mrs. Meldrum's knowledge (I had told her of the young man's visit) had attached himself on the way back from Italy to the Hammond Synge group. My informant was in a position to be definite about this dangler; she knew about his people: she had heard of him before. Hadn't he been, at Oxford, a friend of one of her nephews? Hadn't he spent the Christmas holidays precisely three years before at her brother-in-law's in Yorkshire, taking that occasion to get himself refused with derision by wilful

Betty, the second daughter of the house? Her sister, who liked the floundering youth, had written to her to complain of Betty, and that the young man should now turn up as an appendage of Flora's was one of those oft-cited proofs that the world is small and that there are not enough people to go round. His father had been something or other in the Treasury; his grandfather, on the mother's side, had been something or other in the Church. He had come into the paternal estate, two or three thousand a year in Hampshire; but he had let the place advantageously and was generous to four ugly sisters who lived at Bournemouth and adored him. The family was hideous all round, but the salt of the earth. He was supposed to be unspeakably clever; he was fond of London, fond of books, of intellectual society and of the idea of a political career. That such a man should be at the same time fond of Flora Saunt attested, as the phrase in the first volume of Gibbon has it, the variety of his inclinations. I was soon to learn that he was fonder of her than of all the other things together. Betty, one of five and with views above her station, was at any rate felt at home to have dished herself by her perversity. Of course no one had looked at her since and no one would ever look at her again. It would be eminently desirable that Flora should learn the lesson of Betty's fate.

I was not struck, I confess, with all this in my mind, by any symptoms on our young lady's part of that sort of meditation. The only moral she saw in anything was that of her incomparable countenance, which Mr. Dawling, smitten even like the railway porters and the cabmen by the doom-dealing gods, had followed from London to Venice and from Venice back to London again. I afterwards learned that her version of this episode was profusely inexact: his personal acquaintance with her had been determined by an accident remarkable enough, I admit, in connection with what had gone before—a coincidence at all events superficially striking. At Munich, returning from a tour in the Tyrol with two of his sisters, he had found himself at the *table d'hôte* of his inn opposite to the full presentment of that face of which the mere clumsy copy had made him dream and desire. He had been tossed by it to a height so vertiginous as to involve a retreat from the table; but the next day he had dropped with a resounding thud at the very feet of his apparition. On the following, with an equal incoherence, a sacrifice even of his bewildered sisters, whom he left behind, he made an heroic effort to escape by flight from a fate of which he already felt the cold breath. That fate, in London, very little later, drove him straight before it—drove him one Sunday afternoon, in the rain, to the door of the Hammond Synges. He marched in other words close up to the cannon that was to blow him to pieces. But three weeks, when he reappeared to me, had elapsed since then, yet (to vary my metaphor) the burden he was to carry for the rest of his days was firmly lashed to his back. I don't mean by this that Flora had been persuaded to contract her scope; I mean that he had been treated to the unconditional snub which, as the event was to show, couldn't have been bettered as a means of securing him. She hadn't calculated, but she had said "Never!" and that word had made a bed big enough for his long-legged patience. He became from this moment to my mind the interesting figure in the piece.

Now that he had acted without my aid I was free to show him this, and having on his own side something to show me he repeatedly knocked at my door. What he brought with him on these occasions was a simplicity so huge that, as I turn my ear to the past, I seem even now to hear it bumping up and down my stairs. That was really what I saw of him in the light of his behaviour. He had fallen in love as he might have broken his leg, and the fracture was of a sort that would make him permanently lame. It was the whole man who limped and lurched, with nothing of him left in the same position as before. The tremendous cleverness, the literary society, the political ambition, the Bournemouth sisters all seemed to flop with his every movement a little nearer to the floor. I hadn't had an Oxford training and I had never encountered the great man at whose feet poor Dawling had most submissively sat and who had addressed him his most destructive sniffs; but I remember asking myself if such privileges had been an indispensable preparation to the career on which my friend appeared now to have embarked. I remember too making up my mind about the cleverness, which had its uses and I suppose in impenetrable shades even its critics, but from which the friction of mere personal intercourse was not the sort of process to extract a revealing spark. He accepted without a question both his fever and his chill, and the only thing he showed any subtlety about was this convenience of my friendship. He doubtless told me his simple story, but the matter comes back to me in a kind of sense of *my* being rather the mouthpiece, of my having had to thresh it out for him. He took it from me without a groan, and I gave it to him, as we used to say, pretty hot; he took it again and again, spending his odd half-hours with me as if for the very purpose of learning how idiotically he was in love. He told me I made him see things: to begin with, hadn't I first made him see Flora Saunt? I wanted him to give her up and luminously informed him why; on which he never protested nor contradicted, never was even so alembicated as to declare just for the sake of the drama that he wouldn't. He simply and undramatically didn't, and when at the end of three months I asked him what was the use of talking with such a fellow his nearest approach to a justification was to say that what made him want to help her was just the deficiencies I dwelt on. I could only reply without pointing the moral: "Oh, if you're as sorry for her as that!" I too was nearly as sorry for her as that, but it only led me to be sorrier still for other victims of this compassion. With Dawling as with me the compassion was at first in excess of any visible motive; so that when eventually the motive was supplied each could to a certain extent compliment the other on the fineness of his foresight.

After he had begun to haunt my studio Miss Saunt quite gave it up, and I finally learned that she accused me of conspiring with him to put pressure on her to marry him. She didn't know I would take it that way; else she wouldn't have brought him to see me. It was in her view a part of the conspiracy; that to show him a kindness I asked him at last to sit to me. I daresay moreover she was disgusted to hear that I had ended by attempting almost as many sketches of his beauty as I had attempted of hers. What was the value of tributes to beauty by a hand that luxuriated in ugliness? My relation to poor Dawling's want of modelling was simple enough. I was really digging in that sandy desert for the buried treasure of his soul.

VI

It befell at this period, just before Christmas, that on my having gone under pressure of the season into a great shop to buy a toy or two, my eye, fleeing from superfluity, lighted at a distance on the bright concretion of Flora Saunt, an exhibitability that held its own even against the most plausible pinkness of the most developed dolls. A huge quarter of the place, the biggest bazaar "on earth," was peopled with these and other effigies and fantasies, as well as with purchasers and vendors, haggard alike in the blaze of the gas with hesitations. I was just about to appeal to Flora to avert that stage of my errand when I saw that she was accompanied by a gentleman whose identity, 'though more than a year had elapsed, came back to me from the Folkestone cliff.' It had been associated in that scene with showy knickerbockers; at present it overflowed more splendidly into a fur-trimmed overcoat. Lord Iffield's presence made me waver an instant before crossing over; and during that instant Flora, blank and undistinguishing, as if she too were after all weary of alternatives, looked straight across at me. I was on the point of raising my hat to her when I observed that her face gave no sign. I was exactly in the line of her vision, but she either didn't see me or didn't recognise me, or else had a reason to pretend she didn't. Was her reason that I had displeased her and that she wished to punish me? I had always thought it one of her merits that she wasn't vindictive. She at any rate simply looked away; and at this moment one of the shop-girls, who had apparently gone off in search of it, bustled up to her with a small mechanical toy. It so happened that I followed closely what then took place, afterwards recognising that I had been led to do so, led even through the crowd to press nearer for the purpose, by an impression of which in the act I was not fully conscious.

Flora, with the toy in her hand, looked round at her companion; then seeing his attention had been solicited in another quarter she moved away with the shop-girl, who had evidently offered to conduct her into the presence of more objects of the same sort. When she reached the indicated spot I was in a position still to observe her. She had asked some question about the working of the toy, and the girl, taking it herself, began to explain the little secret. Flora bent her head over it, but she clearly didn't understand. I saw her, in a manner that quickened my curiosity, give a glance back at the place from which she had come. Lord Iffield was talking with another young person: she satisfied herself of this by the aid of a question addressed to her own attendant. She then drew closer to the table near which she stood and, turning her back to me, bent her head lower over the collection of toys and more particularly over the small object the girl had attempted to explain.

She took it back and, after a moment, with her face well averted, made an odd motion of her arms and a significant little duck of her head. These slight signs, singular as it may appear, produced in my bosom an agitation so great that I failed to notice Lord Iffield's whereabouts. He had rejoined her; he was close upon her before I knew it or before she knew it herself. I felt at that instant the strangest of all impulses: if it could have operated more rapidly it would have caused me to dash between them in some such manner as to give Flora a warning. In fact as it was I think I could have done this in time had I not been checked by a curiosity stronger still than my impulse. There were three seconds during which I saw the young man and yet let him come on. Didn't I make the quick calculation that if he didn't catch what Flora was doing I too might perhaps not catch it? She at any rate herself took the alarm. On perceiving her companion's nearness she made, still averted, another duck of her head and a shuffle of her hands so precipitate that a little tin steamboat she had been holding escaped from them and rattled down to the floor with a sharpness that I hear at this hour. Lord Iffield had already seized her arm; with a violent jerk he brought her round toward him. Then it was that there met my eyes a quite distressing sight: this exquisite creature, blushing, glaring, exposed, with a pair of big black-rimmed eyeglasses, defacing her by their position, crookedly astride of her beautiful nose. She made a grab at them with her free hand while I turned confusedly away.

VII

I don't remember how soon it was I spoke to Geoffrey Dawling; his sittings were irregular, but it was certainly the very next time he gave me one.

"Has any rumour ever reached you of Miss Saunt's having anything the matter with her eyes?" He stared with a candour that was a sufficient answer to my question, backing it up with a shocked and mystified "Never!" Then I asked him if he had observed in her any symptom, however disguised, of embarrassed sight: on which, after a moment's thought, he exclaimed "Disguised?" as if my use of that word had vaguely awakened a train. "She's not a bit myopic," he said; "she doesn't blink or contract her lids." I fully recognised this and I mentioned that she altogether denied the impeachment; owing it to him moreover to explain the ground of my inquiry, I gave him a sketch of the incident that had taken place before me at the shop. He knew all about Lord Iffield: that nobleman had figured freely in our conversation as his preferred, his injurious rival. Poor Daw-ling's contention was that if there had been a definite engagement between his lordship and the young lady, the sort of thing that was announced in *The Morning Post*, renunciation and retirement would be comparatively easy to him; but that having waited in vain for any such assurance he was entitled to act as if the door were not really closed or were at any rate not cruelly locked. He was naturally much struck with my anecdote and still more with my interpretation of it.

"There *is* something, there *is* something—possibly something very grave, certainly something that requires she should make use of artificial aids. She won't admit it publicly, because with her idolatry of her beauty, the feeling she is all made up of, she sees in such aids nothing but the humiliation and the disfigurement. She has used them in secret, but that is evidently not enough, for the affection she suffers from, apparently some definite ailment, has lately grown much worse. She looked straight at me in the shop, which was violently lighted, without seeing it was I. At the same distance, at Folkestone, where as you know I first met her, where I heard this mystery hinted at and where she indignantly denied the thing, she appeared easily enough to recognise people. At present she couldn't really make out anything the shop-girl showed her. She has successfully concealed from the man I saw her with that she resorts in private to a pince-nez and that she does so not only under the strictest orders from an oculist, but because literally the poor thing can't accomplish without such help half the business of life. Iffield however has suspected something, and his suspicions, whether expressed or kept to himself, have put him on the watch. I happened to have a glimpse of the movement at which he pounced on her and caught her in the act."

I had thought it all out; my idea explained many things, and Dawling turned pale as he listened to me.

"Was he rough with her?" he anxiously asked.

"How can I tell what passed between them? I fled from the place."

My companion stared at me a moment. "Do you mean to say her eyesight's going?"

"Heaven forbid! In that case how could she take life as she does?"

"How *does* she take life? That's the question!" He sat there bewilderedly brooding; the tears had come into his eyes; they reminded me of those I had seen in Flora's the day I risked my inquiry. The question he had asked was one that to my own satisfaction I was ready to answer, but I hesitated to let him hear as yet all that my reflections had suggested. I was indeed privately astonished at their ingenuity. For the present I only rejoined that it struck me she was playing a particular game; at which he went on as if he hadn't heard me, suddenly haunted with a fear, lost in the dark possibility I had opened up: "Do you mean there's a danger of anything very bad?" "My dear fellow, you must ask her oculist." "Who in the world *is* her oculist?" "I haven't a conception. But we mustn't get too excited. My impression would be that she has only to observe a few ordinary rules, to exercise a little common sense."

Dawling jumped at this. "I see—to stick to the pince-nez."

"To follow to the letter her oculist's prescription, whatever it is and at whatever cost to her prettiness. It's not a thing to be trifled with."

"Upon my honour it *shan't* be trifled with!" he roundly declared; and he adjusted himself to his position again as if we had quite settled the business. After a considerable interval, while I botched away, he suddenly said: "Did they make a great difference?"

"A great difference?"

"Those things she had put on."

"Oh, the glasses—in her beauty? She looked queer of course, but it was partly because one was unaccustomed. There are women who look charming in nippers. What, at any rate, if she does look queer? She must be mad not to accept that alternative."

"She *is* mad," said Geoffrey Dawling.

"Mad to refuse you, I grant. Besides," I went on, "the pince-nez, which was a large and peculiar one, was all awry: she had half pulled it off, but it continued to stick, and she was crimson, she was angry."

"It must have been horrible!" my companion murmured.

"It *was* horrible. But it's still more horrible to defy all warnings; it's still more horrible to be landed in—" Without saying in what I disgustedly shrugged my shoulders.

After a glance at me Dawling jerked round. "Then you do believe that she may be?"

I hesitated. "The thing would be to make *her* believe it. She only needs a good scare."

"But if that fellow is shocked at the precautions she does take?"

"Oh, who knows?" I rejoined with small sincerity. "I don't suppose Iffield is absolutely a brute."

"I would take her with leather blinders, like a shying mare!" cried Geoffrey Dawling.

I had an impression that Iffield wouldn't, but I didn't communicate it, for I wanted to pacify my friend, whom I had discomposed too much for the purposes of my sitting. I recollect that I did some good work that morning, but it also comes back to me that before we separated he had practically revealed to me that my anecdote, connecting itself in his mind with a series of observations at the time unconscious and unregistered, had covered with light the subject of our colloquy. He had had a formless perception of some secret that drove Miss Saunt to subterfuges, and the more he thought of it the more he guessed this secret to be the practice of making believe she saw when she didn't and of cleverly keeping people from finding out how little she saw. When one patched things together it was astonishing what ground they covered. Just as he was going away he asked me from what source, at Folkestone, the horrid tale had proceeded. When I had given him, as I saw no reason not to do, the name of Mrs. Meldrum, he exclaimed: "Oh, I know all about her; she's a friend of some friends of mine!" At this I remembered wilful Betty and said to myself that I knew some one who would probably prove more wilful still.

VIII

A few days later I again heard Dawling on my stairs, and even before he passed my threshold I knew he had something to tell me.

"I've been down to Folkestone—it was necessary I should see her!" I forget whether he had come straight from the station; he was at any rate out of breath with his news, which it took me however a minute to interpret.

"You mean that you've been with Mrs. Meldrum?"

"Yes; to ask her what she knows and how she comes to know it. It worked upon me awfully—I mean what you told me." He made a visible effort to seem quieter than he was, and it showed me sufficiently that he had not been reassured. I laid, to comfort him and smiling at a venture, a friendly hand on his arm, and he dropped into my eyes, fixing them an instant, a strange, distended look which might have expressed the cold clearness of all that was to come. "I *know*—now!" he said with an emphasis he rarely used.

"What then did Mrs. Meldrum tell you?"

"Only one thing that signified, for she has no real knowledge. But that one thing was everything."

"What is it then?"

"Why, that she can't bear the sight of her." His pronouns required some arranging, but after I had successfully dealt with them I replied that I knew perfectly Miss Saunt had a trick of turning her back on the good lady of Folkestone. But what did that prove? "Have you never guessed? I guessed as soon as she spoke!" Dawling towered over me in dismal triumph. It was the first time in our acquaintance that, intellectually speaking, this had occurred;

but even so remarkable an incident still left me sufficiently at sea to cause him to continue: "Why, the effect of those spectacles!"

I seemed to catch the tail of his idea. "Mrs. Meldrum's?"

"They're so awfully ugly and they increase so the dear woman's ugliness." This remark began to flash a light, and when he quickly added "She sees herself, she sees her own fate!" my response was so immediate that I had almost taken the words out of his mouth. While I tried to fix this sudden image of Flora's face glazed in and cross-barred even as Mrs. Meldrum's was glazed and barred, he went on to assert that only the horror of that image, looming out at herself, could be the reason of her avoiding such a monitress. The fact he had encountered made everything hideously vivid and more vivid than anything else that just such another pair of goggles was what would have been prescribed to Flora.

"I see—I see," I presently rejoined. "What would become of Lord Iffield if she were suddenly to come out in them? What indeed would become of every one, what would become of *everything?*" This was an inquiry that Dawling was evidently unprepared to meet, and I completed it by saying at last: "My dear fellow, for that matter, what would become of *you?*"

Once more he turned on me his good green eyes. "Oh, I shouldn't mind!"

The tone of his words somehow made his ugly face beautiful, and I felt that there dated from this moment in my heart a confirmed affection for him. None the less, at the same time, perversely and rudely, I became aware of a certain drollery in our discussion of such alternatives. It made me laugh out and say to him while I laughed: "You'd take her even with those things of Mrs. Meldrum's?"

He remained mournfully grave; I could see that he was surprised at my rude mirth. But he summoned back a vision of the lady at Folkestone and conscientiously replied: "Even with those things of Mrs. Meldrum's." I begged him not to think my laughter in bad taste: it was only a practical recognition of the fact that we had built a monstrous castle in the air. Didn't he see on what flimsy ground the structure rested? The evidence was preposterously small. He believed the worst, but we were utterly ignorant.

"I shall find out the truth," he promptly replied.

"How can you? If you question her you'll simply drive her to perjure herself. Wherein after all does it concern you to know the truth? It's the girl's own affair."

"Then why did you tell me your story?"

I was a trifle embarrassed. "To warn you off," I returned smiling. He took no more notice of these words than presently to remark that Lord Iffield had no serious intentions. "Very possibly," I said. "But you mustn't speak as if Lord Iffield and you were her only alternatives."

Dawling thought a moment. "Wouldn't the people she has consulted give some information? She must have been to people. How else can she have been condemned?"

"Condemned to what? Condemned to perpetual nippers? Of course she has consulted some of the big specialists, but she has done it, you may be sure, in the most clandestine manner; and even if it were supposable that they would tell you anything—which I altogether doubt—you would have great difficulty in finding out which men they are. Therefore leave it alone; never show her what you suspect."

I even, before he quitted me, asked him to promise me this. "All right, I promise," he said gloomily enough. He was a lover who could tacitly grant the proposition that there was no limit to the deceit his loved one was ready to practise: it made so remarkably little difference. I could see that from this moment he would be filled with a passionate pity ever so little qualified by a sense of the girl's fatuity and folly. She was always accessible to him—that I knew; for if she had told him he was an idiot to dream she could dream of him, she would have resented the imputation of having failed to make it clear that she would always be glad to regard him as a friend. What were most of her friends—what were all of them—but repudiated idiots? I was perfectly aware that in her conversations and confidences I myself for instance had a niche in the gallery. As regards poor Dawling I knew how often he still called on the Hammond Synges. It was not there but under the wing of the Floyd-Taylors that her intimacy with Lord Iffield most flourished. At all events when a week after the visit I have just summarised Flora's name was one morning brought up to me I jumped at the conclusion that Dawling had been with her and even I fear briefly entertained the thought that he had broken his word.

IX

She left me, after she had been introduced, in no suspense about her present motive; she was on the contrary in a visible fever to enlighten me; but I promptly learned that for the alarm with which she pitiably panted our young man was not accountable. She had but one thought in the world, and that thought was for Lord Iffield. I had the strangest, saddest scene with her, and if it did me no other good it at least made me at last completely understand why insidiously, from the first, she had struck me as a creature of tragedy. In showing me the whole of her folly it lifted the curtain of her misery. I don't know how much she meant to tell me when she came—I think she had had plans of elaborate misrepresentation; at any rate she found it at the end of ten minutes the simplest way to break down and sob, to be wretched and true. When she had once begun to let herself go the movement took her off her feet: the relief of it was like the cessation of a cramp. She shared in a word her long secret; she shifted her sharp pain. She brought, I confess, tears to my own eyes, tears of helpless tenderness for her helpless poverty. Her visit however was not quite so memorable in itself as in some of its consequences, the most immediate of which was that I went that afternoon to see Geoffrey Dawling, who had in those days rooms in Welbeck Street, where I presented myself at an hour late enough to warrant the supposition that he might have come in. He had not come in, but he was expected, and I was invited to enter and wait for him: a lady, I was informed, was already in his sitting-room. I hesitated, a little at a loss: it had wildly coursed through my brain that the lady was perhaps Flora Saunt. But when I asked if she were young and remarkably pretty I received so significant a "No, sir!" that I risked an advance and after a minute in this manner found myself, to my astonishment, face to face with Mrs. Meldrum. "Oh, you dear thing," she exclaimed, "I'm delighted to see you: you spare me another compromising *démarche!* But for this I should have called on you also. Know the worst at once: if you see me here it's at least deliberate—it's planned, plotted, shameless. I came up on purpose to see him; upon my word, I'm in love with him. Why, if you valued my peace of mind, did you let him, the other day at Folkestone, dawn upon my delighted eyes? I took there in half an hour the most extraordinary fancy to him. With a perfect sense of everything that can be urged against him, I find him none the less the very pearl of men. However, I haven't come up to declare my passion—I've come to bring him news that will interest him much more. Above all I've come to urge upon him to be careful."

"About Flora Saunt?"

"About what he says and does: he must be as still as a mouse! She's at last really engaged."

"But it's a tremendous secret?" I was moved to merriment.

"Precisely: she telegraphed me this noon, and spent another shilling to tell me that not a creature in the world is yet to know it."

"She had better have spent it to tell you that she had just passed an hour with the creature you see before you."

"She has just passed an hour with every one in the place!" Mrs. Meldrum cried. "They've vital reasons, she wired, for it's not coming out for a month. Then it will be formally announced, but meanwhile her happiness is delirious. I daresay Mr. Dawling already knows, and he may, as it's nearly seven o'clock, have jumped off London Bridge; but an effect of the talk I had with him the other day was to make me, on receipt of my telegram, feel it to be my duty to warn him in person against taking action, as it were, on the horrid certitude which I could see he carried away with him. I had added somehow to that certitude. He told me what you had told him you had seen in your shop."

Mrs. Meldrum, I perceived, had come to Welbeck Street on an errand identical with my own—a circumstance indicating her rare sagacity, inasmuch as her ground for undertaking it was a very different thing from what Flora's wonderful visit had made of mine. I remarked to her that what I had seen in the shop was sufficiently striking, but that I had seen a great deal more that morning in my studio. "In short," I said, "I've seen everything."

She was mystified. "Everything?"

"The poor creature is under the darkest of clouds. Oh, she came to triumph, but she remained to talk something approaching to sense! She put herself completely in my hands—she does me the honour to intimate that of all her friends I'm the most disinterested. After she had announced to me that Lord Iffield was bound hands and feet and that for the present I was absolutely the only person in the secret, she arrived at her real business. She had had a suspicion of me ever since the day, at Folkestone, I asked her for the truth about her eyes. The truth is what you and I both guessed. She has no end of a danger hanging over her."

"But from what cause? I, who by God's mercy have kept mine, know everything that can be known about eyes," said Mrs. Meldrum.

"She might have kept hers if she had profited by God's mercy, if she had done in time, done years ago, what was imperatively ordered her; if she hadn't in fine been cursed with the loveliness that was to make her behaviour a thing of fable. She may keep them still if she'll sacrifice—and after all so little—that purely superficial charm. She must do as you've done; she must wear, dear lady, what you wear!"

What my companion wore glittered for the moment like a melon-frame in August. "Heaven forgive her—now I understand!" She turned pale.

But I wasn't afraid of the effect on her good nature of her thus seeing, through her great goggles, why it had always been that Flora held her at such a distance. "I can't tell you," I said, "from what special affection, what state of the eye, her danger proceeds: that's the one thing she succeeded this morning in keeping from me. She knows it herself perfectly; she has had the best advice in Europe. 'It's a thing that's awful, simply awful'—that was the only account she would give me. Year before last, while she was at Boulogne, she went for three days with Mrs. Floyd-Taylor to Paris. She there surreptitiously consulted the greatest man—even Mrs. Floyd-Taylor doesn't know. Last autumn, in Germany, she did the same. 'First put on certain special spectacles with a straight bar in the middle: then we'll talk'—that's practically what they say. What *she* says is that she'll put on anything in nature when she's married, but that she must get married first. She has always meant to do everything as soon as she's married. Then and then only she'll be safe. How will any one ever look at her if she makes herself a fright? How could she ever have got engaged if she had made herself a fright from the first? It's no use to insist that with her beauty she can never *be* a fright. She said to me this morning, poor girl, the most characteristic, the most harrowing things. 'My face is all I have—and *such* a face! I knew from the first I could do anything with it. But I needed it all—I need it still, every exquisite inch of it. It isn't as if I had a figure or anything else. Oh, if God had only given me a figure too, I don't say! Yes, with a figure, a really good one, like Fanny Floyd-Taylor's, who's hideous, I'd have risked plain glasses. *Que voulez-vous?* No one is perfect.' She says she still has money left, but I don't believe a word of it. She has been speculating on her impunity, on the idea that her danger would hold off: she has literally been running a race with it. Her theory has been, as you from the first so clearly saw, that she'd get in ahead. She swears to me that though the 'bar' is too cruel she wears when she's alone what she has been ordered to wear. But when the deuce is she alone? It's herself of course that she has swindled worst: she has put herself off, so insanely that even her vanity but half accounts for it, with little inadequate concessions, little false measures and preposterous evasions and childish hopes. Her great terror is now that Iffield, who already has suspicions, who has found out her pince-nez but whom she has beguiled with some unblushing hocus-pocus, may discover the dreadful facts; and the essence of what she wanted this morning was in that interest to square me, to get me to deny indignantly and authoritatively (for isn't she my 'favourite sitter'?) that she has anything whatever the matter with any part of her. She sobbed, she 'went on,' she entreated; after we got talking her extraordinary nerve left her and she showed me what she has been through—showed me also all her terror of the harm I could do her. 'Wait till I'm married! wait till I'm married!' She took hold of me, she almost sank on her knees. It seems to me highly immoral, one's participation in her fraud; but there's no doubt that she *must* be married: I don't know what I don't see behind it! Therefore," I wound up, "Dawling must keep his hands off."

Mrs. Meldrum had held her breath; she exhaled a long moan. "Well, that's exactly what I came here to tell him."

"Then here he is." Our unconscious host had just opened the door. Immensely startled at finding us he turned a frightened look from one to the other, as if to guess what disaster we were there to announce or avert.

Mrs. Meldrum, on the spot, was all gaiety. "I've come to return your sweet visit. Ah," she laughed, "I mean to keep up the acquaintance!"

"Do—do," he murmured mechanically and absently, continuing to look at us. Then abruptly he broke out: "He's going to marry her."

I was surprised. "You already know?"

He had had in his hand an evening newspaper; he tossed it down on the table. "It's in that."

"Published—already?" I was still more surprised.

"Oh, Flora can't keep a secret!" Mrs. Meldrum humorously declared. She went up to poor Dawling and laid a motherly hand upon him. "It's all right—it's just as it ought to be: don't think about her ever any more." Then as he met this adjuration with a dismal stare in which the thought of her was as abnormally vivid as the colour of the pupil, the excellent woman put up her funny face and tenderly kissed him on the cheek.

X

I have spoken of these reminiscences as of a row of coloured beads, and I confess that as I continue to straighten out my chaplet I am rather proud of the comparison. The beads are all there, as I said—they slip along the string in their small, smooth roundness. Geoffrey Daw-ling accepted like a gentleman the event his evening paper had proclaimed; in view of which I snatched a moment to murmur him a hint to offer Mrs. Meldrum his hand. He returned me a heavy head-shake, and I judged that marriage would henceforth strike him very much as the traffic of the street may strike some poor incurable at the window of an hospital. Circumstances arising at this time promptly led to my making an absence from England, and circumstances already existing offered him a solid basis for similar action. He had after all the usual resource of a Briton—he could take to his boats.

He started on a journey round the globe, and I was left with nothing but my inference as to what might have happened. Later observation however only confirmed my belief that if at any time during the couple of months that followed Flora Saunt's brilliant engagement he had made up, as they say, to the good lady of Folkestone, that good lady would not have pushed him over the cliff. Strange as she was to behold I knew of cases in which she had been obliged to administer that shove. I went to New York to paint a couple of portraits; but I found, once on the spot, that I had counted without Chicago, where I was invited to blot out this harsh discrimination by the production of no less than ten. I spent a year in America and should probably have spent a second had I not been summoned back to England by alarming news from my mother. Her strength had failed, and as soon as I reached London I hurried down to Folkestone, arriving just at the moment to offer a welcome to some slight symptom of a rally. She had been much worse, but she was now a little better; and though I found nothing but satisfaction in having come to her I saw after a few hours that my London studio, where arrears of work had already met me, would be my place to await whatever might next occur. Before returning to town however I had every reason to sally forth in search of Mrs. Meldrum, from whom, in so many months, I had not had a line, and my view of whom, with the adjacent objects, as I had left them, had been intercepted by a luxuriant foreground.

Before I had gained her house I met her, as I supposed, coming toward me across the down, greeting me from afar with the familiar twinkle of her great vitreous badge; and as it was late in the autumn and the esplanade was a blank I was free to acknowledge this signal by cutting a caper on the grass.

My enthusiasm dropped indeed the next moment, for it had taken me but a few seconds to perceive that the person thus assaulted had by no means the figure of my military friend. I felt a shock much greater than any I should have thought possible as on this person's drawing near I identified her as poor little Flora Saunt. At what moment Flora had recognised me belonged to an order of mysteries over which, it quickly came home to me, one would never linger again: I could intensely reflect that once we were face to face it chiefly mattered that I should succeed in looking still more intensely unastonished. All I saw at first was the big gold bar crossing each of her lenses, over which something convex and grotesque, like the eyes of a large insect, something that now represented her whole personality, seemed, as out of the orifice of a prison, to strain forward and press. The face had shrunk away: it looked smaller, appeared even to look plain; it was at all events, so far as the effect on a spectator was concerned, wholly sacrificed to this huge apparatus of sight. There was no smile in it, and she made no motion to take my offered hand.

"I had no idea you were down here!" I exclaimed; and I wondered whether she didn't know me at all or knew me only by my voice.

"You thought I was Mrs. Meldrum," she very quietly remarked.

It was the quietness itself that made me feel the necessity of an answer almost violently gay. "Oh yes," I laughed, "you have a tremendous deal in common with Mrs. Meldrum! I've just returned to England after a long absence and I'm on my way to see her. Won't you come with me?" It struck me that her old reason for keeping clear of our friend was well disposed of now.

"I've just left her; I'm staying with her." She stood solemnly fixing me with her goggles. "Would you like to paint me *now?*" she asked. She seemed to speak, with intense gravity, from behind a mask or a cage.

There was nothing to do but to treat the question with the same exuberance. "It would be a fascinating little artistic problem!" That something was wrong it was not difficult to perceive; but a good deal more than met the eye might be presumed to be wrong if Flora was under Mrs. Meldrum's roof. I had not for a year had much time to think of her, but my imagination had had sufficient warrant for lodging her in more gilded halls. One of the last things I had heard before leaving England was that in commemoration of the new relationship she had gone to stay with Lady Considine. This had made me take everything else for granted, and the noisy American world had deafened my ears to possible contradictions. Her spectacles were at present a direct contradiction; they seemed a negation not only of new relationships but of every old one as well. I remember nevertheless that when after a moment she walked beside me on the grass I found myself nervously hoping she wouldn't as yet at any rate tell me anything very dreadful; so that to stave off this danger I harried her with questions about Mrs. Meldrum and, without waiting for replies, became profuse on the subject of my own doings. My companion was completely silent, and I felt both as if she were watching my nervousness with a sort of sinister irony and as if I were talking to some different, strange person. Flora plain and obscure and soundless was no Flora at all. At Mrs. Meldrum's door she turned off with the observation that as there was certainly a great deal I should have to say to our friend she had better not go in with me. I looked at her again—I had been keeping my eyes away from her— but only to meet her magnified stare. I greatly desired in truth to see Mrs. Meldrum alone, but there was something so pitiful in the girl's predicament that I hesitated to fall in with this idea of dropping her. Yet one couldn't express a compassion without seeming to take too much wretchedness for granted. I reflected that I must really figure to her as a fool, which was an entertainment I had never expected to give her. It rolled over me there for the first time—it has come back to me since—that there is, strangely, in very deep misfortune a dignity finer even than in the most inveterate habit of being all right. I couldn't have to her the manner of treating it as a mere detail that I was face to face with a part of what, at our last meeting, we had had such a scene about; but while I was trying to think of some manner that I *could* have she said quite colourlessly, yet somehow as if she might never see me again: "Goodbye. I'm going to take my walk."

"All alone?"

She looked round the great bleak cliff-top. "With whom should I go? Besides, I like to be alone—for the present."

This gave me the glimmer of a vision that she regarded her disfigurement as temporary, and the confidence came to me that she would never, for her happiness, cease to be a creature of illusions. It enabled me to exclaim, smiling brightly and feeling indeed idiotic: "Oh, I shall see you again! But I hope you'll have a very pleasant walk."

"All my walks are very pleasant, thank you—they do me such a lot of good." She was as quiet as a mouse, and her words seemed to me stupendous in their wisdom. "I take several a day," she continued. She might have been an ancient woman responding with humility at the church door to the patronage of the parson. "The more I take the better I feel. I'm ordered by the doctors to keep all the while in the air and go in for plenty of exercise. It keeps up my general health, you know, and if that goes on improving as it has lately done everything will soon be all right. All that was the matter with me before—and always; it was too reckless!—was that I neglected my general health. It acts directly on the state of the particular organ. So I'm going three miles."

I grinned at her from the doorstep while Mrs. Meldrum's maid stood there to admit me. "Oh, I'm so glad," I said, looking at her as she paced away with the pretty flutter she had kept and remembering the day when, while she rejoined Lord Iffield, I had indulged in the same observation. Her air of assurance was on this occasion not less than it had been on that; but I recalled that she had then struck me as marching off to her doom. Was she really now marching away from it?

XI

As soon as I saw Mrs. Meldrum I broke out to her. "Is there anything in it? *Is* her general health—?"

Mrs. Meldrum interrupted me with her great amused blare. "You've already seen her and she has told you her wondrous tale? What's 'in it' is what has been in everything she has ever done—the most comical, tragical belief in herself. She thinks she's doing a 'cure.'"

"And what does her husband think?"

"Her husband? What husband?"

"Hasn't she then married Lord Iffield?"

"*Vous-en-êtes là?*" cried my hostess. "He behaved like a regular beast."

"How should I know? You never wrote to me."

Mrs. Meldrum hesitated, covering me with what poor Flora called the particular organ. "No, I didn't write to you; and I abstained on purpose. If I didn't I thought you mightn't, over there, hear what had happened. If you should hear I was afraid you would stir up Mr. Dawling."

"Stir him up?"

"Urge him to fly to the rescue; write out to him that there was another chance for him."

"I wouldn't have done it," I said.

"Well," Mrs. Meldrum replied, "it was not my business to give you an opportunity."

"In short you were afraid of it."

Again she hesitated and though it may have been only my fancy I thought she considerably reddened. At all events she laughed out. Then "I was afraid of it!" she very honestly answered.

"But doesn't he know? Has he given no sign?"

"Every sign in life—he came straight back to her. He did everything to get her to listen to him; but she hasn't the smallest idea of it."

"Has he seen her as she is now?" I presently and just a trifle awkwardly inquired.

"Indeed he has, and borne it like a hero. He told me all about it."

"How much you've all been through!" I ventured to ejaculate. "Then what has become of him?"

"He's at home in Hampshire. He has got back his old place and I believe by this time his old sisters. It's not half a bad little place."

"Yet its attractions say nothing to Flora?"

"Oh, Flora's by no means on her back!" my interlocutress laughed.

"She's not on her back because she's on yours. Have you got her for the rest of your life?"

Once more my hostess genially glared at me. "Did she tell you how much the Hammond Synges have kindly left her to live on? Not quite eighty pounds a year."

"That's a good deal, but it won't pay the oculist. What was it that at last induced her to submit to him?"

"Her general collapse after that brute of an Iffield's rupture. She cried her eyes out—she passed through a horror of black darkness. Then came a gleam of light, and the light appears to have broadened. She went into goggles as repentant Magdalens go into the Catholic Church."

"Yet you don't think she'll be saved?"

"*She* thinks she will—that's all I can tell you. There's no doubt that when once she brought herself to accept her real remedy, as she calls it, she began to enjoy a relief that she had never known. That feeling, very new and in spite of what she pays for it most refreshing, has given her something to hold on by, begotten in her foolish little mind a belief that, as she says, she's on the mend and that in the course of time, if she leads a tremendously healthy life, she'll be able to take off her muzzle and become as dangerous again as ever. It keeps her going."

"And what keeps *you?* You're good until the parties begin again."

"Oh, she doesn't object to me now!" smiled Mrs. Meldrum. "I'm going to take her abroad; we shall be a pretty pair." I was struck with this energy and after a moment I inquired the reason of it. "It's to divert her mind," my friend replied, reddening again, I thought, a little. "We shall go next week: I've only waited, to start, to see how your mother would be." I expressed to her hereupon my sense of her extraordinary merit and also that of the inconceivability of Flora's fancying herself still in a situation not to jump at the chance of marrying a man like Dawling. "She says he's too ugly; she says he's too dreary; she says in fact he's 'nobody,'" Mrs. Meldrum pursued. "She says above all that he's not 'her own sort.' She doesn't deny that he's good, but she insists on the fact that he's grotesque. He's quite the last person she would ever dream of." I was almost disposed on hearing this to protest that if the girl had so little proper feeling her noble suitor had perhaps served her right; but after a while my curiosity as to just how her noble suitor *had* served her got the better of that emotion, and I asked a question or two which led my companion again to apply to him the invidious epithet I have already quoted. What had happened was simply that Flora had at the eleventh hour broken down in the attempt to put him off with an uncandid account of her infirmity and that his lordship's interest in her had not been proof against the discovery of the way she had practised on him. Her dissimulation, he was obliged to perceive, had been infernally deep. The future in short assumed a new complexion for him when looked at through the grim glasses of a bride who, as he had said to some one, couldn't really, when you came to find out, see her hand before her face. He had conducted himself like any other jockeyed customer—he had returned the animal as unsound. He had backed out in his own way, giving the business, by some sharp shuffle, such a turn as to make the rupture ostensibly Flora's, but he had none the less remorselessly and basely backed out. He had cared for her lovely face, cared for it in the amused and haunted way it had been her poor little delusive gift to make men care; and her lovely face, damn it, with the monstrous gear she had begun to rig upon it, was just what had let him in. He had in the judgment of his family done everything that could be expected of him; he had made— Mrs. Meldrum had herself seen the letter—a "handsome" offer of pecuniary compensation. Oh, if Flora, with her incredible buoyancy, was in a manner on her feet again now, it was not that she had not for weeks and weeks been prone in the dust. Strange were the humiliations, the prostrations it was given to some natures to survive. That Flora had survived was perhaps after all a sort of sign that she was reserved for some final mercy. "But she has been in the abysses at any rate," said Mrs. Meldrum, "and I really don't think I can tell you what pulled her through."

"I think I can tell *you*," I said. "What in the world but Mrs. Meldrum?"

At the end of an hour Flora had not come in, and I was obliged to announce that I should have but time to reach the station, where, in charge of my mother's servant, I was to find my luggage. Mrs. Meldrum put before me the question of waiting till a later train, so as not to lose our young lady; but I confess I gave this alternative a consideration less profound than I pretended. Somehow I didn't care if I did lose our young lady. Now that I knew the worst that had befallen her it struck me still less as possible to meet her on the ground of condolence; and with the melancholy aspect she wore to me what other ground was left? I lost her, but I caught my train. In truth she was so changed that one hated to see it; and now that she was in charitable hands one didn't feel compelled to make great efforts. I had studied her face for a particular beauty; I had lived with that beauty and reproduced it; but I knew what belonged to my trade well enough to be sure it was gone for ever.

XII

I was soon called back to Folkestone; but Mrs. Meldrum and her young friend had already left England, finding to that end every convenience on the spot and not having had to come up to town. My thoughts however were so painfully engaged there that I should in any case have had little attention for them: the event occurred that was to bring my series of visits to a close. When this high tide had ebbed I returned to America and to my interrupted work, which had opened out on such a scale that, with a deep plunge into a great chance, I was three good years in rising again to the surface. There are nymphs and naiads moreover in the American depths: they may have had something to do with the duration of my dive. I mention them to account for a grave misdemeanour—the fact that after the first year I rudely neglected

Mrs. Meldrum. She had written to me from Florence after my mother's death and had mentioned in a postscript that in our young lady's calculations the lowest numbers were now Italian counts. This was a good omen, and if in subsequent letters there was no news of a sequel I was content to accept small things and to believe that grave tidings, should there be any, would come to me in due course. The gravity of what might happen to a featherweight became indeed with time and distance less appreciable, and I was not without an impression that Mrs. Meldrum, whose sense of proportion was not the least of her merits, had no idea of boring the world with the ups and downs of her pensioner. The poor girl grew dusky and dim, a small fitful memory, a regret tempered by the comfortable consciousness of how kind Mrs. Meldrum would always be to her. I was professionally more preoccupied than I had ever been, and I had swarms of pretty faces in my eyes and a chorus of high voices in my ears. Geoffrey Dawling had on his return to England written me two or three letters: his last information had been that he was going into the figures of rural illiteracy. I was delighted to receive it and had no doubt that if he should go into figures they would, as they are said to be able to prove anything, prove at least that my advice was sound and that he had wasted time enough. This quickened on my part another hope, a hope suggested by some roundabout rumour—I forget how it reached me—that he was engaged to a girl down in Hampshire. He turned out not to be, but I felt sure that if only he went into figures deep enough he would become, among the girls down in Hampshire or elsewhere, one of those numerous prizes of battle whose defences are practically not on the scale of their provocations. I nursed in short the thought that it was probably open to him to become one of the types as to which, as the years go on, frivolous and superficial spectators lose themselves in the wonder that they ever succeeded in winning even the least winsome mates. He never alluded to Flora Saunt; and there was in his silence about her, quite as in Mrs. Meldrum's, an element of instinctive tact, a brief implication that if you didn't happen to have been in love with her she was not an inevitable topic.

Within a week after my return to London I went to the opera, of which I had always been much of a devotee. I arrived too late for the first act of "Lohengrin," but the second was just beginning, and I gave myself up to it with no more than a glance at the house. When it was over I treated myself, with my glass, from my place in the stalls, to a general survey of the boxes, making doubtless on their contents the reflections, pointed by comparison, that are most familiar to the wanderer restored to London. There was a certain proportion of pretty women, but I suddenly became aware that one of these was far prettier than the others. This lady, alone in one of the smaller receptacles of the grand tier and already the aim of fifty tentative glasses, which she sustained with admirable serenity—this single exquisite figure, placed in the quarter furthest removed from my stall, was a person, I immediately felt, to cause one's curiosity to linger. Dressed in white, with diamonds in her hair and pearls on her neck, she had a pale radiance of beauty which even at that distance made her a distinguished presence and, with the air that easily attaches to lonely loveliness in public places, an agreeable mystery. A mystery however she remained to me only for a minute after I had levelled my glass at her: I feel to this moment the startled thrill, the shock almost of joy with which I suddenly encountered in her vague brightness a rich revival of Flora Saunt. I say a revival because, to put it crudely, I had on that last occasion left poor Flora for dead. At present perfectly alive again, she was altered only, as it were, by resurrection. A little older, a little quieter, a little finer and a good deal fairer, she was simply transfigured by recovery. Sustained by the reflection that even recovery wouldn't enable her to distinguish me in the crowd, I was free to look at her well. Then it was it came home to me that my vision of her in her great goggles had been cruelly final. As her beauty was all there was of her, that machinery had extinguished her, and so far as I had thought of her in the interval I had thought of her as buried in the tomb her stern specialist had built. With the sense that she had escaped from it came a lively wish to return to her; and if I didn't straightway leave my place and rush round the theatre and up to her box it was because I was fixed to the spot some moments longer by the simple inability to cease looking at her.

She had been from the first of my seeing her practically motionless, leaning back in her chair with a kind of thoughtful grace and with her eyes vaguely directed, as it seemed to me, to one of the boxes on my side of the house and consequently over my head and out of my sight. The only movement she made for some time was to finger with an ungloved hand

and as if with the habit of fondness the row of pearls on her neck, which my glass showed me to be large and splendid. Her diamonds and pearls, in her solitude, mystified me, making me, as she had had no such brave jewels in the days of the Hammond Synges, wonder what undreamt-of improvement had taken place in her fortunes. The ghost of a question hovered there a moment: could anything so prodigious have happened as that on her tested and proved amendment Lord Iffield had taken her back? This could not have occurred without my hearing of it; and moreover if she had become a person of such fashion where was the little court one would naturally see at her elbow? Her isolation was puzzling, though it could easily suggest that she was but momentarily alone. If she had come with Mrs. Meldrum that lady would have taken advantage of the interval to pay a visit to some other box— doubtless the box at which Flora had just been looking. Mrs. Meldrum didn't account for the jewels, but the refreshment of Flora's beauty accounted for anything. She presently moved her eyes over the house, and I felt them brush me again like the wings of a dove. I don't know what quick pleasure flickered into the hope that she would at last see me. She did see me: she suddenly bent forward to take up the little double-barrelled ivory glass that rested on the edge of the box and, to all appearance, fix me with it. I smiled from my place straight up at the searching lenses, and after an instant she dropped them and smiled as straight back at me. Oh, her smile: it was her old smile, her young smile, her peculiar smile made perfect! I instantly left my stall and hurried off for a nearer view of it; quite flushed, I remember, as I went, with the annoyance of having happened to think of the idiotic way I had tried to paint her. Poor Iffield with his sample of that error, and still poorer Dawling in particular with his! I hadn't touched her, I was professionally humiliated, and as the attendant in the lobby opened her box for me I felt that the very first thing I should have to say to her would be that she must absolutely sit to me again.

XIII

She gave me the smile once more as over her shoulder, from her chair, she turned her face to me. "Here you are again!" she exclaimed with her disgloved hand put up a little backward for me to take. I dropped into a chair just behind her and, having taken it and noted that one of the curtains of the box would make the demonstration sufficiently private, bent my lips over it and impressed them on its finger-tips. It was given me however, to my astonishment, to feel next that all the privacy in the world couldn't have sufficed to mitigate the start with which she greeted this free application of my moustache: the blood had jumped to her face, she quickly recovered her hand and jerked at me, twisting herself round, a vacant, challenging stare. During the next few instants several extraordinary things happened, the first of which was that now I was close to them the eyes of loveliness I had come up to look into didn't show at all the conscious light I had just been pleased to see them flash across the house: they showed on the contrary, to my confusion, a strange, sweet blankness, an expression I failed to give a meaning to until, without delay, I felt on my arm, directed to it as if instantly to efface the effect of her start, the grasp of the hand she had impulsively snatched from me. It was the irrepressible question in this grasp that stopped on my lips all sound of salutation. She had mistaken my entrance for that of another person, a pair of lips without a moustache. She was feeling me to see who I was! With the perception of this and of her not seeing me I sat gaping at her and at the wild word that didn't come, the right word to express or to disguise my stupefaction. What was the right word to commemorate one's sudden discovery, at the very moment too at which one had been most encouraged to count on better things, that one's dear old friend had gone blind? Before the answer to this question dropped upon me—and the moving moments, though few, seemed many—I heard, with the sound of voices, the click of the attendant's key on the other side of the door. Poor Flora heard also, and with the hearing, still with her hand on my arm, she brightened again as I had a minute since seen her brighten across the house: she had the sense of the return of the person she had taken me for—the person with the right pair of lips, as to whom I was for that matter much more in the dark than she. I gasped, but my word had come: if she had lost her sight it was in this very loss that she had found again her beauty. I managed to speak while we were still alone, before her companion had appeared. "You're lovelier at this day than you have ever been in your life!" At the sound of my voice and that of the opening of the door her excitement broke into audible joy. She sprang up, recognising me, always holding me, and gleefully cried to a gentleman who was arrested in the doorway by the sight of me: "He has come back, he has come back, and you should have heard what he says of me!" The gentleman was Geoffrey Dawling, and I thought it best to let him hear on the spot. "How beautiful she is, my dear man—but how extraordinarily beautiful! More beautiful at this hour than ever, ever before!"

It gave them almost equal pleasure and made Dawling blush up to his eyes; while this in turn produced, in spite of deepened astonishment, a blessed snap of the strain that I had been under for some moments. I wanted to embrace them both, and while the opening bars of another scene rose from the orchestra I almost did embrace Dawling, whose first emotion on beholding me had visibly and ever so oddly been a consciousness of guilt. I had caught him somehow in the act, though that was as yet all I knew; but by the time we had sunk noiselessly into our chairs again (for the music was supreme, Wagner passed first) my demonstration ought pretty well to have given him the limit of the criticism he had to fear. I myself indeed, while the opera blazed, was only too afraid he might divine in our silent closeness the very moral of my optimism, which was simply the comfort I had gathered from seeing that if our companion's beauty lived again her vanity partook of its life. I had hit on the right note—that was what eased me off: it drew all pain for the next half-hour from the sense of the deep darkness in which the stricken woman sat there. If the music, in that darkness, happily soared and swelled for her, it beat its wings in unison with those of a gratified passion. A great deal came and went between us without profaning the occasion, so that I could feel at the end of twenty minutes as if I knew almost everything he might in kindness have to tell me; knew even why Flora, while I stared at her from the stalls, had misled me by the use of ivory and crystal and by appearing to recognise me and smile. She leaned back in her chair in luxurious ease: I had from the first become aware that the way she fingered her pearls was a sharp image of the wedded state. Nothing of old had seemed wanting to her assurance; but I hadn't then dreamed of the art with which she would wear that assurance as a married woman. She had taken him when everything had failed; he had taken her when she herself had done so. His embarrassed eyes confessed it all, confessed the deep peace he found in it. They only didn't tell me why he had not written to me, nor clear up as yet a minor obscurity. Flora after a while again lifted the glass from the ledge of the box and elegantly swept the house with it. Then, by the mere instinct of her grace, a motion but half conscious, she inclined her head into the void with the sketch of a salute, producing, I could see, a perfect imitation of a response to some homage. Dawling and I looked at each other again: the tears came into his eyes. She was playing at perfection still, and her misfortune only simplified the process.

I recognised that this was as near as I should ever come, certainly as I should come that night, to pressing on her misfortune. Neither of us would name it more than we were doing then, and Flora would never name it at all. Little by little I perceived that what had occurred was, strange as it might appear, the best thing for her happiness. The question was now only of her beauty and her being seen and marvelled at: with Dawling to do for her everything in life her activity was limited to that. Such an activity was all within her scope: it asked nothing of her that she couldn't splendidly give. As from time to time in our delicate communion she turned her face to me with the parody of a look I lost none of the signs of its strange new glory. The expression of the eyes was a bit of pastel put in by a master's thumb; the whole head, stamped with a sort of showy suffering, had gained a fineness from what she had passed through. Yes, Flora was settled for life—nothing could hurt her further. I foresaw the particular praise she would mostly incur—she would be incomparably "interesting." She would charm with her pathos more even than she had charmed with her pleasure. For herself above all she was fixed for ever, rescued from all change and ransomed from all doubt. Her old certainties, her old vanities were justified and sanctified, and in the darkness that had closed upon her one object remained clear. That object, as unfading as a mosaic mask, was fortunately the loveliest she could possibly look upon. The greatest blessing of all was of course that Dawling thought so. Her future was ruled with the straightest line, and so for that matter was his. There were two facts to which before I left my friends I gave time to sink into my spirit. One of them was that he had changed by some process as effective as Flora's change; had been simplified somehow into service as she had been simplified into success. He was such a picture of inspired intervention as I had never yet encountered: he would exist henceforth for the sole purpose of rendering unnecessary, or rather impossible, any reference even on her own part to his wife's infirmity. Oh yes, how little desire he would ever give *me* to refer to it! He principally after a while made me feel—and this was my second lesson—that, good-natured as he was, my being there to see it all oppressed him; so that by the time the act ended I recognised that I too had filled out my hour. Dawling remembered things; I think he caught in my very face the irony of old judgments: they made him thresh about in his chair. I said to Flora as I took leave of her that I would come to see her; but I may mention that I never went. I'll go to-morrow if I hear she wants me; but what in the world can she ever want? As I quitted them I laid my hand on Dawling's arm and drew him for a moment into the lobby.

"Why did you never write to me of your marriage?"

He smiled uncomfortably, showing his long yellow teeth and something more. "I don't know—the whole thing gave me such a tremendous lot to do."

This was the first dishonest speech I had heard him make: he really hadn't written to me because he had an idea I would think him a still bigger fool than before. I didn't insist, but I tried there, in the lobby, so far as a pressure of his hand could serve me, to give him a notion of what I thought him. "I can't at any rate make out," I said, "why I didn't hear from Mrs. Meldrum."

"She didn't write to you?"

"Never a word. What has become of her?"

"I think she's at Folkestone," Dawling returned; "but I'm sorry to say that practically she has ceased to see us."

"You haven't quarrelled with her?"

"How *could* we? Think of all we owe her. At the time of our marriage, and for months before, she did everything for us: I don't know how we should have managed without her. But since then she has never been near us and has given us rather markedly little encouragement to try and keep up our relations with her."

I was struck with this though of course I admit I am struck with all sorts of things. "Well," I said after a moment, "even if I could imagine a reason for that attitude it wouldn't explain why she shouldn't have taken account of *my* natural interest."

"Just so." Dawling's face was a windowless wall. He could contribute nothing to the mystery, and, quitting him, I carried it away. It was not till I went down to see Mrs. Meldrum that it was really dispelled. She didn't want to hear of them or to talk of them, not a bit, and it was just in the same spirit that she hadn't wanted to write of them. She had done everything in the world for them, but now, thank heaven, the hard business was over. After I had taken this in, which I was quick to do, we quite avoided the subject. She simply couldn't bear it.

THE NEXT TIME

Mrs. Highmore's errand this morning was odd enough to deserve commemoration: she came to ask me to write a notice of her great forthcoming work. Her great works have come forth so frequently without my assistance that I was sufficiently entitled on this occasion to open my eyes; but what really made me stare was the ground on which her request reposed, and what leads me to record the incident is the train of memory lighted by that explanation. Poor Ray Limbert, while we talked, seemed to sit there between us: she reminded me that my acquaintance with him had begun, eighteen years ago, with her having come in precisely as she came in this morning to bespeak my charity for him. If she didn't know then how little my charity was worth she is at least enlightened about it to-day, and this is just the circumstance that makes the drollery of her visit. As I hold up the torch to the dusky years—by which I mean as I cipher up with a pen that stumbles and stops the figured column of my reminiscences—I see that Limbert's public hour, or at least my small apprehension of it, is rounded by those two occasions. It was *finis*, with a little moralising flourish, that Mrs. Highmore seemed to trace to-day at the bottom of the page. "One of the most voluminous writers of the time," she has often repeated this sign; but never, I daresay, in spite of her professional command of appropriate emotion, with an equal sense of that mystery and that sadness of things which to people of imagination generally hover over the close of human histories. This romance at any rate is bracketed by her early and her late appeal; and when its melancholy protrusions had caught the declining light again from my half-hour's talk with her I took a private vow to recover while that light still lingers something of the delicate flush, to pick out with a brief patience the perplexing lesson.

It was wonderful to observe how for herself Mrs. Highmore had already done so: she wouldn't have hesitated to announce to me what was the matter with Ralph Limbert, or at all events to give me a glimpse of the high admonition she had read in his career. There could have been no better proof of the vividness of this parable, which we were really in our pleasant sympathy quite at one about, than that Mrs. Highmore, of all hardened sinners, should have been converted. This indeed was not news to me: she impressed upon me that for the last ten years she had wanted to do something artistic, something as to which she was prepared not to care a rap whether or no it should sell. She brought home to me further that it had been mainly seeing what her brother-in-law did and how he did it that had wedded her to this perversity. As *he* didn't sell, dear soul, and as several persons, of whom I was one, thought highly of that, the fancy had taken her—taken her even quite early in her prolific course—of reaching, if only once, the same heroic eminence. She yearned to be, like Limbert, but of course only once, an exquisite failure. There was something a failure was, a failure in the market, that a success somehow wasn't. A success was as prosaic as a good dinner: there was nothing more to be said about it than that you had had it. Who but vulgar people, in such a case, made gloating remarks about the courses? It was often by such vulgar people that a success was attested. It made if you came to look at it nothing but money; that is it made so much that any other result showed small in comparison. A failure now could make—oh, with the aid of immense talent of course, for there were failures and failures—such a reputation! She did me the honour—she had often done it—to intimate that what she meant by reputation was seeing *me* toss a flower. If it took a failure to catch a failure I was by my own admission well qualified to place the laurel. It was because she had made so much money and Mr. Highmore had taken such care of it that she could treat herself to an hour of pure glory. She perfectly remembered that as often as I had heard her heave that sigh I had been prompt with my declaration that a book sold might easily be as glorious as a book unsold. Of course she knew this, but she knew also that it was the age of trash triumphant and that she had never heard me speak of anything that had "done well" exactly as she had sometimes heard me speak of something that hadn't—with just two or three words of respect which, when I used them, seemed to convey more than they commonly stood for, seemed to hush up the discussion a little, as if for the very beauty of the secret.

I may declare in regard to these allusions that, whatever I then thought of myself as a holder of the scales I had never scrupled to laugh out at the humour of Mrs. Highmore's pursuit of quality at any price. It had never rescued her even for a day from the hard doom of popularity, and though I never gave her my word for it there was no reason at all why it should. The public *would* have her, as her husband used roguishly to remark; not indeed that, making her bargains, standing up to her publishers and even, in his higher flights, to her reviewers, he ever had a glimpse of her attempted conspiracy against her genius, or rather as I may say against mine. It was not that when she tried to be what she called subtle (for wasn't Limbert subtle, and wasn't I?) her fond consumers, bless them, didn't suspect the trick nor show what they thought of it: they straightway rose on the contrary to the morsel she had hoped to hold too high, and, making but a big, cheerful bite of it, wagged their great collective tail artlessly for more. It was not given to her not to please, nor granted even to her best refinements to affright. I have always respected the mystery of those humiliations, but I was fully aware this morning that they were practically the reason why she had come to me. Therefore when she said with the flush of a bold joke in her kind, coarse face "What I feel is, you know, that *you* could settle me if you only would." I knew quite well what she meant. She meant that of old it had always appeared to be the fine blade, as some one had hyperbolically called it, of my particular opinion that snapped the silken thread by which Limbert's chance in the market was wont to hang. She meant that my favour was compromising, that my praise indeed was fatal. I had made myself a little specialty of seeing nothing in certain celebrities, of seeing overmuch in an occasional nobody, and of judging from a point of view that, say what I would for it (and I had a monstrous deal to say) remained perverse and obscure. Mine was in short the love that killed, for my subtlety, unlike Mrs. Highmore's, produced no tremor of the public tail. She had not forgotten how, toward the end, when his case was worst, Limbert would absolutely come to me with a funny, shy pathos in his eyes and say: "My dear fellow, I think I've done it this time, if you'll only keep quiet." If my keeping quiet in those days was to help him to appear to have hit the usual taste, for the want of which he was starving, so now my breaking out was to help Mrs. Highmore to appear to have hit the unusual.

The moral of all this was that I had frightened the public too much for our late friend, but that as she was not starving this was exactly what her grosser reputation required. And then, she good-naturedly and delicately intimated, there would always be, if further reasons were wanting, the price of my clever little article. I think she gave that hint with a flattering impression—spoiled child of the booksellers as she is—that the price of my clever little articles is high. Whatever it is, at any rate, she had evidently reflected that poor Limbert's anxiety for his own profit used to involve my sacrificing mine. Any inconvenience that my obliging her might entail would not in fine be pecuniary. Her appeal, her motive, her fantastic thirst for quality and her ingenious theory of my influence struck me all as excellent comedy, and when I consented contingently to oblige her she left me the sheets of her new novel. I could plead no inconvenience and have been looking them over; but I am frankly appalled at what she expects of me. What is she thinking of, poor dear, and what has put it into her head that "quality" has descended upon her? Why does she suppose that she has been "artistic"? She hasn't been anything whatever, I surmise, that she has not inveterately been. What does she imagine she has left out? What does she conceive she has put in? She has neither left out nor put in anything. I shall have to write her an embarrassed note. The book doesn't exist, and there's nothing in life to say about it. How can there be anything but the same old faithful rush for it?

I

This rush had already begun when, early in the seventies, in the interest of her prospective brother-in-law, she approached me on the singular ground of the unencouraged sentiment I had entertained for her sister. Pretty pink Maud had cast me out, but I appear to have passed in the flurried little circle for a magnanimous youth. Pretty pink Maud, so lovely then, before her troubles, that dusky Jane was gratefully conscious of all she made up for, Maud Stannace, very literary too, very languishing and extremely bullied by her mother, had yielded, invidiously as it might have struck me, to Ray Limbert's suit, which Mrs. Stannace was not the woman to stomach. Mrs.

Stannace was seldom the woman to do anything: she had been shocked at the way her children, with the grubby taint of their father's blood (he had published pale Remains or flat Conversations of *his* father) breathed the alien air of authorship. If not the daughter, nor even the niece, she was, if I am not mistaken, the second cousin of a hundred earls and a great stickler for relationship, so that she had other views for her brilliant child, especially after her quiet one (such had been her original discreet forecast of the producer of eighty volumes) became the second wife of an ex-army-surgeon, already the father of four children. Mrs. Stannace had too manifestly dreamed it would be given to pretty pink Maud to detach some one of the hundred, who wouldn't be missed, from the cluster. It was because she cared only for cousins that I unlearnt the way to her house, which she had once reminded me was one of the few paths of gentility I could hope to tread. Ralph Limbert, who belonged to nobody and had done nothing—nothing even at Cambridge— had only the uncanny spell he had cast upon her younger daughter to recommend him; but if her younger daughter had a spark of filial feeling she wouldn't commit the indecency of deserting for his sake a deeply dependent and intensely aggravated mother.

These things I learned from Jane Highmore, who, as if her books had been babies (they remained her only ones) had waited till after marriage to show what she could do and now bade fair to surround her satisfied spouse (he took for some mysterious reason, a part of the credit) with a little family, in sets of triplets, which properly handled would be the support of his declining years. The young couple, neither of whom had a penny, were now virtually engaged: the thing was subject to Ralph's putting his hand on some regular employment. People more enamoured couldn't be conceived, and Mrs. Highmore, honest woman, who had moreover a professional sense for a love-story, was eager to take them under her wing. What was wanted was a decent opening for Limbert, which it had occurred to her I might assist her to find, though indeed I had not yet found any such matter for myself. But it was well known that I was too particular, whereas poor Ralph, with the easy manners of genius, was ready to accept almost anything to which a salary, even a small one, was attached. If he could only for instance get a place on a newspaper the rest of his maintenance would come freely enough. It was true that his two novels, one of which she had brought to leave with me, had passed unperceived and that to her, Mrs. Highmore personally, they didn't irresistibly appeal; but she could all the same assure me that I should have only to spend ten minutes with him (and our encounter must speedily take place) to receive an impression of latent power.

Our encounter took place soon after I had read the volumes Mrs. Highmore had left with me, in which I recognised an intention of a sort that I had then pretty well given up the hope of meeting. I daresay that without knowing it I had been looking out rather hungrily for an altar of sacrifice: however that may be I submitted when I came across Ralph Limbert to one of the rarest emotions of my literary life, the sense of an activity in which I could critically rest. The rest was deep and salutary, and it has not been disturbed to this hour. It has been a long, large surrender, the luxury of dropped discriminations. He couldn't trouble me, whatever he did, for I practically enjoyed him as much when he was worse as when he was better. It was a case, I suppose, of natural prearrangement, in which, I hasten to add, I keep excellent company. We are a numerous band, partakers of the same repose, who sit together in the shade of the tree, by the plash of the fountain, with the glare of the desert around us and no great vice that I know of but the habit perhaps of estimating people a little too much by what they think of a certain style. If it had been laid upon these few pages, none the less, to be the history of an enthusiasm, I should not have undertaken them: they are concerned with Ralph Limbert in relations to which I was a stranger or in which I participated only by sympathy. I used to talk about his work, but I seldom talk now: the brotherhood of the faith have become, like the Trappists, a silent order. If to the day of his death, after mortal disenchantments, the impression he first produced always evoked the word "ingenuous," those to whom his face was familiar can easily imagine what it must have been when it still had the light of youth. I had never seen a man of genius look so passive, a man of experience so off his guard. At the period I made his acquaintance this freshness was all un-brushed. His foot had begun to stumble, but he was full of big intentions and of sweet Maud Stannace. Black-haired and pale, deceptively languid, he had the eyes of a clever child and the voice of a bronze bell. He saw more even than I had done in the girl he was engaged to;

as time went on I became conscious that we had both, properly enough, seen rather more than there was. Our odd situation, that of the three of us, became perfectly possible from the moment I observed that he had more patience with her than I should have had. I was happy at not having to supply this quantity, and she, on her side, found pleasure in being able to be impertinent to me without incurring the reproach of a bad wife.

Limbert's novels appeared to have brought him no money: they had only brought him, so far as I could then make out, tributes that took up his time. These indeed brought him from several quarters some other things, and on my part at the end of three months *The Blackport Beacon*. I don't to-day remember how I obtained for him the London correspondence of the great northern organ, unless it was through somebody's having obtained it for myself. I seem to recall that I got rid of it in Limbert's interest, persuaded the editor that he was much the better man. The better man was naturally the man who had pledged himself to support a charming wife. We were neither of us good, as the event proved, but he had a finer sort of badness. *The Blackport Beacon* had two London correspondents—one a supposed haunter of political circles, the other a votary of questions sketchily classified as literary. They were both expected to be lively, and what was held out to each was that it was honourably open to him to be livelier than the other. I recollect the political correspondent of that period and how the problem offered to Ray Limbert was to try to be livelier than Pat Moyle. He had not yet seemed to me so candid as when he undertook this exploit, which brought matters to a head with Mrs. Stannace, inasmuch as her opposition to the marriage now logically fell to the ground. It's all tears and laughter as I look back upon that admirable time, in which nothing was so romantic as our intense vision of the real. No fool's paradise ever rustled such a cradle-song. It was anything but Bohemia—it was the very temple of Mrs. Grundy. We knew we were too critical, and that made us sublimely indulgent; we believed we did our duty or wanted to, and that made us free to dream. But we dreamed over the multiplication-table; we were nothing if not practical. Oh, the long smokes and sudden ideas, the knowing hints and banished scruples! The great thing was for Limbert to bring out his next book, which was just what his delightful engagement with the *Beacon* would give him leisure and liberty to do. The kind of work, all human and elastic and suggestive, was capital experience: in picking up things for his bi-weekly letter he would pick up life as well, he would pick up literature. The new publications, the new pictures, the new people—there would be nothing too novel for us and nobody too sacred. We introduced everything and everybody into Mrs. Stannace's drawing-room, of which I again became a familiar.

Mrs. Stannace, it was true, thought herself in strange company; she didn't particularly mind the new books, though some of them seemed queer enough, but to the new people she had decided objections. It was notorious however that poor Lady Robeck secretly wrote for one of the papers, and the thing had certainly, in its glance at the doings of the great world, a side that might be made attractive. But we were going to make every side attractive, and we had everything to say about the sort of thing a paper like the *Beacon* would want. To give it what it would want and to give it nothing else was not doubtless an inspiring, but it was a perfectly respectable task, especially for a man with an appealing bride and a contentious mother-in-law. I thought Lambert's first letters as charming as the type allowed, though I won't deny that in spite of my sense of the importance of concessions I was just a trifle disconcerted at the way he had caught the tone. The tone was of course to be caught, but need it have been caught so in the act? The creature was even cleverer, as Maud Stannace said, than she had ventured to hope. Verily it was a good thing to have a dose of the wisdom of the serpent. If it had to be journalism—well, it *was* journalism. If he had to be "chatty "—well, he *was* chatty. Now and then he made a hit that—it was stupid of me—brought the blood to my face. I hated him to be so personal; but still, if it would make his fortune—! It wouldn't of course directly, but the book would, practically and in the sense to which our pure ideas of fortune were confined; and these things were all for the book. The daily balm meanwhile was in what one knew of the book—there were exquisite things to know; in the quiet monthly cheques from Blackport and in the deeper rose of Maud's little preparations, which were as dainty, on their tiny scale, as if she had been a humming-bird building a nest. When at the end of three months her betrothed had fairly settled down to his correspondence—in which Mrs. Highmore was the only person, so far as we could discover, disappointed, even she moreover being in this particular tortuous and possibly jealous; when the situation had assumed such a comfortable shape it was quite time to prepare. I published at that moment my first volume, mere faded ink to-day, a little collection of literary impressions, odds and ends of criticism contributed to a journal less remunerative but also less chatty than the *Beacon*, small ironies and ecstasies, great phrases and mistakes; and the very week it came out poor Limbert devoted half of one of his letters to it, with the happy sense this time of gratifying both himself and me as well as the Blackport breakfast-tables. I remember his saying it wasn't literature, the stuff, superficial stuff, he had to write about me; but what did that matter if it came back, as we knew, to the making for literature in the roundabout way? I sold the thing, I remember, for ten pounds, and with the money I bought in Vigo Street a quaint piece of old silver for Maud Stannace, which I carried to her with my own hand as a wedding-gift. In her mother's small drawing-room, a faded bower of photography fenced in and bedimmed by folding screens out of which sallow persons of fashion with dashing signatures looked at you from retouched eyes and little windows of plush, I was left to wait long enough to feel in the air of the house a hushed vibration of disaster. When our young lady came in she was very pale and her eyes too had been retouched.

"Something horrid has happened," I immediately said; and having really all along but half believed in her mother's meagre permission I risked with an unguarded groan the introduction of Mrs. Stannace's name.

"Yes, she has made a dreadful scene; she insists on our putting it off again. We're very unhappy: poor Ray has been turned off." Her tears began to flow again.

I had such a good conscience that I stared. "Turned off what?"

"Why, his paper of course. The *Beacon* has given him what he calls the sack. They don't like his letters: they're not the style of thing they want."

My blankness could only deepen. "Then what style of thing *do* they want?"

"Something more chatty."

"More?" I cried, aghast.

"More gossipy, more personal. They want 'journalism.' They want tremendous trash."

"Why, that's just what his letters have *been!*" I broke out.

This was strong, and I caught myself up, but the girl offered me the pardon of a beautiful wan smile. "So Ray himself declares. He says he has stooped so low."

"Very well—he must stoop lower. He *must* keep the place."

"He can't!" poor Maud wailed. "He says he has tried all he knows, has been abject, has gone on all fours, and that if they don't like that—"

"He accepts his dismissal?" I interposed in dismay.

She gave a tragic shrug. "What other course is open to him? He wrote to them that such work as he has done is the very worst he can do for the money."

"Therefore," I inquired with a flash of hope, "they'll offer him more for worse?"

"No indeed," she answered, "they haven't even offered him to go on at a reduction. He isn't funny enough."

I reflected a moment. "But surely such a thing as his notice of my book—!"

"It was your wretched book that was the last straw! He should have treated it superficially."

"Well, if he didn't—!" I began. Then I checked myself. "*Je vous porte malheur.*"

She didn't deny this; she only went, on: "What on earth is he to do?"

"He's to do better than the monkeys! He's to write!"

145

"But what on earth are we to marry on?"

I considered once more. "You're to marry on *The Major Key*."

II

The Major Key was the new novel, and the great thing accordingly was to finish it; a consummation for which three months of the *Beacon* had in some degree prepared the way. The action of that journal was indeed a shock, but I didn't know then the worst, didn't know that in addition to being a shock it was also a symptom. It was the first hint of the difficulty to which poor Limbert was eventually to succumb. His state was the happier of a truth for his not immediately seeing all that it meant. Difficulty was the law of life, but one could thank heaven it was exceptionally present in that horrid quarter. There was the difficulty that inspired, the difficulty of *The Major Key* to wit, which it was after all base to sacrifice to the turning of somersaults for pennies. These convictions Ray Limbert beguiled his fresh wait by blandly entertaining: not indeed, I think, that the failure of his attempt to be chatty didn't leave him slightly humiliated. If it was bad enough to have grinned through a horse-collar it was very bad indeed to have grinned in vain. Well, he would try no more grinning or at least no more horse-collars. The only success worth one's powder was success in the line of one's idiosyncrasy. Consistency was in itself distinction, and what was talent but the art of being completely whatever it was that one happened to be? One's things were characteristic or they were nothing. I look back rather fondly on our having exchanged in those days these admirable remarks and many others; on our having been very happy too, in spite of postponements and obscurities, in spite also of such occasional hauntings as could spring from our lurid glimpse of the fact that even twaddle cunningly calculated was far above people's heads. It was easy to wave away spectres by the reflection that all one had to do was not to write for people; it was certainly not for people that Limbert wrote while he hammered at *The Major Key*. The taint of literature was fatal only in a certain kind of air, which was precisely the kind against which we had now closed our window. Mrs. Stannace rose from her crumpled cushions as soon as she had obtained an adjournment, and Maud looked pale and proud, quite victorious and superior, at her having obtained nothing more. Maud behaved well, I thought, to her mother, and well indeed for a girl who had mainly been taught to be flowerlike to every one. What she gave Ray Limbert her fine, abundant needs made him then and ever pay for; but the gift was liberal, almost wonderful—an assertion I make even while remembering to how many clever women, early and late, his work has been dear. It was not only that the woman he was to marry was in love with him, but that (this was the strangeness) she had really seen almost better than any one what he could do. The greatest strangeness was that she didn't want him to do something different. This boundless belief was indeed the main way of her devotion; and as an act of faith it naturally asked for miracles. She was a rare wife for a poet if she was not perhaps the best who could have been picked out for a poor man.

Well, we were to have the miracles at all events and we were in a perfect state of mind to receive them. There were more of us every day, and we thought highly even of our friend's odd jobs and pot-boilers. The *Beacon* had had no successor, but he found some quiet comers and stray chances. Perpetually poking the fire and looking out of the window, he was certainly not a monster of facility, but he was, thanks perhaps to a certain method in that madness, a monster of certainty. It wasn't every one however who knew him for this: many editors printed him but once. He was getting a small reputation as a man it was well to have the first time; he created obscure apprehensions as to what might happen the second. He was good for making an impression, but no one seemed exactly to know what the impression was good for when made. The reason was simply that they had not seen yet *The Major Key* that fiery-hearted rose as to which we watched in private the formation of petal after petal and flame after flame. Nothing mattered but this, for it had already elicited a splendid bid, much talked about in Mrs. Highmore's drawing-room, where at this point my reminiscences grow particularly thick. *Her* roses bloomed all the year and her sociability increased with her row of prizes. We had an idea that we "met every one" there—so we naturally thought when we met each other. Between our hostess and Ray Limbert flourished the happiest relation, the only cloud on which was that her husband eyed him rather askance. When he was called clever this personage wanted to know what he had to "show;" and it was certain that he showed nothing that could compare with Jane Highmore. Mr. Highmore took his stand on accomplished work and, turning up his coat-tails, warmed his rear with a good conscience at the neat bookcase in which the generations of triplets were chronologically arranged. The harmony between his companions rested on the fact that, as I have already hinted, each would have liked so much to be the other. Limbert couldn't but have a feeling about a woman who in addition to being the best creature and her sister's backer would have made, could she have condescended, such a success with the *Beacon*. On the other hand Mrs. Highmore used freely to say: "Do you know, he'll do exactly the thing that *I* want to do? I shall never do it myself, but he'll do it instead. Yes, he'll do *my* thing, and I shall hate him for it—the wretch." Hating him was her pleasant humour, for the wretch was personally to her taste.

She prevailed on her own publisher to promise to take *The Major Key* and to engage to pay a considerable sum down, as the phrase is, on the presumption of its attracting attention. This was good news for the evening's end at Mrs. Highmore's when there were only four or five left and cigarettes ran low; but there was better news to come, and I have never forgotten how, as it was I who had the good fortune to bring it, I kept it back on one of those occasions, for the sake of my effect, till only the right people remained. The right people were now more and more numerous, but this was a revelation addressed only to a choice residuum—a residuum including of course Limbert himself, with whom I haggled for another cigarette before I announced that as a consequence of an interview I had had with him that afternoon, and of a subtle argument I had brought to bear, Mrs. Highmore's pearl of publishers had agreed to put forth the new book as a serial. He was to "run" it in his magazine and he was to pay ever so much more for the privilege. I produced a fine gasp which presently found a more articulate relief, but poor Limbert's voice failed him once for all (he knew he was to walk away with me) and it was some one else who asked me in what my subtle argument had resided. I forget what florid description I then gave of it: to-day I have no reason not to confess that it had resided in the simple plea that the book was exquisite. I had said: "Come, my dear friend, be original; just risk it for that!" My dear friend seemed to rise to the chance, and I followed up my advantage, permitting him honestly no illusion as to the quality of the work. He clutched interrogatively at two or three attenuations, but I dashed them aside, leaving him face to face with the formidable truth. It was just a pure gem: was he the man not to flinch? His danger appeared to have acted upon him as the anaconda acts upon the rabbit; fascinated and paralysed, he had been engulfed in the long pink throat. When a week before, at my request, Limbert had let me possess for a day the complete manuscript, beautifully copied out by Maud Stannace, I had flushed with indignation at its having to be said of the author of such pages that he hadn't the common means to marry. I had taken the field in a great glow to repair this scandal, and it was therefore quite directly my fault if three months later, when *The Major Key* began to run, Mrs. Stannace was driven to the wall. She had made a condition of a fixed income; and at last a fixed income was achieved.

She had to recognise it, and after much prostration among the photographs she recognised it to the extent of accepting some of the convenience of it in the form of a project for a common household, to the expenses of which each party should proportionately contribute. Jane Highmore made a great point of her not being left alone, but Mrs. Stannace herself determined the proportion, which on Limbert's side at least and in spite of many other fluctuations was never altered. His income had been "fixed" with a vengeance: having painfully stooped to the comprehension of it Mrs. Stannace rested on this effort to the end and asked no further question on the subject. *The Major Key* in other words ran ever so long, and before it was half out Limbert and Maud had been married and the common household set up. These first months were probably the happiest in the family annals, with wedding-bells and budding laurels, the quiet, assured course of the book and the friendly, familiar note, round the corner, of Mrs. Highmore's big guns. They gave Ralph time to block in another picture as well as to let me know after a while that he had the happy prospect of becoming a father. We had at times some dispute as to whether *The Major Key* was making an impression, but our contention could only be futile so long as we were not agreed as to what an impression consisted of. Several persons wrote to the author and several others asked to be introduced to him:

wasn't that an impression? One of the lively "weeklies," snapping at the deadly "monthlies," said the whole thing was "grossly inartistic"—wasn't that? It was somewhere else proclaimed "a wonderfully subtle character-study"—wasn't that too? The strongest effect doubtless was produced on the publisher when, in its lemon-coloured volumes, like a little dish of three custards, the book was at last served cold: he never got his money back and so far as I know has never got it back to this day. *The Major Key* was rather a great performance than a great success. It converted readers into friends and friends into lovers; it placed the author, as the phrase is—placed him all too definitely; but it shrank to obscurity in the account of sales eventually rendered. It was in short an exquisite thing, but it was scarcely a thing to have published and certainly not a thing to have married on. I heard all about the matter, for my intervention had much exposed me. Mrs. Highmore said the second volume had given her ideas, and the ideas are probably to be found in some of her works, to the circulation of which they have even perhaps contributed. This was not absolutely yet the very thing she wanted to do, but it was on the way to it. So much, she informed me, she particularly perceived in the light of a critical study which I put forth in a little magazine; which the publisher in his advertisements quoted from profusely; and as to which there sprang up some absurd story that Limbert himself had written it. I remember that on my asking some one why such an idiotic thing had been said my interlocutor replied: "Oh, because, you know, it's just the way he *would* have written!" My spirit sank a little perhaps as I reflected that with such analogies in our manner there might prove to be some in our fate.

It was during the next four or five years that our eyes were open to what, unless something could be done, that fate, at least on Limbert's part, might be. The thing to be done was of course to write the book, the book that would make the difference, really justify the burden he had accepted and consummately express his power. For the works that followed upon *The Major Key* he had inevitably to accept conditions the reverse of brilliant, at a time too when the strain upon his resources had begun to show sharpness. With three babies in due course, an ailing wife and a complication still greater than these, it became highly important that a man should do only his best. Whatever Limbert did was his best; so at least each time I thought and so I unfailingly said somewhere, though it was not my saying it, heaven knows, that made the desired difference. Every one else indeed said it, and there was among multiplied worries always the comfort that his position was quite assured. The two books that followed *The Major Key* did more than anything else to assure it, and Jane Highmore was always crying out: "You stand alone, dear Ray; you stand absolutely alone!" Dear Ray used to tell me that he felt the truth of this in feebly attempted discussions with his bookseller. His sister-in-law gave him good advice into the bargain; she was a repository of knowing hints, of esoteric learning. These things were doubtless not the less valuable to him for bearing wholly on the question of how a reputation might be with a little gumption, as Mrs. Highmore said, "worked." Save when she occasionally bore testimony to her desire to do, as Limbert did, something some day for her own very self, I never heard her speak of the literary motive as if it were distinguishable from the pecuniary. She cocked up his hat, she pricked up his prudence for him, reminding him that as one seemed to take one's self so the silly world was ready to take one. It was a fatal mistake to be too candid even with those who were all right—not to look and to talk prosperous, not at least to pretend that one had beautiful sales. To listen to her you would have thought the profession of letters a wonderful game of bluff. Wherever one's idea began it ended somehow in inspired paragraphs in the newspapers. "*I* pretend, I assure you, that you are going off like wildfire—I can at least do that for you!" she often declared, prevented as she was from doing much else by Mr. Highmore's insurmountable objection to *their* taking Mrs. Stannace.

I couldn't help regarding the presence of this latter lady in Limbert's life as the major complication: whatever he attempted it appeared given to him to achieve as best he could in the mere margin of the space in which she swung her petticoats. I may err in the belief that she practically lived on him, for though it was not in him to follow adequately Mrs. Highmore's counsel there were exasperated confessions he never made, scanty domestic curtains he rattled on their rings. I may exaggerate in the retrospect his apparent anxieties, for these after all were the years when his talent was freshest and when as a writer he most laid down his line. It wasn't of Mrs. Stannace nor even as time went on of Mrs. Limbert that we mainly talked when I got at longer intervals a smokier hour in the little grey den from which we could step out, as we used to say, to the lawn. The lawn was the back-garden, and Limbert's study was behind the dining-room, with folding doors not impervious to the clatter of the children's tea. We sometimes took refuge from it in the depths—a bush and a half deep—of the shrubbery, where was a bench that gave us a view while we gossiped of Mrs. Stannace's tiara-like headdress nodding at an upper window. Within doors and without Limbert's life was overhung by an awful region that figured in his conversation, comprehensively and with unpremeditated art, as Upstairs. It was Upstairs that the thunder gathered, that Mrs. Stannace kept her accounts and her state, that Mrs. Limbert had her babies and her headaches, that the bells for ever jangled at the maids, that everything imperative in short took place—everything that he had somehow, pen in hand, to meet and dispose of in the little room on the garden-level. I don't think he liked to go Upstairs, but no special burst of confidence was needed to make me feel that a terrible deal of service went. It was the habit of the ladies of the Stannace family to be extremely waited on, and I've never been in a house where three maids and a nursery-governess gave such an impression of a retinue. "Oh, they're so deucedly, so hereditarily fine!"—I remember how that dropped from him in some worried hour. Well, it was because Maud was so universally fine that we had both been in love with her. It was not an air moreover for the plaintive note: no private inconvenience could long outweigh for him the great happiness of these years—the happiness that sat with us when we talked and that made it always amusing to talk, the sense of his being on the heels of success, coming closer and closer, touching it at last, knowing that he should touch it again and hold it fast and hold it high. Of course when we said success we didn't mean exactly what Mrs. Highmore for instance meant. He used to quote at me as a definition something from a nameless page of my own, some stray dictum to the effect that the man of his craft had achieved it when of a beautiful subject his expression was complete. Well, wasn't Limbert's in all conscience complete?

III

It was bang upon this completeness all the same that the turn arrived, the turn I can't say of his fortune—for what was that?—but of his confidence, of his spirits and, what was more to the point, of his system. The whole occasion on which the first symptom flared out is before me as I write. I had met them both at dinner: they were diners who had reached the penultimate stage—the stage which in theory is a rigid selection and in practice a wan submission. It was late in the season and stronger spirits than theirs were broken; the night was close and the air of the banquet such as to restrict conversation to the refusal of dishes and consumption to the sniffing of a flower. It struck me all the more that Mrs. Limbert was flying her flag. As vivid as a page of her husband's prose, she had one of those flickers of freshness that are the miracle of her sex and one of those expensive dresses that are the miracle of ours. She had also a neat brougham in which she had offered to rescue an old lady from the possibilities of a queer cab-horse; so that when she had rolled away with her charge I proposed a walk home with her husband, whom I had overtaken on the doorstep. Before I had gone far with him he told me he had news for me—he had accepted, of all people and of all things, an "editorial position." It had come to pass that very day, from one hour to another, without time for appeals or ponderations: Mr. Bousefield, the proprietor of a "high-class monthly," making, as they said, a sudden change, had dropped on him heavily out of the blue. It was all right—there was a salary and an idea, and both of them, as such things went, rather high. We took our way slowly through the vacant streets, and in the explanations and revelations that as we lingered under lamp-posts I drew from him I found with an apprehension that I tried to gulp down a foretaste of the bitter end. He told me more than he had ever told me yet. He couldn't balance accounts—that was the trouble: his expenses were too rising a tide. It was absolutely necessary that he should at last make money, and now he must work only for that. The need this last year had gathered the force of a crusher: it had rolled over him and laid him on his back. He had his scheme; this time he knew what he was about; on some good occasion, with leisure to talk it over, he would tell me the blessed whole. His editorship would help him, and for the rest he must help himself. If he couldn't they would have to do something fundamental— change their life altogether, give up London, move into the country, take a house at thirty pounds a year, send their children to the Board-school. I saw that he was excited, and he admitted that he was: he had waked out of a trance. He had been on the wrong tack; he had piled mistake on mistake. It was the vision of his remedy that now excited him: ineffably, grotesquely simple, it had yet come to him only within a day or two. No, he wouldn't tell me what it was; he would give me the night to guess, and if I shouldn't guess it would be because I was as big an ass as himself. However, a lone man might be an ass: he had room in his life for his ears. Ray had a burden that demanded a back: the back must therefore now be properly instituted. As to the editorship, it was simply heaven-sent, being not at all another case of *The Blackport Beacon* but a case of the very opposite. The proprietor, the great Mr. Bousefield, had approached him precisely because his name, which was to be on the cover, *didn't* represent the chatty. The whole thing was to be—oh, on fiddling little lines of course—a protest against the chatty. Bousefield wanted him to be himself; it was for himself Bousefield had picked him out. Wasn't it beautiful and brave of Bousefield? He wanted literature, he saw the great reaction coming, the way the cat was going to jump. "Where will you get literature?" I wofully asked; to which he replied with a laugh that what he had to get was not literature but only what Bousefield would take for it.

In that single phrase without more ado I discovered his famous remedy. What was before him for the future was not to do his work but to do what somebody else would take for it. I had the question out with him on the next opportunity, and of all the lively discussions into which we had been destined to drift it lingers in my mind as the liveliest. This was not, I hasten to add, because I disputed his conclusions: it was an effect of the very force with which, when I had fathomed his wretched premises, I took them to my soul. It was very well to talk with Jane Highmore about his standing alone: the eminent relief of this position had brought him to the verge of ruin. Several persons admired his books—nothing was less contestable; but they appeared to have a mortal objection to acquiring them by subscription or by purchase: they begged or borrowed or stole, they delegated one of the party perhaps to commit the volumes to memory and repeat them, like the bards of old, to listening multitudes. Some ingenious theory was required at any rate to account for the inexorable limits of his circulation. It wasn't a thing for five people to live on; therefore either the objects circulated must change their nature or the organisms to be nourished must. The former change was perhaps the easier to consider first. Limbert considered it with extraordinary ingenuity from that time on, and the ingenuity, greater even than any I had yet had occasion to admire in him, made the whole next stage of his career rich in curiosity and suspense.

"I have been butting my skull against a wall," he had said in those hours of confidence; "and, to be as sublime a blockhead, if you'll allow me the word, you, my dear fellow, have kept sounding the charge. We've sat prating here of 'success,' heaven help us, like chanting monks in a cloister, hugging the sweet delusion that it lies somewhere in the work itself, in the expression, as you said, of one's subject or the intensification, as somebody else somewhere says, of one's note. One has been going on in short as if the only thing to do were to accept the law of one's talent and thinking that if certain consequences didn't follow it was only because one wasn't logical enough. My disaster has served me right—I mean for using that ignoble word at all. It's a mere distributor's, a mere hawker's word. What *is* 'success' anyhow? When a book's right, it's right—shame to it surely if it isn't. When it sells it sells—it brings money like potatoes or beer. If there's dishonour one way and inconvenience the other, it certainly is comfortable, but it as certainly isn't glorious to have escaped them. People of delicacy don't brag either about their probity or about their luck. Success be hanged!—I want to sell. It's a question of life and death. I must study the way. I've studied too much the other way—I know the other way now, every inch of it. I must cultivate the market—it's a science like another. I must go in for an infernal cunning. It will be very amusing, I foresee that; I shall lead a dashing life and drive a roaring trade. I haven't been obvious—I must *be* obvious. I haven't been popular—I must *be* popular. It's another art—or perhaps it isn't an art at all. It's something else; one must find out what it is. Is it something awfully queer?—you blush!—something barely decent? All the greater incentive to curiosity! Curiosity's an immense motive; we shall have tremendous sport. They all do it; it's only a question of how. Of course I've everything to unlearn; but what is life, as Jane Highmore says, but a lesson? I must get all I can, all she can give me, from Jane. She can't explain herself much; she's all intuition; her processes are obscure; it's the spirit that swoops down and catches her up. But I must study her reverently in her works. Yes, you've defied me before, but now my loins are girded: I declare I'll read one of them—I really will: I'll put it through if I perish!"

I won't pretend that he made all these remarks at once; but there wasn't one that he didn't make at one time or another, for suggestion and occasion were plentiful enough, his life being now given up altogether to his new necessity. It wasn't a question of his having or not having, as they say, my intellectual sympathy: the brute force of the pressure left no room for judgment; it made all emotion a mere recourse to the spyglass. I watched him as I should have watched a long race or a long chase, irresistibly siding with him but much occupied with the calculation of odds. I confess indeed that my heart, for the endless stretch that he covered so fast, was often in my throat. I saw him peg away over the sun-dappled plain, I saw him double and wind and gain and lose; and all the while I secretly entertained a conviction. I wanted him to feed his many mouths, but at the bottom of all things was my sense that if he should succeed in doing so in this particular way I should think less well of him. Now I had an absolute terror of that. Meanwhile so far as I could I backed him up, I helped him: all the more that I had warned him immensely at first, smiled with a compassion it was very good of him not to have found exasperating over the complacency of his assumption that a man could escape from himself. Ray Limbert at all events would certainly never escape; but one could make believe for him, make believe very hard—an undertaking in which at first Mr. Bousefield was visibly a blessing. Limbert was delightful on the business of this being at last my chance too—my chance, so miraculously vouchsafed, to appear with a certain luxuriance. He didn't care how often he printed me, for wasn't it exactly in my direction Mr. Bousefield held that the cat was going to jump? This was the least he could do for me. I might write on anything I liked—on anything at least but Mr. Limbert's second manner. He didn't wish attention strikingly called to his second manner; it was to operate insidiously; people were to be left to believe they had discovered it long ago. "Ralph Limbert? Why, when did we ever live without him?"—that's what he wanted them to say. Besides, they hated manners—let sleeping dogs lie. His understanding with Mr. Bousefield—on which he had had not at all to insist; it was the excellent man who insisted—was that he should run one of his beautiful stories in the magazine. As to the beauty of his story however Limbert was going to be less admirably straight than as to the beauty of everything else. That was another reason why I mustn't write about his new line: Mr. Bousefield was not to be too definitely warned that such a periodical was exposed to prostitution. By the time he should find it out for himself the public—*le gros public*—would have bitten, and then perhaps he would be conciliated and forgive. Everything else would be literary in short, and above all *I* would be; only Ralph Limbert wouldn't—he'd chuck up the whole thing sooner. He'd be vulgar, he'd be rudimentary, he'd be atrocious: he'd be elaborately what he hadn't been before. I duly noticed that he had more trouble in making "everything else" literary than he had at first allowed for; but this was largely counteracted by the ease with which he was able to obtain that his mark should not be overshot. He had taken well to heart the old lesson of the *Beacon*; he remembered that he was after all there to keep his contributors down much rather than to keep them up. I thought at times that he kept them down a trifle too far, but he assured me that I needn't be nervous: he had his limit—his limit was inexorable. He would reserve pure vulgarity for his serial, over which he was sweating blood and water; elsewhere it should be qualified by the prime qualification, the mediocrity that attaches, that endears. Bousefield, he allowed, was proud, was difficult: nothing was really good enough for him but the middling good; but he himself was prepared for adverse comment, resolute for his noble course. Hadn't Limbert moreover in the event of a charge of laxity from headquarters the great strength of being able to point to my contributions? Therefore I must let myself go, I must abound in my peculiar sense, I must be a resource in case of accidents. Limbert's vision of accidents hovered mainly over the sudden awakening of Mr. Bousefield to the stuff that in the department of fiction his editor was palming off. He would then have to confess in all humility that this was not what the good old man wanted, but I should be all the more there as a salutary specimen. I would cross the scent with something showily impossible, splendidly unpopular—I must be sure to have something on hand. I always had plenty on hand—poor Limbert needn't have worried: the magazine was forearmed each month by my care with a retort to any possible accusation of trifling with Mr. Bousefield's standard. He had admitted to Limbert, after much consideration indeed, that he was prepared to be perfectly human; but he had added that he was not prepared for an abuse of this admission. The thing in the world I think I least felt myself was an abuse, even though (as I had never mentioned to my friendly editor) I too had my project for a bigger reverberation. I daresay I trusted mine more than I trusted Limbert's; at all events the golden mean in which in the special case he saw his salvation as an editor was something I should be most sure of if I were to exhibit it myself. I exhibited it month after month in the form of a monstrous levity, only praying heaven that my editor might now not tell me, as he had so often told me, that my result was awfully good. I knew what that would signify—it would signify, sketchily speaking, disaster. What he did tell me heartily was that it was just what his game required: his new line had brought with it an earnest assumption—earnest save when we privately laughed about it—of the locutions proper to real bold enterprise. If I tried to keep him in the dark even as he kept Mr. Bousefield there was nothing to show that I was not tolerably successful: each case therefore presented a promising analogy for the other. He never noticed my descent, and it was accordingly possible that Mr. Bousefield would never notice his.

But would nobody notice it at all?—that was a question that added a prospective zest to one's possession of a critical sense. So much depended upon it that I was rather relieved than otherwise not to know the answer too soon. I waited in fact a year—the year for which Limbert had cannily engaged on trial with Mr. Bousefield; the year as to which through the same sharpened shrewdness it had been conveyed in the agreement between them that Mr. Bousefield was not to intermeddle. It had been Limbert's general prayer that we would during this period let him quite alone. His terror of my direct rays was a droll, dreadful force that always operated: he explained it by the fact that I understood him too well, expressed too much of his intention, saved him too little from himself. The less he was saved the more he didn't sell: I literally interpreted, and that was simply fatal.

I held my breath accordingly; I did more—I closed my eyes, I guarded my treacherous ears. He induced several of us to do that (of such devotions we were capable) so that not even glancing at the thing from month to month, and having nothing but his shamed, anxious silence to go by, I participated only vaguely in the little hum that surrounded his act of sacrifice. It was blown about the town that the public would be surprised; it was hinted, it was printed that he was making a desperate bid. His new work was spoken of as "more calculated for general acceptance." These tidings produced in some quarters much reprobation, and nowhere more, I think, than on the part of certain persons who had never read a word of him, or assuredly had never spent a shilling on him, and who hung for hours over the other attractions of the newspaper that announced his abasement. So much asperity cheered me a little—seemed to signify that he might really be doing something. On the other hand I had a distinct alarm; some one sent me for some alien reason an American journal (containing frankly more than that source of affliction) in which was quoted a passage from our friend's last instalment. The passage—I couldn't for my life help reading it—was simply superb. Ah, he *would* have to move to the country if that was the worst he could do! It gave me a pang to see how little after all he had improved since the days of his competition with Pat Moyle. There was nothing in the passage quoted in the American paper that Pat would for a moment have owned. During the last weeks, as the opportunity of reading the complete thing drew near, one's suspense was barely endurable, and I shall never forget the July evening on which I put it to rout. Coming home to dinner I found the two volumes on my table, and I sat up with them half the night, dazed, bewildered, rubbing my eyes, wondering at the monstrous joke. *Was* it a monstrous joke, his second manner—was *this* the new line, the desperate bid, the scheme for more general acceptance and the remedy for material failure? Had he made a fool of all his following, or had he most injuriously made a still bigger fool of himself? Obvious?—where the deuce was it obvious? Popular?—how on earth could it be popular? The thing was charming with all his charm and powerful with all his power: it was an unscrupulous, an unsparing, a shameless, merciless masterpiece. It was, no doubt, like the old letters to the *Beacon*, the worst he could do; but the perversity of the effort, even though heroic, had been frustrated by the purity of the gift. Under what illusion had he laboured, with what wavering, treacherous compass had he steered? His honour was inviolable, his measurements were all wrong. I was thrilled with the whole impression and with all that came crowding in its train. It was too grand a collapse—it was too hideous a triumph; I exalted almost with tears—I lamented with a strange delight. Indeed as the short night waned and, threshing about in my emotion, I fidgeted to my high-perched window for a glimpse of the summer dawn, I became at last aware that I was staring at it out of eyes that had compassionately and admiringly filled. The eastern sky, over the London housetops, had a wonderful tragic crimson. That was the colour of his magnificent mistake.

IV

If something less had depended on my impression I daresay I should have communicated it as soon as I had swallowed my breakfast; but the case was so embarrassing that I spent the first half of the day in reconsidering it, dipping into the book again, almost feverishly turning its leaves and trying to extract from them, for my friend's benefit, some symptom of reassurance, some ground for felicitation. This rash challenge had consequences merely dreadful; the wretched volumes, imperturbable and impeccable, with their shyer secrets and their second line of defence, were like a beautiful woman more denuded or a great symphony on a new hearing. There was something quite sinister in the way they stood up to me. I couldn't however be dumb— that was to give the wrong tinge to my disappointment; so that later in the afternoon, taking my courage in both hands, I approached with a vain tortuosity poor Limbert's door. A smart victoria waited before it in which from the bottom of the street I saw that a lady who had apparently just issued from the house was settling herself. I recognised Jane Highmore and instantly paused till she should drive down to me. She presently met me half-way and as soon as she saw me stopped her carriage in agitation. This was a relief—it postponed a moment the sight of that pale, fine face of our friend's fronting me for the right verdict. I gathered from the flushed eagerness with which Mrs. Highmore asked me if I had heard the news that a verdict of some sort had already been rendered.

"What news?—about the book?"

"About that horrid magazine. They're shockingly upset. He has lost his position—he has had a fearful flare-up with Mr. Bousefield."

I stood there blank, but not unaware in my blankness of how history repeats itself. There came to me across the years Maud's announcement of their ejection from the *Beacon*, and dimly, confusedly the same explanation was in the air. This time however I had been on my guard; I had had my suspicion. "He has made it too flippant?" I found breath after an instant to inquire.

Mrs. Highmore's vacuity exceeded my own. "Too 'flippant'? He has made it too oracular. Mr. Bousefield says he has killed it." Then perceiving my stupefaction: "Don't you know what has happened?" she pursued; "isn't it because in his trouble, poor love, he has sent for you that you've come? You've heard nothing at all? Then you had better know before you see them. Get in here with me—I'll take you a turn and tell you." We were close to the Park, the Regent's, and when with extreme alacrity I had placed myself beside her and the carriage had begun to enter it she went on: "It was what I feared, you know. It reeked with culture. He keyed it up too high."

I felt myself sinking in the general collapse. "What are you talking about?"

"Why, about that beastly magazine. They're all on the streets. I shall have to take mamma."

I pulled myself together. "What on earth then did Bousefield want? He said he wanted intellectual power."

"Yes, but Ray overdid it."

"Why, Bousefield said it was a thing he *couldn't* overdo."

"Well, Ray managed: he took Mr. Bousefield too literally. It appears the thing has been doing dreadfully, but the proprietor couldn't say anything, because he had covenanted to leave the editor quite free. He describes himself as having stood there in a fever and seen his ship go down. A day or two ago the year was up, so he could at last break out. Maud says he did break out quite fearfully; he came to the house and let poor Ray have it. Ray gave it to him back; he reminded him of his own idea of the way the cat was going to jump."

I gasped with dismay. "Has Bousefield abandoned that idea? Isn't the cat going to jump?"

Mrs. Highmore hesitated. "It appears that she doesn't seem in a hurry. Ray at any rate has jumped too far ahead of her. He should have temporised a little, Mr. Bousefield says; but I'm beginning to think, you know," said my companion, "that Ray *can't* temporise." Fresh from my emotions of the previous twenty-four hours I was scarcely in a position to disagree with her. "He published too much pure thought."

"Pure thought?" I cried. "Why, it struck me so often—certainly in a due proportion of cases—as pure drivel!"

"Oh, you're more keyed up than he! Mr. Bousefield says that of course he wanted things that were suggestive and clever, things that he could point to with pride. But he contends that Ray didn't allow for human weakness. He gave everything in too stiff doses."

Sensibly, I fear, to my neighbour I winced at her words; I felt a prick that made me meditate. Then I said: "Is that, by chance, the way he gave *me?*" Mrs. Highmore remained silent so long that I had somehow the sense of a fresh pang; and after a minute, turning in my seat, I laid my hand on her arm, fixed my eyes upon her face and pursued pressingly: "Do you suppose it to be to my 'Occasional Remarks' that Mr. Bousefield refers?"

At last she met my look. "Can you bear to hear it?"

"I think I can bear anything now."

"Well then, it was really what I wanted to give you an inkling of. It's largely over you that they've quarrelled. Mr. Bousefield wants him to chuck you."

I grabbed her arm again. "And Limbert *won't?*"

"He seems to cling to you. Mr. Bousefield says no magazine can afford you."

I gave a laugh that agitated the very coachman. "Why, my dear lady, has he any idea of my price?"

"It isn't your price—he says you're dear at any price; you do so much to sink the ship. Your 'Remarks' are called 'Occasional,' but nothing could be more deadly regular: you're there month after month and you're never anywhere else. And you supply no public want."

"I supply the most delicious irony."

"So Ray appears to have declared. Mr. Bousefield says that's not in the least a public want. No one can make out what you're talking about and no one would care if he could. I'm only quoting *him*, mind."

"Quote, quote—if Limbert holds out. I think I must leave you now, please: I must rush back to express to him what I feel."

"I'll drive you to his door. That isn't all," said Mrs. Highmore. And on the way, when the carriage had turned, she communicated the rest. "Mr. Bousefield really arrived with an ultimatum: it had the form of something or other by Minnie Meadows."

"Minnie Meadows?" I was stupefied.

"The new lady-humourist every one is talking about. It's the first of a series of screaming sketches for which poor Ray was to find a place."

"Is *that* Mr. Bousefield's idea of literature?"

"No, but he says it's the public's, and you've got to take *some* account of the public. *Aux grands maux les grands remèdes.* They had a tremendous lot of ground to make up, and no one would make it up like Minnie. She would be the best concession they could make to human weakness; she would strike at least this note of showing that it was not going to be quite all—well, all *you*. Now Ray draws the line at Minnie; he won't stoop to Minnie; he declines to touch, to look at Minnie. When Mr. Bousefield—rather imperiously, I believe—made Minnie a *sine quâ non* of his retention of his post he said something rather violent, told him to go to some unmentionable place and take Minnie with him. That of course put the fat on the fire. They had really a considerable scene."

163

"So had he with the *Beacon* man," I musingly replied. "Poor dear, he seems born for considerable scenes! It's on Minnie, then, that they've really split?" Mrs. Highmore exhaled her despair in a sound which I took for an assent, and when we had rolled a little further I rather in-consequently and to her visible surprise broke out of my reverie. "It will never do in the world—he *must* stoop to Minnie!"

"It's too late—and what I've told you still isn't all. Mr. Bousefield raises another objection."

"What other, pray?"

"Can't you guess?"

I wondered. "No more of Ray's fiction?"

"Not a line. That's something else no magazine can stand. Now that his novel has run its course Mr. Bousefield is distinctly disappointed."

I fairly bounded in my place. "Then it may do?"

Mrs. Highmore looked bewildered. "Why so, if he finds it too dull?"

"Dull? Ralph Limbert? He's as fine as a needle!"

"It comes to the same thing—he won't penetrate leather. Mr. Bousefield had counted on something that *would*, on something that would have a wider acceptance. Ray says he wants iron pegs." I collapsed again; my flicker of elation dropped to a throb of quieter comfort; and after a moment's silence I asked my neighbour if she had herself read the work our friend had just put forth. "No," she replied, "I gave him my word at the beginning, on his urgent request, that I wouldn't."

"Not even as a book?"

"He begged me never to look at it at all. He said he was trying a low experiment. Of course I knew what he meant and I entreated him to let me just for curiosity take a peep. But he was firm, he declared he couldn't bear the thought that a woman like me should see him in the depths."

"He's only, thank God, in the depths of distress," I replied. "His experiment's nothing worse than a failure."

"Then Bousefield *is* right—his circulation won't budge?"

"It won't move one, as they say in Fleet Street. The book has extraordinary beauty."

"Poor duck—after trying so hard!" Jane Highmore sighed with real tenderness. "What *will* then become of them?"

I was silent an instant. "You must take your mother."

She was silent too. "I must speak of it to Cecil!" she presently said. Cecil is Mr. Highmore, who then entertained, I knew, strong views on the inadjustability of circumstances in general to the idiosyncrasies of Mrs. Stannace. He held it supremely happy that in an important relation she should have met her match. Her match was Ray Limbert—not much of a writer but a practical man. "The dear things still think, you know," my companion continued, "that the book will be the beginning of their fortune. Their illusion, if you're right, will be rudely dispelled."

"That's what makes me dread to face them. I've just spent with his volumes an unforgettable night. His illusion has lasted because so many of us have been pledged till this moment to turn our faces the other way. We haven't known the truth and have therefore had nothing to say. Now that we do know it indeed we have practically quite as little. I hang back from the threshold. How can I follow up with a burst of enthusiasm such a catastrophe as Mr. Bousefield's visit?"

As I turned uneasily about my neighbour more comfortably snuggled. "Well, I'm glad then I haven't read him and have nothing unpleasant to say!" We had come back to Limbert's door, and I made the coachman stop short of it. "But he'll try again, with that determination of his: he'll build his hopes on the next time."

"On what else has he built them from the very first? It's never the present for him that bears the fruit; that's always postponed and for somebody else:

there has always to be another try. I admit that his idea of a 'new line' has made him try harder than ever. It makes no difference," I brooded, still timorously lingering; "his achievement of his necessity, his hope of a market will continue to attach themselves to the future. But the next time will disappoint him as each last time has done—and then the next and the next and the next!"

I found myself seeing it all with a clearness almost inspired: it evidently cast a chill on Mrs. Highmore. "Then what on earth will become of him?" she plaintively asked.

"I don't think I particularly care what may become of *him*," I returned with a conscious, reckless increase of my exaltation; "I feel it almost enough to be concerned with what may become of one's enjoyment of him. I don't know in short what will become of his circulation; I am only quite at my ease as to what will become of his work. It will simply keep all its quality. He'll try again for the common with what he'll believe to be a still more infernal cunning, and again the common will fatally elude him, for his infernal cunning will have been only his genius in an ineffectual disguise." We sat drawn up by the pavement, facing poor Limbert's future as I saw it. It relieved me in a manner to know the worst, and I prophesied with an assurance which as I look back upon it strikes me as rather remarkable. "*Que voulez-vous?*" I went on; "you can't make a sow's ear of a silk purse! It's grievous indeed if you like—there are people who can't be vulgar for trying. *He* can't—it wouldn't come off, I promise you, even once. It takes more than trying—it comes by grace. It happens not to be given to Limbert to fall. He belongs to the heights—he breathes there, he lives there, and it's accordingly to the heights I must ascend," I said as I took leave of my conductress, "to carry him this wretched news from where *we* move!"

V

A few months were sufficient to show how right I had been about his circulation. It didn't move one, as I had said; it stopped short in the same place, fell off in a sheer descent, like some precipice gaped up at by tourists. The public in other words drew the line for him as sharply as he had drawn it for Minnie Meadows. Minnie has skipped with a flouncing caper over his line, however; whereas the mark traced by a lustier cudgel has been a barrier insurmountable to Limbert. Those next times I had spoken of to Jane Highmore, I see them simplified by retrocession. Again and again he made his desperate bid—again and again he tried to. His rupture with Mr. Bousefield caused him, I fear, in professional circles to be thought impracticable, and I am perfectly aware, to speak candidly, that no sordid advantage ever accrued to him from such public patronage of my performances as he had occasionally been in a position to offer. I reflect for my comfort that any injury I may have done him by untimely application of a faculty of analysis which could point to no converts gained by honourable exercise was at least equalled by the injury he did himself. More than once, as I have hinted, I held my tongue at his request, but my frequent plea that such favours weren't politic never found him, when in other connections there was an opportunity to give me a lift, anything but indifferent to the danger of the association. He let them have me in a word whenever he could; sometimes in periodicals in which he had credit, sometimes only at dinner. He talked about me when he couldn't get me in, but it was always part of the bargain that I shouldn't make him a topic. "How can I successfully serve you if you do?" he used to ask: he was more afraid than I thought he ought to have been of the charge of tit for tat. I didn't care, for I never could distinguish tat from tit; but as I have intimated I dropped into silence really more than anything else because there was a certain fascinated observation of his course which was quite testimony enough and to which in this huddled conclusion of it he practically reduced me.

I see it all foreshortened, his wonderful remainder—see it from the end backward, with the direction widening toward me as if on a level with the eye. The migration to the country promised him at first great things—smaller expenses, larger leisure, conditions eminently conducive on each occasion to the possible triumph of the next time. Mrs. Stannace, who altogether disapproved of it, gave as one of her reasons that her son-in-law, living mainly in a village on the edge of a goose-green, would be deprived of that contact with the great world which was indispensable to the painter of manners. She had the showiest arguments for keeping him in touch, as she called it, with good society; wishing to know with some force where, from the moment he ceased to represent it from observation, the novelist could be said to be. In London fortunately a clever man was just a clever man; there were charming houses in which a person of Ray's undoubted ability, even though without the knack of making the best use of it, could always be sure of a quiet corner for watching decorously the social kaleidoscope. But the kaleidoscope of the goose-green, what in the world was that, and what such delusive thrift as drives about the land (with a fearful account for flys from the inn) to leave cards on the country magnates? This solicitude for Limbert's subject-matter was the specious colour with which, deeply determined not to affront mere tolerance in a cottage, Mrs. Stannace overlaid her indisposition to place herself under the heel of Cecil Highmore. She knew that he ruled Upstairs as well as down, and she clung to the fable of the association of interests in the north of London. The Highmores had a better address—they lived now in Stanhope Gardens; but Cecil was fearfully artful—he wouldn't hear of an association of interests nor treat with his mother-in-law save as a visitor. She didn't like false positions; but on the other hand she didn't like the sacrifice of everything she was accustomed to. Her universe at all events was a universe full of card-leavings and charming houses, and it was fortunate that she couldn't Upstairs catch the sound of the doom to which, in his little grey den, describing to me his diplomacy, Limbert consigned alike the country magnates and the opportunities of London. Despoiled of every guarantee she went to Stanhope Gardens like a mere maidservant, with restrictions on her very luggage, while during the year that followed this upheaval Limbert, strolling with me on the goose-green, to which I often ran down, played extravagantly over the theme that with what he was now going in for it was a positive comfort not to have the social kaleidoscope. With a cold-blooded trick in view what had life or manners or the best society or flys from the inn to say to the question? It was as good a place as another to play his new game. He had found a quieter corner than any corner of the great world, and a damp old house at sixpence a year, which, beside leaving him all his margin to educate his children, would allow of the supreme luxury of his frankly presenting himself as a poor man. This was a convenience that *ces dames*, as he called them, had never yet fully permitted him.

It rankled in me at first to see his reward so meagre, his conquest so mean; but the simplification effected had a charm that I finally felt; it was a forcing-house for the three or four other fine miscarriages to which his scheme was evidently condemned. I limited him to three or four, having had my sharp impression, in spite of the perpetual broad joke of the thing, that a spring had really snapped in him on the occasion of that deeply disconcerting sequel to the episode of his editorship. He never lost his sense of the grotesque want, in the difference made, of adequate relation to the effort that had been the intensest of his life. He had from that moment a charge of shot in him, and it slowly worked its way to a vital part. As he met his embarrassments each year with his punctual false remedy I wondered periodically where he found the energy to return to the attack. He did it every time with a rage more blanched, but it was clear to me that the tension must finally snap the cord. We got again and again the irrepressible work of art, but what did *he* get, poor man, who wanted something so different? There were likewise odder questions than this in the matter, phenomena more curious and mysteries more puzzling, which often for sympathy if not for illumination I intimately discussed with Mrs. Limbert. She had her burdens, dear lady: after the removal from London and a considerable interval she twice again became a mother. Mrs. Stannace too, in a more restricted sense, exhibited afresh, in relation to the home she had abandoned, the same exemplary character. In her poverty of guarantees at Stanhope Gardens there had been least of all, it appeared, a proviso that she shouldn't resentfully revert again from Goneril to Regan. She came down to the goose-green like Lear himself, with fewer knights, or at least baronets, and the joint household was at last patched up. It fell to pieces and was put together on various occasions before Ray Limbert died. He was ridden to the end by the superstition that he had broken up Mrs. Stannace's original home on pretences that had proved hollow and that if he hadn't given Maud what she might have had he could at least give her back her mother. I was always sure that a sense of the compensations he owed was half the motive of the dogged pride with which he tried to wake up the libraries. I believed Mrs. Stannace still had money, though she pretended that, called upon at every turn to retrieve deficits, she had long since poured it into the general fund. This conviction haunted me; I suspected her of secret hoards, and I said to myself that she couldn't be so infamous as not some day on her deathbed to leave everything to her less opulent daughter. My compassion for the Limberts led me to hover perhaps indiscreetly round that closing scene, to dream of some happy time when such an accession of means would make up a little for their present penury.

This however was crude comfort, as in the first place I had nothing definite to go by and in the second I held it for more and more indicated that Ray wouldn't outlive her. I never ventured to sound him as to what in this particular he hoped or feared, for after the crisis marked by his leaving London I had new scruples about suffering him to be reminded of where he fell short. The poor man was in truth humiliated, and there were things as to which that kept us both silent. In proportion as he tried more fiercely for the market the old plaintiff arithmetic, fertile in jokes, dropped from our conversation. We joked immensely still about the process, but our treatment of the results became sparing and superficial. He talked as much as ever, with monstrous arts and borrowed hints, of the traps he kept setting, but we all agreed to take merely for granted that the animal was caught. This propriety had really dawned upon me the day that after Mr. Bousefield's visit Mrs. Highmore put me down at his door. Mr. Bousefield in that juncture had been served up to me anew, but after we had disposed of him we came to the book, which I was obliged to confess I had already rushed through. It was from this moment—the moment at which my terrible impression of it had blinked out at his anxious query—that the image of his scared face was to abide with me. I couldn't attenuate then—the cat was out of the bag; but later, each of the next times, I did, I acknowledge, attenuate. We all did religiously, so far as was possible; we cast ingenious ambiguities over the strong places, the beauties that betrayed him most, and found ourselves in the queer position of admirers banded to mislead a confiding artist. If we stifled our cheers however and dissimulated our joy our fond hypocrisy accomplished little, for Limbert's finger was on a pulse that told a plainer story. It was a satisfaction to have secured a greater freedom with his wife, who at last, much to her honour, entered into the conspiracy and whose sense of responsibility was flattered by the frequency of our united appeal to her for some answer to the marvellous riddle. We had all turned it over till we were tired of it, threshing out the question why the note he strained every chord to pitch for common ears should invariably insist on addressing itself to the angels. Being, as it were, ourselves the angels we had only a limited quarrel in each case with the event; but its inconsequent character, given the forces set in motion, was peculiarly baffling. It was like an interminable sum that wouldn't come straight; nobody had the time to handle so many figures. Limbert gathered, to make his pudding, dry bones and dead husks; how then was one to formulate the law that made the dish prove a feast? What was the cerebral treachery that defied his own vigilance? There was some obscure interference of taste, some obsession of the exquisite. All one could say was that genius was a fatal disturber or that the unhappy man had no effectual *flair*. When he went abroad to gather garlic he came home with heliotrope.

I hasten to add that if Mrs. Limbert was not directly illuminating she was yet rich in anecdote and example, having found a refuge from mystification exactly where the rest of us had found it, in a more devoted embrace and the sense of a finer glory. Her disappointments and eventually her privations had been many, her discipline severe; but she had ended by accepting the long grind of life and was now quite willing to take her turn at the mill. She was essentially one of us—she always understood. Touching and admirable at the last, when through the unmistakable change in Limbert's health her troubles were thickest, was the spectacle of the particular pride that she wouldn't have exchanged for prosperity. She had said to me once—only once, in a gloomy hour in London days when things were not going at all—that one really had to think him a very great man because if one didn't one would be rather ashamed of him. She had distinctly felt it at first—and in a very tender place—that almost every one passed him on the road; but I believe that in these final years she would almost have been ashamed of him if he had suddenly gone into editions. It is certain indeed that her complacency was not subjected to that shock. She would have liked the money immensely, but she would have missed something she had taught herself to regard as rather rare. There is another remark I remember her making, a remark to the effect that of course if she could have chosen she would have liked him to be Shakespeare or Scott,

171

but that failing this she was very glad he wasn't—well, she named the two gentlemen, but I won't. I daresay she sometimes laughed out to escape an alternative. She contributed passionately to the capture of the second manner, foraging for him further afield than he could conveniently go, gleaning in the barest stubble, picking up shreds to build the nest and in particular in the study of the great secret of how, as we always said, they all did it laying waste the circulating libraries. If Limbert had a weakness he rather broke down in his reading. It was fortunately not till after the appearance of *The Hidden Heart* that he broke down in everything else. He had had rheumatic fever in the spring, when the book was but half finished, and this ordeal in addition to interrupting his work had enfeebled his powers of resistance and greatly reduced his vitality. He recovered from the fever and was able to take up the book again, but the organ of life was pronounced ominously weak and it was enjoined upon him with some sharpness that he should lend himself to no worries. It might have struck me as on the cards that his worries would now be surmountable, for when he began to mend he expressed to me a conviction almost contagious that he had never yet made so adroit a bid as in the idea of *The Hidden Heart*. It is grimly droll to reflect that this superb little composition, the shortest of his novels but perhaps the loveliest, was planned from the first as an "adventure-story" on approved lines. It was the way they all did the adventure-story that he tried most dauntlessly to emulate. I wonder how many readers ever divined to which of their bookshelves *The Hidden Heart* was so exclusively addressed. High medical advice early in the summer had been quite viciously clear as to the inconvenience that might ensue to him should he neglect to spend the winter in Egypt. He was not a man to neglect anything; but Egypt seemed to us all then as unattainable as a second edition. He finished *The Hidden Heart* with the energy of apprehension and desire, for if the book should happen to do what "books of that class," as the publisher said, sometimes did he might well have a fund to draw on. As soon as I read the deep and delicate thing I knew, as I had known in each case before, exactly how well it would do. Poor Limbert in this long business always figured to me an undiscourageable parent to whom only girls kept being born. A bouncing boy, a son and heir was devoutly prayed for and almanacks and old wives consulted; but the spell was inveterate, incurable, and *The Hidden Heart* proved, so to speak, but another female child. When the winter arrived accordingly Egypt was out of the question. Jane Highmore, to my knowledge, wanted to lend him money, and there were even greater devotees who did their best to induce him to lean on them. There was so marked a "movement" among his friends that a very considerable sum would have been at his disposal; but his stiffness was invincible: it had its root, I think, in his sense, on his own side, of sacrifices already made. He had sacrificed honour and pride, and he had sacrificed them precisely to the question of money. He would evidently, should he be able to go on, have to continue to sacrifice them, but it must be all in the way to which he had now, as he considered, hardened himself. He had spent years in plotting for favour, and since on favour he must live it could only be as a bargain and a price.

He got through the early part of the season better than we feared, and I went down in great elation to spend Christmas on the goose-green.

He told me late on Christmas eve, after our simple domestic revels had sunk to rest and we sat together by the fire, that he had been visited the night before in wakeful hours by the finest fancy for a really good thing that he had ever felt descend in the darkness. "It's just the vision of a situation that contains, upon my honour, everything," he said, "and I wonder that I've never thought of it before." He didn't describe it further, contrary to his common practice, and I only knew later, by Mrs. Limbert, that he had begun *Derogation* and that he was completely full of his subject. It was a subject however that he was not to live to treat. The work went on for a couple of months in happy mystery, without revelations even to his wife. He had not invited her to help him to get up his case—she had not taken the field with him as on his previous campaigns. We only knew he was at it again but that less even than ever had been said about the impression to be made on the market. I saw him in February and thought him sufficiently at ease. The great thing was that he was immensely interested and was pleased with the omens. I got a strange, stirring sense that he had not consulted the usual ones and indeed that he had floated away into a grand indifference, into a reckless consciousness of art. The voice of the market had suddenly grown faint and far: he had come back at the last, as people so often do, to one of the moods, the sincerities of his prime. Was he really with a blurred sense of the urgent doing something now only for himself? We wondered and waited— we felt that he was a little confused. What had happened, I was afterwards satisfied, was that he had quite forgotten whether he generally sold or not. He had merely waked up one morning again in the country of the blue and had stayed there with a good conscience and a great idea. He stayed till death knocked at the gate, for the pen dropped from his hand only at the moment when from sudden failure of the heart his eyes, as he sank back in his chair, closed for ever. *Derogation* is a splendid fragment; it evidently would have been one of his high successes. I am not prepared to say it would have waked up the libraries.

THE WAY IT CAME

I find, as you prophesied, much that's interesting, but little that helps the delicate question—the possibility of publication. Her diaries are less systematic than I hoped; she only had a blessed habit of noting and narrating. She summarised, she saved; she appears seldom indeed to have let a good story pass without catching it on the wing. I allude of course not so much to things she heard as to things she saw and felt. She writes sometimes of herself, sometimes of others, sometimes of the combination. It's under this last rubric that she's usually most vivid. But it's not, you will understand, when she's most vivid that she's always most publish-able. To tell the truth she's fearfully indiscreet, or has at least all the material for making me so. Take as an instance the fragment I send you, after dividing it for your convenience into several small chapters. It is the contents of a thin blank-book which I have had copied out and which has the merit of being nearly enough a rounded thing, an intelligible whole. These pages evidently date from years ago. I've read with the liveliest wonder the statement they so circumstantially make and done my best to swallow the prodigy they leave to be inferred. These things would be striking, wouldn't they? to any reader; but can you imagine for a moment my placing such a document before the world, even though, as if she herself had desired the world should have the benefit of it, she has given her friends neither name nor initials? Have you any sort of clue to their identity? I leave her the floor.

I

I know perfectly of course that I brought it upon myself; but that doesn't make it any better. I was the first to speak of her to him—he had never even heard her mentioned. Even if I had happened not to speak some one else would have made up for it: I tried afterwards to find comfort in that reflection. But the comfort of reflections is thin: the only comfort that counts in life is not to have been a fool. That's a beatitude I shall doubtless never enjoy. "Why, you ought to meet her and talk it over," is what I immediately said. "Birds of a feather flock together." I told him who she was and that they were birds of a feather because if he had had in youth a strange adventure she had had about the same time just such another. It was well known to her friends—an incident she was constantly called on to describe. She was charming, clever, pretty, unhappy; but it was none the less the thing to which she had originally owed her reputation.

Being at the age of eighteen somewhere abroad with an aunt she had had a vision of one of her parents at the moment of death. The parent was in England, hundreds of miles away and so far as she knew neither dying nor dead. It was by day, in the museum of some great foreign town. She had passed alone, in advance of her companions, into a small room containing some famous work of art and occupied at that moment by two other persons. One of these was an old custodian; the second, before observing him, she took for a stranger, a tourist. She was merely conscious that he was bareheaded and seated on a bench. The instant her eyes rested on him however she beheld to her amazement her father, who, as if he had long waited for her, looked at her in singular distress, with an impatience that was akin to reproach. She rushed to him with a bewildered cry, "Papa, what *is* it?" but this was followed by an exhibition of still livelier feeling when on her movement he simply vanished, leaving the custodian and her relations, who were at her heels, to gather round her in dismay. These persons, the official, the aunt, the cousins were therefore in a manner witnesses of the fact—the fact at least of the impression made on her; and there was the further testimony of a doctor who was attending one of the party and to whom it was immediately afterwards communicated. He gave her a remedy for hysterics but said to the aunt privately: "Wait and see if something doesn't happen at home." Something *had* happened—the poor father, suddenly and violently seized, had died that morning. The aunt, the mother's sister, received before the day was out a telegram announcing the event and requesting her to prepare her niece for it. Her niece was already prepared, and the girl's sense of this visitation remained of course indelible. We had all as her friends had it conveyed to us and had conveyed it creepily to each other. Twelve years had elapsed and as a woman who had made an unhappy marriage and lived apart from her husband she had become interesting from other sources; but since the name she now bore was a name frequently borne, and since moreover her judicial separation, as things were going, could hardly count as a distinction, it was usual to qualify her as "the one, you know, who saw her father's ghost."

As for him, dear man, he had seen his mother's. I had never heard of that till this occasion on which our closer, our pleasanter acquaintance led him, through some turn of the subject of our talk, to mention it and to inspire me in so doing with the impulse to let him know that he had a rival in the field—a person with whom he could compare notes. Later on his story became for him, perhaps because of my unduly repeating it, likewise a convenient wordly label; but it had not a year before been the ground on which he was introduced to me. He had other merits, just as she, poor thing! had others. I can honestly say that I was quite aware of them from the first—I discovered them sooner than he discovered mine. I remember how it struck me even at the time that his sense of mine was quickened by my having been able to match, though not indeed straight from my own experience, his curious anecdote. It dated, this anecdote, as hers did, from some dozen years before—a year in which, at Oxford, he had for some reason of his own been staying on into the "Long." He had been in the August afternoon on the river. Coming back into his room while it was still distinct daylight he found his mother standing there as if her eyes had been fixed on the door. He had had a letter from her that morning out of Wales, where she was staying with her father. At the sight of him she smiled with extraordinary radiance and extended her arms to him, and then as he sprang forward and joyfully opened his own he vanished from the place. He wrote to her that night, telling her what had happened; the letter had been carefully preserved. The next morning he heard of her death. He was through this chance of our talk extremely struck with the little prodigy I was able to produce for him. He had never encountered another case. Certainly they ought to meet, my friend and he; certainly they would have something in common. I would arrange this, wouldn't I?—if *she* didn't mind; for himself he didn't mind in the least. I had promised to speak to her of the matter as soon as possible, and within the week I was able to do so. She "minded" as little as he; she was perfectly willing to see him. And yet no meeting was to occur—as meetings are commonly understood.

II

That's just half my tale—the extraordinary way it was hindered. This was the fault of a series of accidents; but the accidents continued for years and became, for me and for others, a subject of hilarity with either party. They were droll enough at first; then they grew rather a bore. The odd thing was that both parties were amenable: it wasn't a case of their being indifferent, much less of their being indisposed. It was one of the caprices of chance, aided I suppose by some opposition of their interests and habits. His were centred in his office, his eternal inspectorship, which left him small leisure, constantly calling him away and making him break engagements. He liked society, but he found it everywhere and took it at a run. I never knew at a given moment where he was, and there were times when for months together I never saw him. She was on her side practically suburban: she lived at Richmond and never went "out." She was a woman of distinction, but not of fashion, and felt, as people said, her situation. Decidedly proud and rather whimsical she lived her life as she had planned it. There were things one could do with her, but one couldn't make her come to one's parties. One went indeed a little more than seemed quite convenient to hers, which consisted of her cousin, a cup of tea and the view. The tea was good; but the view was familiar, though perhaps not, like the cousin—a disagreeable old maid who had been of the group at the museum and with whom she now lived—offensively so. This connection with an inferior relative, which had partly an economical motive—she proclaimed her companion a marvellous manager—was one of the little perversities we had to forgive her. Another was her estimate of the proprieties created by her rupture with her husband. That was extreme—many persons called it even morbid. She made no advances; she cultivated scruples; she suspected, or I should perhaps rather say she remembered slights: she was one of the few women I have known whom that particular predicament had rendered modest rather than bold. Dear thing! she had some delicacy.

Especially marked were the limits she had set to possible attentions from men: it was always her thought that her husband was waiting to pounce on her. She discouraged if she didn't forbid the visits of male persons not senile: she said she could never be too careful.

When I first mentioned to her that I had a friend whom fate had distinguished in the same weird way as herself I put her quite at liberty to say "Oh, bring him out to see me!" I should probably have been able to bring him, and a situation perfectly innocent or at any rate comparatively simple would have been created. But she uttered no such word; she only said: "I must meet him certainly; yes, I shall look out for him!" That caused the first delay, and meanwhile various things happened. One of them was that as time went on she made, charming as she was, more and more friends, and that it regularly befell that these friends were sufficiently also friends of his to bring him up in conversation. It was odd that without belonging, as it were, to the same world or, according to the horrid term, the same set, my baffled pair should have happened in so many cases to fall in with the same people and make them join in the funny chorus. She had friends who didn't know each other but who inevitably and punctually recommended *him*. She had also the sort of originality, the intrinsic interest that led her to be kept by each of us as a kind of private resource, cultivated jealously, more or less in secret, as a person whom one didn't meet in society, whom it was not for every one—whom it was not for the vulgar—to approach, and with whom therefore acquaintance was particularly difficult and particularly precious. We saw her separately, with appointments and conditions, and found it made on the whole for harmony not to tell each other. Somebody had always had a note from her still later than somebody else. There was some silly woman who for a long time, among the unprivileged, owed to three simple visits to Richmond a reputation for being intimate with "lots of awfully clever out-of-the-way people."

Every one has had friends it has seemed a happy thought to bring together, and every one remembers that his happiest thoughts have not been his greatest successes; but I doubt if there was ever a case in which the failure was in such direct proportion to the quantity of influence set in motion. It is really perhaps here the quantity of influence that was most remarkable. My lady and gentleman each declared to me and others that it was like the subject of a roaring farce. The reason first given had with time dropped-out of sight and fifty better ones flourished on top of it. They were so awfully alike: they had the same ideas and tricks and tastes, the same prejudices and superstitions and heresies; they said the same things and sometimes did them; they liked and disliked the same persons and places, the same books, authors and styles; any one could see a certain identity even in their looks and their features. It established much of a propriety that they were in common parlance equally "nice" and almost equally handsome. But the great sameness, for wonder and chatter, was their rare perversity in regard to being photographed. They were the only persons ever heard of who had never been "taken" and who had a passionate objection to it. They just *wouldn't* be, for anything any one could say. I had loudly complained of this; him in particular I had so vainly desired to be able to show on my drawing-room chimney-piece in a Bond Street frame. It was at any rate the very liveliest of all the reasons why they ought to know each other—all the lively reasons reduced to naught by the strange law that had made them bang so many doors in each other's face, made them the buckets in the well, the two ends of the see-saw, the two parties in the state, so that when one was up the other was down, when one was out the other was in; neither by any possibility entering a house till the other had left it, or leaving it, all unawares, till the other was at hand. They only arrived when they had been given up, which was precisely also when they departed. They were in a word alternate and incompatible; they missed each other with an inveteracy that could be explained only by its being preconcerted. It was however so far from preconcerted that it had ended—literally after several years—by disappointing and annoying them. I don't think their curiosity was lively till it had been proved utterly vain. A great deal was of course done to help them, but it merely laid wires for them to trip. To give examples I should have to have taken notes; but I happen to remember that neither had ever been able to dine on the right occasion. The right occasion for each was the occasion that would be wrong for the other. On the wrong one they were most punctual, and there were never any but wrong ones. The very elements conspired and the constitution of man reinforced them. A cold, a headache, a bereavement, a storm, a fog, an earthquake, a cataclysm infallibly intervened. The whole business was beyond a joke.

Yet as a joke it had still to be taken, though one couldn't help feeling that the joke had made the situation serious, had produced on the part of each a consciousness, an awkwardness, a positive dread of the last accident of all, the only one with any freshness left, the accident that would bring them face to face. The final effect of its predecessors had been to kindle this instinct. They were quite ashamed—perhaps even a little of each other. So much preparation, so much frustration: what indeed could be good enough for it all to lead up to? A mere meeting would be mere flatness. Did I see them at the end of years, they often asked, just stupidly confronted? If they were bored by the joke they might be worse bored by something else. They made exactly the same reflections, and each in some manner was sure to hear of the other's.

I really think it was this peculiar diffidence that finally controlled the situation. I mean that if they had failed for the first year or two because they couldn't help it they kept up the habit because they had—what shall I call it?—grown nervous. It really took some lurking volition to account for anything so absurd

III

When to crown our long acquaintance I accepted his renewed offer of marriage it was humorously said, I know, that I had made the gift of his photograph a condition. This was so far true that I had refused to give him mine without it. At any rate I had him at last, in his high distinction, on the chimney-piece, where the day she called to congratulate me she came nearer than she had ever done to seeing him. He had set her in being taken an example which I invited her to follow; he had sacrificed his perversity—wouldn't she sacrifice hers? She too must give me something on my engagement—wouldn't she give me the companion-piece? She laughed and shook her head; she had headshakes whose impulse seemed to come from as far away as the breeze that stirs a flower. The companion-piece to the portrait of my future husband was the portrait of his future wife. She had taken her stand—she could depart from it as little as she could explain it. It was a prejudice, an *entêtement*, a vow—she would live and die unphotographed. Now too she was alone in that state: this was what she liked; it made her so much more original. She rejoiced in the fall of her late associate and looked a long time at his picture, about which she made no memorable remark, though she even turned it over to see the back. About our engagement she was charming—full of cordiality and sympathy. "You've known him even longer than I've *not?*" she said, "and that seems a very long time." She understood how we had jogged together over hill and dale and how inevitable it was that we should now rest together. I'm definite about all this because what followed is so strange that it's a kind of relief to me to mark the point up to which our relations were as natural as ever. It was I myself who in a sudden madness altered and destroyed them. I see now that she gave me no pretext and that I only found one in the way she looked at the fine face in the Bond Street frame. How then would I have had her look at it? What I had wanted from the first was to make her care for him. Well, that was what I still wanted—up to the moment of her having promised me that he would on this occasion really aid me to break the silly spell that had kept them asunder. I had arranged with him to do his part if she would as triumphantly do hers. I was on a different footing now—I was on a footing to answer for him. I would positively engage that at five on the following Saturday he would be on that spot. He was out of town on pressing business; but pledged to keep his promise to the letter he would return on purpose and in abundant time. "Are you perfectly sure?" I remember she asked, looking grave and considering: I thought she had turned a little pale. She was tired, she was indisposed: it was a pity he was to see her after all at so poor a moment. If he only *could* have seen her five years before! However, I replied that this time I was sure and that success therefore depended simply on herself. At five o'clock on the Saturday she would find him in a particular chair I pointed out, the one in which he usually sat and in which—though this I didn't mention—he had been sitting when, the week before, he put the question of our future to me in the way that had brought me round. She looked at it in silence, just as she had looked at the photograph, while

I repeated for the twentieth time that it was too preposterous it shouldn't somehow be feasible to introduce to one's dearest friend one's second self. "*Am* I your dearest friend?" she asked with a smile that for a moment brought back her beauty. I replied by pressing her to my bosom; after which she said: "Well, I'll come. I'm extraordinarily afraid, but you may count on me."

When she had left me I began to wonder what she was afraid of, for she had spoken as if she fully meant it. The next day, late in the afternoon, I had three lines from her: she had found on getting home the announcement of her husband's death. She had not seen him for seven years, but she wished me to know it in this way before I should hear of it in another. It made however in her life, strange and sad to say, so little difference that she would scrupulously keep her appointment. I rejoiced for her—I supposed it would make at least the difference of her having more money; but even in this diversion, far from forgetting that she had said she was afraid, I seemed to catch sight of a reason for her being so. Her fear as the evening went on became contagious, and the contagion took in my breast the form of a sudden panic. It wasn't jealousy—it was the dread of jealousy. I called myself a fool for not having been quiet till we were man and wife. After that I should somehow feel secure. It was only a question of waiting another month—a trifle surely for people who had waited so long. It had been plain enough she was nervous, and now that she was free she naturally wouldn't be less so. What was her nervousness therefore but a presentiment? She had been hitherto the victim of interference, but it was quite possible she would henceforth be the source of it. The victim in that case would be my simple self. What had the interference been but the finger of providence pointing out a danger? The danger was of course for poor *me*. It had been kept at bay by a series of accidents unexampled in their frequency; but the reign of accident was now visibly at an end. I had an intimate conviction that both parties would keep the tryst. It was more and more impressed upon me that they were approaching, converging. We had talked about breaking the spell; well, it would be effectually broken—unless indeed it should merely take another form and overdo their encounters as it had overdone their escapes.

This was something I couldn't sit still for thinking of; it kept me awake—at midnight I was full of unrest. At last I felt there was only one way of laying the ghost. If the reign of accident was over I must just take up the succession. I sat down and wrote a hurried note which would meet him on his return and which as the servants had gone to bed I sallied forth bareheaded into the empty, gusty street to drop into the nearest pillar-box. It was to tell him that I shouldn't be able to be at home in the afternoon as I had hoped and that he must postpone his visit till dinner-time. This was an implication that he would find me alone.

IV

When accordingly at five she presented herself I naturally felt false and base. My act had been a momentary madness, but I had at least to be consistent. She remained an hour; he of course never came; and I could only persist in my perfidy. I had thought it best to let her come; singular as this now seems to me I thought it diminished my guilt. Yet as she sat there so visibly white and weary, stricken with a sense of everything her husband's death had opened up, I felt an almost intolerable pang of pity and remorse. If I didn't tell her on the spot what I had done it was because I was too ashamed. I feigned astonishment—I feigned it to the end; I protested that if ever I had had confidence I had had it that day. I blush as I tell my story—I take it as my penance. There was nothing indignant I didn't say about him; I invented suppositions, attenuations; I admitted in stupefaction, as the hands of the clock travelled, that their luck hadn't turned. She smiled at this vision of their "luck," but she looked anxious—she looked unusual: the only thing that kept me up was the fact that, oddly enough, she wore mourning—no great depths of crape, but simple and scrupulous black. She had in her bonnet three small black feathers. She carried a little muff of astrachan. This put me by the aid of some acute reflection a little in the right. She had written to me that the sudden event made no difference for her, but apparently it made as much difference as that. If she was inclined to the usual forms why didn't she observe that of not going the first day or two out to tea? There was some one she wanted so much to see that she couldn't wait till her husband was buried. Such a betrayal of eagerness made me hard and cruel enough to practise my odious deceit, though at the same time, as the hour waxed and waned, I suspected in her something deeper still than disappointment and somewhat less successfully concealed. I mean a strange underlying relief, the soft, low emission of the breath that comes when a danger is past. What happened as she spent her barren hour with me was that at last she gave him up. She let him go for ever. She made the most graceful joke of it that I've ever seen made of anything; but it was for all that a great date in her life. She spoke with her mild gaiety of all the other vain times, the long game of hide-and-seek, the unprecedented queerness of such a relation. For it was, or had been, a relation, wasn't it, hadn't it? That was just the absurd part of it. When she got up to go I said to her that it was more a relation than ever, but that I hadn't the face after what had occurred to propose to her for the present another opportunity. It was plain that the only valid opportunity would be my accomplished marriage. Of course she would be at my wedding? It was even to be hoped that *he* would.

"If *I* am, he won't be!" she declared with a laugh. I admitted there might be something in that. The thing was therefore to get us safely married first. "That won't help us. Nothing will help us!" she said as she kissed me farewell. "I shall never, never see him!" It was with those words she left me.

I could bear her disappointment as I've called it; but when a couple of hours later I received him at dinner I found that I couldn't bear his. The way my manoeuvre might have affected him had not been particularly present to me; but the result of it was the first word of reproach that had ever yet dropped from him. I say "reproach" because that expression is scarcely too strong for the terms in which he conveyed to me his surprise that under the extraordinary circumstances I should not have found some means not to deprive him of such an occasion. I might really have managed either not to be obliged to go out or to let their meeting take place all the same. They would probably have got on in my drawing-room without me. At this I quite broke down—I confessed my iniquity and the miserable reason of it. I had not put her off and I had not gone out; she had been there and after waiting for him an hour had departed in the belief that he had been absent by his own fault.

"She must think me a precious brute!" he exclaimed. "Did she say of me—what she had a right to say?"

"I assure you she said nothing that showed the least feeling. She looked at your photograph, she even turned round the back of it, on which your address happens to be inscribed. Yet it provoked her to no demonstration. She doesn't care so much as all that."

"Then why are you afraid of her?"

"It was not of her I was afraid. It was of you."

"Did you think I would fall in love with her? You never alluded to such a possibility before," he went on as I remained silent. "Admirable person as you pronounced her, that wasn't the light in which you showed her to me."

"Do you mean that if it *had* been you would have managed by this time to catch a glimpse of her? I didn't fear things then," I added. "I hadn't the same reason."

He kissed me at this, and when I remembered that she had done so an hour or two before I felt for an instant as if he were taking from my lips the very pressure of hers. In spite of kisses the incident had shed a certain chill, and I suffered horribly from the sense that he had seen me guilty of a fraud. He had seen it only through my frank avowal, but I was as unhappy as if I had a stain to efface. I couldn't get over the manner of his looking at me when I spoke of her apparent indifference to his not having come.

For the first time since I had known him he seemed to have expressed a doubt of my word. Before we parted I told him that I would undeceive her, start the first thing in the morning for Richmond and there let her know that he had been blameless. At this he kissed me again. I would expiate my sin, I said; I would humble myself in the dust; I would confess and ask to be forgiven. At this he kissed me once more.

V

In the train the next day this struck me as a good deal for him to have consented to; but my purpose was firm enough to carry me on. I mounted the long hill to where the view begins, and then I knocked at her door. I was a trifle mystified by the fact that her blinds were still drawn, reflecting that if in the stress of my compunction I had come early I had certainly yet allowed people time to get up.

"At home, mum? She has left home for ever."

I was extraordinarily startled by this announcement of the elderly parlour-maid. "She has gone away?"

"She's dead, mum, please." Then as I gasped at the horrible word: "She died last night."

The loud cry that escaped me sounded even in my own ears like some harsh violation of the hour. I felt for the moment as if I had killed her; I turned faint and saw through a vagueness the woman hold out her arms to me. Of what next happened I have no recollection, nor of anything but my friend's poor stupid cousin, in a darkened room, after an interval that I suppose very brief, sobbing at me in a smothered accusatory way. I can't say how long it took me to understand, to believe and then to press back with an immense effort that pang of responsibility which, superstitiously, insanely had been at first almost all I was conscious of. The doctor, after the fact, had been superlatively wise and clear: he was satisfied of a long-latent weakness of the heart, determined probably years before by the agitations and terrors to which her marriage had introduced her. She had had in those days cruel scenes with her husband, she had been in fear of her life. All emotion, everything in the nature of anxiety and suspense had been after that to be strongly deprecated, as in her marked cultivation of a quiet life she was evidently well aware; but who could say that any one, especially a "real lady," could be successfully protected from every little rub? She had had one a day or two before in the news of her husband's death; for there were shocks of all kinds, not only those of grief and surprise. For that matter she had never dreamed of so near a release; it had looked uncommonly as if he would live as long as herself. Then in the evening, in town, she had manifestly had another: something must have happened there which it would be indispensable to clear up. She had come back very late—it was past eleven o'clock, and on being met in the hall by her cousin, who was extremely anxious, had said that she was tired and must rest a moment before mounting the stairs. They had passed together into the dining-room, her companion proposing a glass of wine and bustling to the sideboard to pour it out. This took but a moment, and when my informant turned round our poor friend had not had time to seat herself. Suddenly, with a little moan that was barely audible, she dropped upon the sofa. She was dead. What unknown "little rub" had dealt her the blow? What shock, in the name of wonder, *had* she had in town? I mentioned immediately the only one I could imagine—her having failed to meet at my house, to which by invitation for the purpose she had come at five o'clock, the gentleman I was to be married to, who had been accidentally kept away and with whom she had no acquaintance whatever. This obviously counted for little; but something else might easily have occurred; nothing in the London streets was more possible than an accident, especially an accident in those desperate cabs. What had she done, where had she gone on leaving my house? I had taken for granted she had gone straight home. We both presently remembered that in her excursions to town she sometimes, for convenience, for refreshment, spent an hour or two at the "Gentlewomen," the quiet little ladies' club, and I promised that it should be my first care to make at that establishment thorough inquiry. Then we entered the dim and dreadful chamber where she lay locked up in death and where, asking after a little to be left alone with her, I remained for half an hour. Death had made her, had kept her beautiful; but I felt above all, as I knelt at her bed, that it had made her, had kept her silent. It had turned the key on something I was concerned to know.

On my return from Richmond and after another duty had been performed I drove to his chambers. It was the first time, but I had often wanted to see them. On the staircase, which, as the house contained twenty sets of rooms, was unrestrictedly public, I met his servant, who went back with me and ushered me in. At the sound of my entrance he appeared in the doorway of a further room, and the instant we were alone I produced my news: "She's dead!"

"Dead?"

He was tremendously struck, and I observed that he had no need to ask whom, in this abruptness, I meant.

"She died last evening—just after leaving me."

He stared with the strangest expression, his eyes searching mine as if they were looking for a trap. "Last evening—after leaving you?" He repeated my words in stupefaction. Then he brought out so that it was in stupefaction I heard: "Impossible! I saw her."

"You 'saw' her?"

"On that spot—where you stand."

This brought back to me after an instant, as if to help me to take it in, the memory of the strange warning of his youth. "In the hour of death—I understand: as you so beautifully saw your mother."

"Ah! *not* as I saw my mother—not that way, not that way!" He was deeply moved by my news—far more moved, I perceived, than he would have been the day before: it gave me a vivid sense that, as I had then said to myself, there was indeed a relation between them and that he had actually been face to face with her. Such an idea, by its reassertion of his extraordinary privilege, would have suddenly presented him as painfully abnormal had he not so vehemently insisted on the difference. "I saw her living—I saw her to speak to her—I saw her as I see you now!"

It is remarkable that for a moment, though only for a moment, I found relief in the more personal, as it were, but also the more natural of the two phenomena. The next, as I embraced this image of her having come to him on leaving me and of just what it accounted for in the disposal of her time, I demanded with a shade of harshness of which I was aware—"What on earth did she come for?" He had now had a minute to think—to recover himself and judge of effects, so that if it was still with excited eyes he spoke he showed a conscious redness and made an inconsequent attempt to smile away the gravity of his words.

"She came just to see me. She came—after what had passed at your house—so that we *should*, after all, at last meet. The impulse seemed to me exquisite, and that was the way I took it."

I looked round the room where she had been—where she had been and I never had been.

"And was the way you took it the way she expressed it?"

"She only expressed it by being here and by letting me look at her. That was enough!" he exclaimed with a singular laugh.

I wondered more and more. "You mean she didn't speak to you?"

"She said nothing. She only looked at me as I looked at her."

"And *you* didn't speak either?"

He gave me again his painful smile. "I thought of *you*. The situation was every way delicate. I used the finest tact. But she saw she had pleased me." He even repeated his dissonant laugh.

"She evidently pleased you!" Then I thought a moment. "How long did she stay?"

"How can I say? It seemed twenty minutes, but it was probably a good deal less."

"Twenty minutes of silence!" I began to have my definite view and now in fact quite to clutch at it. "Do you know you're telling me a story positively monstrous?"

He had been standing with his back to the fire; at this, with a pleading look, he came to me. "I beseech you, dearest, to take it kindly."

I could take it kindly, and I signified as much; but I couldn't somehow, as he rather awkwardly opened his arms, let him draw me to him. So there fell between us for an appreciable time the discomfort of a great silence.

<u>VI</u>

He broke it presently by saying: "There's absolutely no doubt of her death?"

"Unfortunately none. I've just risen from my knees by the bed where they've laid her out."

He fixed his eyes hard on the floor; then he raised them to mine. "How does she look?"

"She looks—at peace."

He turned away again, while I watched him; but after a moment he began: "At what hour, then——?"

"It must have been near midnight. She dropped as she reached her house—from an affection of the heart which she knew herself and her physician knew her to have, but of which, patiently, bravely she had never spoken to me."

He listened intently and for a minute he was unable to speak. At last he broke out with an accent of which the almost boyish confidence, the really sublime simplicity rings in my ears as I write: "Wasn't she *wonderful!*" Even at the time I was able to do it justice enough to remark in reply that I had always told him so; but the next minute, as if after speaking he had caught a glimpse of what he might have made me feel, he went on quickly: "You see that if she didn't get home till midnight—"

I instantly took him up. "There was plenty of time for you to have seen her? How so," I inquired, "when you didn't leave my house till late? I don't remember the very moment—I was preoccupied. But you know that though you said you had lots to do you sat for some time after dinner. She, on her side, was all the evening at the 'Gentlewomen.' I've just come from there—I've ascertained. She had tea there; she remained a long, long time."

"What was she doing all the long, long time?" I saw that he was eager to challenge at every step my account of the matter; and the more he showed this the more I found myself disposed to insist on that account, to prefer, with apparent perversity, an explanation which only deepened the marvel and the mystery, but which, of the two prodigies it had to choose from, my reviving jealousy found easiest to accept. He stood there pleading with a candour that now seems to me beautiful for the privilege of having in spite of supreme defeat known the living woman; while I, with a passion I wonder at to-day, though it still smoulders in a manner in its ashes, could only reply that, through a strange gift shared by her with his mother and on her own side likewise hereditary, the miracle of his youth had been renewed for him, the miracle of hers for her. She had been to him—yes, and by an impulse as charming as he liked; but oh! she had not been in the body. It was a simple question of evidence. I had had, I assured him, a definite statement of what she had done—most of the time—at the little club. The place was almost empty, but the servants had noticed her. She had sat motionless in a deep chair by the drawing-room fire; she had leaned back her head, she had closed her eyes, she had seemed softly to sleep.

"I see. But till what o'clock?"

"There," I was obliged to answer, "the servants fail me a little. The portress in particular is unfortunately a fool, though even she too is supposed to be a Gentlewoman. She was evidently at that period of the evening, without a substitute and, against regulations, absent for some little time from the cage in which it's her business to watch the comings and goings. She's muddled, she palpably prevaricates; so I can't positively, from her observation, give you an hour. But it was remarked toward half-past ten that our poor friend was no longer in the club."

"She came straight here; and from here she went straight to the train."

"She couldn't have run it so close," I declared. "That was a thing she particularly never did."

"There was no need of running it close, my dear—she had plenty of time. Your memory is at fault about my having left you late: I left you, as it happens, unusually early. I'm sorry my stay with you seemed long; for I was back here by ten."

"To put yourself into your slippers," I rejoined, "and fall asleep in your chair. You slept till morning—you saw her in a dream!" He looked at me in silence and with sombre eyes—eyes that showed me he had some irritation to repress. Presently I went on: "You had a visit, at an extraordinary hour, from a lady—*soit*: nothing in the world is more probable. But there are ladies and ladies. How in the name of goodness, if she was unannounced and dumb and you had into the bargain never seen the least portrait of her—how could you identify the person we're talking of?"

"Haven't I to absolute satiety heard her described? I'll describe her for you in every particular."

"Don't!" I exclaimed with a promptness that made him laugh once more. I coloured at this, but I continued: "Did your servant introduce her?"

"He wasn't here—he's always away when he's wanted. One of the features of this big house is that from the street-door the different floors are accessible practically without challenge. My servant makes love to a young person employed in the rooms above these, and he had a long bout of it last evening. When he's out on that job he leaves my outer door, on the staircase, so much ajar as to enable him to slip back without a sound. The door then only requires a push. She pushed it—that simply took a little courage."

"A little? It took tons! And it took all sorts of impossible calculations."

"Well, she had them—she made them. Mind you, I don't deny for a moment," he added, "that it was very, very wonderful!"

Something in his tone prevented me for a while from trusting myself to speak. At last I said: "How did she come to know where you live?"

"By remembering the address on the little label the shop-people happily left sticking to the frame I had had made for my photograph."

"And how was she dressed?"

"In mourning, my own dear. No great depths of crape, but simple and scrupulous black. She had in her bonnet three small black feathers. She carried a little muff of astrachan. She has near the left eye," he continued, "a tiny vertical scar—"

I stopped him short. "The mark of a caress from her husband." Then I added: "How close you must have been to her!" He made no answer to this, and I thought he blushed, observing which I broke straight off. "Well, goodbye."

"You won't stay a little?" He came to me again tenderly, and this time I suffered him. "Her visit had its beauty," he murmured as he held me, "but yours has a greater one."

I let him kiss me, but I remembered, as I had remembered the day before, that the last kiss she had given, as I supposed, in this world had been for the lips he touched.

"I'm life, you see," I answered. "What you saw last night was death."

"It was life—it was life!"

He spoke with a kind of soft stubbornness, and I disengaged myself. We stood looking at each other hard.

"You describe the scene—so far as you describe it at all—in terms that are incomprehensible. She was in the room before you knew it?"

"I looked up from my letter-writing—at that table under the lamp, I had been wholly absorbed in it—and she stood before me."

"Then what did you do?"

"I sprang up with an ejaculation, and she, with a smile, laid her finger, ever so warningly, yet with a sort of delicate dignity, to her lips. I knew it meant silence, but the strange thing was that it seemed immediately to explain and to justify her. We, at any rate, stood for a time that, as I've told you, I can't calculate, face to face. It was just as you and I stand now."

"Simply staring?"

He impatiently protested. "Ah! *we're* not staring!"

"Yes, but we're talking."

"Well, *we* were—after a fashion." He lost himself in the memory of it. "It was as friendly as this." I had it on my tongue's end to ask if that were saying much for it, but I remarked instead that what they had evidently done was to gaze in mutual admiration. Then I inquired whether his recognition of her had been immediate. "Not quite," he replied, "for, of course, I didn't expect her; but it came to me long before she went who she was—who she could only be."

I thought a little. "And how did she at last go?"

"Just as she arrived. The door was open behind her, and she passed out."

"Was she rapid—slow?"

"Rather quick. But looking behind her," he added, with a smile. "I let her go, for I perfectly understood that I was to take it as she wished."

I was conscious of exhaling a long, vague sigh. "Well, you must take it now as *I* wish—you must let *me* go."

At this he drew near me again, detaining and persuading me, declaring with all due gallantry that I was a very different matter. I would have given anything to have been able to ask him if he had touched her, but the words refused to form themselves: I knew well enough how horrid and vulgar they would sound. I said something else—I forget exactly what; it was feebly tortuous, and intended to make him tell me without my putting the question. But he didn't tell me; he only repeated, as if from a glimpse of the propriety of soothing and consoling me, the sense of his declaration of some minutes before—the assurance that she was indeed exquisite, as I had always insisted, but that I was his "real" friend and his very own for ever. This led me to reassert, in the spirit of my previous rejoinder, that I had at least the merit of being alive; which in turn drew from him again the flash of contradiction I dreaded. "Oh, *she* was alive! she was, she was!"

"She was dead! she was dead!" I asseverated with an energy, a determination that it should be so, which comes back to me now almost as grotesque. But the sound of the word, as it rang out, filled me suddenly with horror, and all the natural emotion the meaning of it might have evoked in other conditions gathered and broke in a flood. It rolled over me that here was a great affection quenched, and how much I had loved and trusted her. I had a vision at the same time of the lonely beauty of her end. "She's gone— she's lost to us for ever!" I burst into sobs.

"That's exactly what I feel," he exclaimed, speaking with extreme kindness and pressing me to him for comfort. "She's gone; she's lost to us for ever: so what does it matter now?" He bent over me, and when his face had touched mine I scarcely knew if it were wet with my tears or with his own.

VII

It was my theory, my conviction, it became, as I may say, my attitude, that they had still never "met;" and it was just on this ground that I said to myself it would be generous to ask him to stand with me beside her grave. He did so, very modestly and tenderly, and I assumed, though he himself clearly cared nothing for the danger, that the solemnity of the occasion, largely made up of persons who had known them both and had a sense of the long joke, would sufficiently deprive his presence of all light association. On the question of what had happened the evening of her death little more passed between us; I had been overtaken by a horror of the element of evidence. It seemed gross and prying on either hypothesis. He, on his side, had none to produce, none at least but a statement of his house-porter—on his own admission a most casual and intermittent personage—that between the hours of ten o'clock and midnight no less than three ladies in deep black had flitted in and out of the place. This proved far too much; we had neither of us any use for three. He knew that I considered I had accounted for every fragment of her time, and we dropped the matter as settled; we abstained from further discussion. What I knew however was that he abstained to please me rather than because he yielded to my reasons. He didn't yield—he was only indulgent; he clung to his interpretation because he liked it better. He liked it better, I held, because it had more to say to his vanity. That, in a similar position, would not have been its effect on me, though I had doubtless quite as much; but these are things of individual humour, as to which no person can judge for another. I should have supposed it more gratifying to be the subject of one of those inexplicable occurrences that are chronicled in thrilling books and disputed about at learned meetings; I could conceive, on the part of a being just engulfed in the infinite and still vibrating with human emotion, of nothing more fine and pure, more high and august than such an impulse of reparation, of admonition or even of curiosity. *That* was beautiful, if one would, and I should in his place have thought more of myself for being so distinguished. It was public that he had already, that he had long been distinguished, and what was this in itself but almost a proof? Each of the strange visitations contributed to establish the other. He had a different feeling; but he had also, I hasten to add, an unmistakable desire not to make a stand or, as they say, a fuss about it. I might believe what I liked—the more so that the whole thing was in a manner a mystery of my producing. It was an event of my history, a puzzle of my consciousness, not of his; therefore he would take about it any tone that struck me as convenient. We had both at all events other business on hand; we were pressed with preparations for our marriage.

Mine were assuredly urgent, but I found as the days went on that to believe what I "liked" was to believe what I was more and more intimately convinced of. I found also that I didn't like it so much as that came to, or that the pleasure at all events was far from being the cause of my conviction. My obsession, as I may really call it and as I began to perceive, refused to be elbowed away, as I had hoped, by my sense of paramount duties. If I had a great deal to do I had still more to think about, and the moment came when my occupations were gravely menaced by my thoughts. I see it all now, I feel it, I live it over. It's terribly void of joy, it's full indeed to overflowing of bitterness; and yet I must do myself justice—I couldn't possibly be other than I was. The same strange impressions, had I to meet them again, would produce the same deep anguish, the same sharp doubts, the same still sharper certainties. Oh, it's all easier to remember than to write, but even if I could retrace the business hour by hour, could find terms for the inexpressible, the ugliness and the pain would quickly stay my hand. Let me then note very simply and briefly that a week before our wedding-day, three weeks after her death, I became fully aware that I had something very serious to look in the face, and that if I was to make this effort I must make it on the spot and before another hour should elapse. My unextinguished jealousy—*that* was the Medusa-mask. It hadn't died with her death, it had lividly survived, and it was fed by suspicions unspeakable. They *would* be unspeakable to-day, that is, if I hadn't felt the sharp need of uttering them at the time.

This need took possession of me—to save me, as it appeared, from my fate. When once it had done so I saw—in the urgency of the case, the diminishing hours and shrinking interval—only one issue, that of absolute promptness and frankness. I could at least not do him the wrong of delaying another day, I could at least treat my difficulty as too fine for a subterfuge. Therefore very quietly, but none the less abruptly and hideously, I put it before him on a certain evening that we must reconsider our situation and recognise that it had completely altered.

He stared bravely. "How has it altered?"

"Another person has come between us."

He hesitated a moment. "I won't pretend not to know whom you mean." He smiled in pity for my aberration, but he meant to be kind. "A woman dead and buried!"

"She's buried, but she's not dead. She's dead for the world—she's dead for me. But she's not dead for *you*."

"You hark back to the different construction we put on her appearance that evening?"

"No," I answered, "I hark back to nothing. I've no need of it. I've more than enough with what's before me."

"And pray, darling, what is that?"

"You're completely changed."

"By that absurdity?" he laughed.

"Not so much by that one as by other absurdities that have followed it."

"And what may they have been?"

We had faced each other fairly, with eyes that didn't flinch; but his had a dim, strange light, and my certitude triumphed in his perceptible paleness. "Do you really pretend," I asked, "not to know what they are?"

"My dear child," he replied, "you describe them too sketchily!"

I considered a moment. "One may well be embarrassed to finish the picture! But from that point of view—and from the beginning—what was ever more embarrassing than your idiosyncrasy?"

He was extremely vague. "My idiosyncrasy?"

"Your notorious, your peculiar power."

He gave a great shrug of impatience, a groan of overdone disdain. "Oh, my peculiar power!"

"Your accessibility to forms of life," I coldly went on, "your command of impressions, appearances, contacts closed—for our gain or our loss—to the rest of us. That was originally a part of the deep interest with which you inspired me—one of the reasons I was amused, I was indeed positively proud to know you. It was a magnificent distinction; it's a magnificent distinction still. But of course I had no prevision then of the way it would operate now; and even had that been the case I should have had none of the extraordinary way in which its action would affect me."

"To what in the name of goodness," he pleadingly inquired, "are you fantastically alluding?" Then as I remained silent, gathering a tone for my charge, "How in the world *does* it operate?" he went on; "and how in the world are you affected?"

"She missed you for five years," I said, "but she never misses you now. You're making it up!"

"Making it up?" He had begun to turn from white to red.

"You see her—you see her: you see her every night!" He gave a loud sound of derision, but it was not a genuine one. "She comes to you as she came that evening," I declared; "having tried it she found she liked it!" I was able, with God's help, to speak without blind passion or vulgar violence; but those were the exact words—and far from "sketchy" they then appeared to me—that I uttered. He had turned away in his laughter, clapping his hands at my folly, but in an instant he faced me again, with a change of expression that struck me. "Do you dare to deny," I asked, "that you habitually see her?"

He had taken the line of indulgence, of meeting me halfway and kindly humouring me. At all events, to my astonishment, he suddenly said: "Well, my dear, what if I do?"

"It's your natural right; it belongs to your constitution and to your wonderful, if not perhaps quite enviable fortune. But you will easily understand that it separates us. I unconditionally release you."

"Release me?"

"You must choose between me and her."

He looked at me hard. "I see." Then he walked away a little, as if grasping what I had said and thinking how he had best treat it. At last he turned upon me afresh. "How on earth do you know such an awfully private thing?"

"You mean because you've tried so hard to hide it? It *is* awfully private, and you may believe I shall never betray you. You've done your best, you've acted your part, you've behaved, poor dear! loyally and admirably. Therefore I've watched you in silence, playing my part too; I've noted every drop in your voice, every absence in your eyes, every effort in your indifferent hand: I've waited till I was utterly sure and miserably unhappy. How *can* you hide it when you're abjectly in love with her, when you're sick almost to death with the joy of what she gives you?" I checked his quick protest with a quicker gesture. "You love her as you've *never* loved, and, passion for passion, she gives it straight back! She rules you, she holds you, she has you all! A woman, in such a case as mine, divines and feels and sees; she's not an idiot who has to be credibly informed. You come to me mechanically, compunctiously, with the dregs of your tenderness and the remnant of your life. I can renounce you, but I can't share you; the best of you is hers; I know what it is and I freely give you up to her for ever!"

He made a gallant fight, but it couldn't be patched up; he repeated his denial, he retracted his admission, he ridiculed my charge, of which I freely granted him moreover the indefensible extravagance. I didn't pretend for a moment that we were talking of common things; I didn't pretend for a moment that he and she were common people. Pray, if they *had* been, how should I ever have cared for them? They had enjoyed a rare extension of being and they had caught me up in their flight; only I couldn't breathe in such an air and I promptly asked to be set down. Everything in the facts was monstrous, and most of all my lucid perception of them; the only thing allied to nature and truth was my having to act on that perception. I felt after I had spoken in this sense that my assurance was complete; nothing had been wanting to it but the sight of my effect on him. He disguised indeed the effect in a cloud of chaff, a diversion that gained him time and covered his retreat. He challenged my sincerity, my sanity, almost my humanity, and that of course widened our breach and confirmed our rupture. He did everything in short but convince me either that I was wrong or that he was unhappy; we separated, and I left him to his inconceivable communion.

He never married, any more than I've done. When six years later, in solitude and silence, I heard of his death I hailed it as a direct contribution to my theory. It was sudden, it was never properly accounted for, it was surrounded by circumstances in which—for oh, I took them to pieces!—I distinctly read an intention, the mark of his own hidden hand. It was the result of a long necessity, of an unquenchable desire. To say exactly what I mean, it was a response to an irresistible call.

THE END

About Author

Henry James OM (15 April 1843 – 28 February 1916) was an American-British author regarded as a key transitional figure between literary realism and literary modernism, and is considered by many to be among the greatest novelists in the English language. He was the son of Henry James Sr. and the brother of renowned philosopher and psychologist William James and diarist Alice James.

He is best known for a number of novels dealing with the social and marital interplay between émigré Americans, English people, and continental Europeans. Examples of such novels include The Portrait of a Lady, The Ambassadors, and The Wings of the Dove. His later works were increasingly experimental. In describing the internal states of mind and social dynamics of his characters, James often made use of a style in which ambiguous or contradictory motives and impressions were overlaid or juxtaposed in the discussion of a character's psyche. For their unique ambiguity, as well as for other aspects of their composition, his late works have been compared to impressionist painting.

His novella The Turn of the Screw has garnered a reputation as the most analysed and ambiguous ghost story in the English language and remains his most widely adapted work in other media. He also wrote a number of other highly regarded ghost stories and is considered one of the greatest masters of the field.

James published articles and books of criticism, travel, biography, autobiography, and plays. Born in the United States, James largely relocated to Europe as a young man and eventually settled in England, becoming a British subject in 1915, one year before his death. James was nominated for the Nobel Prize in Literature in 1911, 1912 and 1916.

Life

Early years, 1843–1883

James was born at 2 Washington Place in New York City on 15 April 1843. His parents were Mary Walsh and Henry James Sr. His father was intelligent and steadfastly congenial. He was a lecturer and philosopher who had inherited independent means from his father, an Albany banker and investor. Mary came from a wealthy family long settled in New York City. Her sister Katherine lived with her adult family for an extended period of time. Henry Jr. had three brothers, William, who was one year his senior, and younger brothers Wilkinson (Wilkie) and Robertson. His younger sister was Alice. Both of his parents were of Irish and Scottish descent.

The family first lived in Albany, at 70 N. Pearl St., and then moved to Fourteenth Street in New York City when James was still a young boy. His education was calculated by his father to expose him to many influences, primarily scientific and philosophical; it was described by Percy Lubbock, the editor of his selected letters, as "extraordinarily haphazard and promiscuous." James did not share the usual education in Latin and Greek classics. Between 1855 and 1860, the James' household traveled to London, Paris, Geneva, Boulogne-sur-Mer and Newport, Rhode Island, according to the father's current interests and publishing ventures, retreating to the United States when funds were low. Henry studied primarily with tutors and briefly attended schools while the family traveled in Europe. Their longest stays were in France, where Henry began to feel at home and became fluent in French. He was afflicted with a stutter, which seems to have manifested itself only when he spoke English; in French, he did not stutter.

In 1860 the family returned to Newport. There Henry became a friend of the painter John La Farge, who introduced him to French literature, and in particular, to Balzac. James later called Balzac his "greatest master," and said that he had learned more about the craft of fiction from him than from anyone else.

In the autumn of 1861 Henry received an injury, probably to his back, while fighting a fire. This injury, which resurfaced at times throughout his life, made him unfit for military service in the American Civil War.

In 1864 the James family moved to Boston, Massachusetts to be near William, who had enrolled first in the Lawrence Scientific School at Harvard and then in the medical school. In 1862 Henry attended Harvard Law School, but realised that he was not interested in studying law. He pursued his interest in literature and associated with authors and critics William Dean Howells and Charles Eliot Norton in Boston and Cambridge, formed lifelong friendships with Oliver Wendell Holmes Jr., the future Supreme Court Justice, and with James and Annie Fields, his first professional mentors.

His first published work was a review of a stage performance, "Miss Maggie Mitchell in Fanchon the Cricket," published in 1863. About a year later, A Tragedy of Error, his first short story, was published anonymously. James's first payment was for an appreciation of Sir Walter Scott's novels, written for the North American Review. He wrote fiction and non-fiction pieces for The Nation and Atlantic Monthly, where Fields was editor. In 1871 he published his first novel, Watch and Ward, in serial form in the Atlantic Monthly. The novel was later published in book form in 1878.

During a 14-month trip through Europe in 1869–70 he met Ruskin, Dickens, Matthew Arnold, William Morris, and George Eliot. Rome impressed him profoundly. "Here I am then in the Eternal City," he wrote to his brother William. "At last—for the first time—I live!" He attempted to support himself as a freelance writer in Rome, then secured a position as Paris correspondent for the New York Tribune, through the influence of its editor John Hay. When these efforts failed he returned to New York City. During 1874 and 1875 he published Transatlantic Sketches, A Passionate Pilgrim, and Roderick Hudson. During this early period in his career he was influenced by Nathaniel Hawthorne.

In 1869 he settled in London. There he established relationships with Macmillan and other publishers, who paid for serial installments that they would later publish in book form. The audience for these serialized novels was largely made up of middle-class women, and James struggled to fashion serious literary work within the strictures imposed by editors' and publishers' notions of what was suitable for young women to read. He lived in rented rooms but was able to join gentlemen's clubs that had libraries and where he could entertain male friends. He was introduced to English society by Henry Adams and Charles Milnes Gaskell, the latter introducing him to the Travellers' and the Reform Clubs.

In the fall of 1875 he moved to the Latin Quarter of Paris. Aside from two trips to America, he spent the next three decades—the rest of his life—in Europe. In Paris he met Zola, Alphonse Daudet, Maupassant, Turgenev, and others. He stayed in Paris only a year before moving to London.

In England he met the leading figures of politics and culture. He continued to be a prolific writer, producing The American (1877), The Europeans (1878), a revision of Watch and Ward (1878), French Poets and Novelists (1878), Hawthorne (1879), and several shorter works of fiction. In 1878 Daisy Miller established his fame on both sides of the Atlantic. It drew notice perhaps mostly because it depicted a woman whose behavior is outside the social norms of Europe. He also began his first masterpiece, The Portrait of a Lady, which would appear in 1881.

In 1877 he first visited Wenlock Abbey in Shropshire, home of his friend Charles Milnes Gaskell whom he had met through Henry Adams. He was much inspired by the darkly romantic Abbey and the surrounding countryside, which features in his essay Abbeys and Castles. In particular the gloomy monastic fishponds behind the Abbey are said to have inspired the lake in The Turn of the Screw.

While living in London, James continued to follow the careers of the "French realists", Émile Zola in particular. Their stylistic methods influenced his own work in the years to come. Hawthorne's influence on him faded during this period, replaced by George Eliot and Ivan Turgenev. 1879–1882 saw the publication of The Europeans, Washington Square, Confidence, and The Portrait of a Lady. He visited America in 1882–1883, then returned to London.

The period from 1881 to 1883 was marked by several losses. His mother died in 1881, followed by his father a few months later, and then by his brother Wilkie. Emerson, an old family friend, died in 1882. His friend Turgenev died in 1883.

Middle years, 1884–1897

In 1884 James made another visit to Paris. There he met again with Zola, Daudet, and Goncourt. He had been following the careers of the French "realist" or "naturalist" writers, and was increasingly influenced by them. In 1886, he published The Bostonians and The Princess Casamassima, both influenced by the French writers he'd studied assiduously. Critical reaction and sales were poor. He wrote to Howells that the books had hurt his career rather than helped because they had "reduced the desire, and demand, for my productions to zero". During this time he became friends with Robert Louis Stevenson, John Singer Sargent, Edmund Gosse, George du Maurier, Paul Bourget, and Constance Fenimore Woolson. His third novel from the 1880s was The Tragic Muse. Although he was following the precepts of Zola in his novels of the '80s, their tone and attitude are closer to the fiction of Alphonse Daudet. The lack of critical and financial success for his novels during this period led him to try writing for the theatre. (His dramatic works and his experiences with theatre are discussed below.)

In the last quarter of 1889, he started translating "for pure and copious lucre" Port Tarascon, the third volume of Alphonse Daudet adventures of Tartarin de Tarascon. Serialized in Harper's Monthly Magazine from June 1890, this translation praised as "clever" by The Spectator was published in January 1891 by Sampson Low, Marston, Searle & Rivington.

After the stage failure of Guy Domville in 1895, James was near despair and thoughts of death plagued him. The years spent on dramatic works were not entirely a loss. As he moved into the last phase of his career he found ways to adapt dramatic techniques into the novel form.

In the late 1880s and throughout the 1890s James made several trips through Europe. He spent a long stay in Italy in 1887. In that year the short novel The Aspern Papers and The Reverberator were published.

Late years, 1898–1916

In 1897–1898 he moved to Rye, Sussex, and wrote The Turn of the Screw. 1899–1900 saw the publication of The Awkward Age and The Sacred

Fount. During 1902–1904 he wrote The Ambassadors, The Wings of the Dove, and The Golden Bowl.

In 1904 he revisited America and lectured on Balzac. In 1906–1910 he published The American Scene and edited the "New York Edition", a 24-volume collection of his works. In 1910 his brother William died; Henry had just joined William from an unsuccessful search for relief in Europe on what then turned out to be his (Henry's) last visit to the United States (from summer 1910 to July 1911), and was near him, according to a letter he wrote, when he died.

In 1913 he wrote his autobiographies, A Small Boy and Others, and Notes of a Son and Brother. After the outbreak of the First World War in 1914 he did war work. In 1915 he became a British subject and was awarded the Order of Merit the following year. He died on 28 February 1916, in Chelsea, London. As he requested, his ashes were buried in Cambridge Cemetery in Massachusetts.

Biographers

James regularly rejected suggestions that he should marry, and after settling in London proclaimed himself "a bachelor". F. W. Dupee, in several volumes on the James family, originated the theory that he had been in love with his cousin Mary ("Minnie") Temple, but that a neurotic fear of sex kept him from admitting such affections: "James's invalidism ... was itself the symptom of some fear of or scruple against sexual love on his part." Dupee used an episode from James's memoir A Small Boy and Others, recounting a dream of a Napoleonic image in the Louvre, to exemplify James's romanticism about Europe, a Napoleonic fantasy into which he fled.

Dupee had not had access to the James family papers and worked principally from James's published memoir of his older brother, William, and the limited collection of letters edited by Percy Lubbock, heavily weighted toward James's last years. His account therefore moved directly from James's childhood, when he trailed after his older brother, to elderly invalidism. As more material became available to scholars, including the diaries of contemporaries and hundreds of affectionate and sometimes erotic letters written by James to younger men, the picture of neurotic celibacy gave way to a portrait of a closeted homosexual.

Between 1953 and 1972, Leon Edel authored a major five-volume biography of James, which accessed unpublished letters and documents after Edel gained the permission of James's family. Edel's portrayal of James included the suggestion he was celibate. It was a view first propounded by critic Saul Rosenzweig in 1943. In 1996 Sheldon M. Novick published Henry James: The Young Master, followed by Henry James: The Mature Master (2007). The first book "caused something of an uproar in Jamesian circles" as it challenged the previous received notion of celibacy, a once-familiar paradigm in biographies of homosexuals when direct evidence was non-existent. Novick also criticised Edel for following the discounted Freudian interpretation of homosexuality "as a kind of failure." The difference of opinion erupted in a series of exchanges between Edel and Novick which were published by the online magazine Slate, with the latter arguing that even the suggestion of celibacy went against James's own injunction "live!"—not "fantasize!"

A letter James wrote in old age to Hugh Walpole has been cited as an explicit statement of this. Walpole confessed to him of indulging in "high jinks", and James wrote a reply endorsing it: "We must know, as much as possible, in our beautiful art, yours & mine, what we are talking about — & the only way to know it is to have lived & loved & cursed & floundered & enjoyed & suffered — I don't think I regret a single 'excess' of my responsive youth".

The interpretation of James as living a less austere emotional life has been subsequently explored by other scholars. The often intense politics of Jamesian scholarship has also been the subject of studies. Author Colm Tóibín has said that Eve Kosofsky Sedgwick's Epistemology of the Closet made a landmark difference to Jamesian scholarship by arguing that he be read as a homosexual writer whose desire to keep his sexuality a secret shaped his layered style and dramatic artistry. According to Tóibín such a reading "removed James from the realm of dead white males who wrote about posh people. He became our contemporary."

James's letters to expatriate American sculptor Hendrik Christian Andersen have attracted particular attention. James met the 27-year-old Andersen in Rome in 1899, when James was 56, and wrote letters to Andersen that are intensely emotional: "I hold you, dearest boy, in my innermost love, & count on your feeling me—in every throb of your soul". In a letter of 6 May 1904, to his brother William, James referred to himself as "always your hopelessly celibate even though sexagenarian Henry". How accurate that description might have been is the subject of contention among James's biographers,   but the letters to Andersen were occasionally quasi-erotic: "I put, my dear boy, my arm around you, & feel the pulsation, thereby, as it were, of our excellent future & your admirable endowment." To his homosexual friend Howard Sturgis, James could write: "I repeat, almost to indiscretion, that I could live with you. Meanwhile I can only try to live without you."

His numerous letters to the many young gay men among his close male friends are more forthcoming. In a letter to Howard Sturgis, following a long visit, James refers jocularly to their "happy little congress of two" and in letters to Hugh Walpole he pursues convoluted jokes and puns about their relationship, referring to himself as an elephant who "paws you oh so benevolently" and winds about Walpole his "well meaning old trunk". His letters to Walter Berry printed by the Black Sun Press have long been celebrated for their lightly veiled eroticism.

He corresponded in almost equally extravagant language with his many female friends, writing, for example, to fellow novelist Lucy Clifford: "Dearest Lucy! What shall I say? when I love you so very, very much, and see you nine times for once that I see Others! Therefore I think that—if you want it made clear to the meanest intelligence—I love you more than I love Others." To his New York friend Mary Cadwalader Jones: "Dearest Mary Cadwalader. I yearn over you, but I yearn in vain; & your long silence really breaks my heart, mystifies, depresses, almost alarms me, to the point even of making me wonder if poor unconscious & doting old Célimare [Jones's pet name for James] has 'done' anything, in some dark somnambulism of the spirit, which has ... given you a bad moment, or a wrong impression, or a 'colourable pretext' ... However these things may be, he loves you as tenderly as ever;

nothing, to the end of time, will ever detach him from you, & he remembers those Eleventh St. matutinal intimes hours, those telephonic matinées, as the most romantic of his life ..." His long friendship with American novelist Constance Fenimore Woolson, in whose house he lived for a number of weeks in Italy in 1887, and his shock and grief over her suicide in 1894, are discussed in detail in Edel's biography and play a central role in a study by Lyndall Gordon. (Edel conjectured that Woolson was in love with James and killed herself in part because of his coldness, but Woolson's biographers have objected to Edel's account.)

Works

Style and themes

James is one of the major figures of trans-Atlantic literature. His works frequently juxtapose characters from the Old World (Europe), embodying a feudal civilisation that is beautiful, often corrupt, and alluring, and from the New World (United States), where people are often brash, open, and assertive and embody the virtues—freedom and a more highly evolved moral character—of the new American society. James explores this clash of personalities and cultures, in stories of personal relationships in which power is exercised well or badly. His protagonists were often young American women facing oppression or abuse, and as his secretary Theodora Bosanquet remarked in her monograph Henry James at Work:

> When he walked out of the refuge of his study and into the world and looked around him, he saw a place of torment, where creatures of prey perpetually thrust their claws into the quivering flesh of doomed, defenseless children of light ... His novels are a repeated exposure of this wickedness, a reiterated and passionate plea for the fullest freedom of development, unimperiled by reckless and barbarous stupidity.

Critics have jokingly described three phases in the development of James's prose: "James I, James II, and The Old Pretender." He wrote short stories and plays. Finally, in his third and last period he returned to the long, serialised novel. Beginning in the second period, but most noticeably in the third, he increasingly abandoned direct statement in favour of frequent

211

double negatives, and complex descriptive imagery. Single paragraphs began to run for page after page, in which an initial noun would be succeeded by pronouns surrounded by clouds of adjectives and prepositional clauses, far from their original referents, and verbs would be deferred and then preceded by a series of adverbs. The overall effect could be a vivid evocation of a scene as perceived by a sensitive observer. It has been debated whether this change of style was engendered by James's shifting from writing to dictating to a typist, a change made during the composition of What Maisie Knew.

In its intense focus on the consciousness of his major characters, James's later work foreshadows extensive developments in 20th century fiction. Indeed, he might have influenced stream-of-consciousness writers such as Virginia Woolf, who not only read some of his novels but also wrote essays about them. Both contemporary and modern readers have found the late style difficult and unnecessary; his friend Edith Wharton, who admired him greatly, said that there were passages in his work that were all but incomprehensible. James was harshly portrayed by H. G. Wells as a hippopotamus laboriously attempting to pick up a pea that had got into a corner of its cage. The "late James" style was ably parodied by Max Beerbohm in "The Mote in the Middle Distance".

More important for his work overall may have been his position as an expatriate, and in other ways an outsider, living in Europe. While he came from middle-class and provincial beginnings (seen from the perspective of European polite society) he worked very hard to gain access to all levels of society, and the settings of his fiction range from working class to aristocratic, and often describe the efforts of middle-class Americans to make their way in European capitals. He confessed he got some of his best story ideas from gossip at the dinner table or at country house weekends. He worked for a living, however, and lacked the experiences of select schools, university, and army service, the common bonds of masculine society. He was furthermore a man whose tastes and interests were, according to the prevailing standards of Victorian era Anglo-American culture, rather feminine, and who was shadowed by the cloud of prejudice that then and later accompanied suspicions of his homosexuality. Edmund Wilson famously compared James's objectivity to Shakespeare's:

One would be in a position to appreciate James better if one compared him with the dramatists of the seventeenth century—Racine and Molière, whom he resembles in form as well as in point of view, and even Shakespeare, when allowances are made for the most extreme differences in subject and form. These poets are not, like Dickens and Hardy, writers of melodrama—either humorous or pessimistic, nor secretaries of society like Balzac, nor prophets like Tolstoy: they are occupied simply with the presentation of conflicts of moral character, which they do not concern themselves about softening or averting. They do not indict society for these situations: they regard them as universal and inevitable. They do not even blame God for allowing them: they accept them as the conditions of life.

It is also possible to see many of James's stories as psychological thought-experiments. In his preface to the New York edition of The American he describes the development of the story in his mind as exactly such: the "situation" of an American, "some robust but insidiously beguiled and betrayed, some cruelly wronged, compatriot..." with the focus of the story being on the response of this wronged man. The Portrait of a Lady may be an experiment to see what happens when an idealistic young woman suddenly becomes very rich. In many of his tales, characters seem to exemplify alternative futures and possibilities, as most markedly in "The Jolly Corner", in which the protagonist and a ghost-doppelganger live alternative American and European lives; and in others, like The Ambassadors, an older James seems fondly to regard his own younger self facing a crucial moment.

Major novels

The first period of James's fiction, usually considered to have culminated in The Portrait of a Lady, concentrated on the contrast between Europe and America. The style of these novels is generally straightforward and, though personally characteristic, well within the norms of 19th-century fiction. Roderick Hudson (1875) is a Künstlerroman that traces the development of the title character, an extremely talented sculptor. Although the book shows some signs of immaturity—this was James's first serious attempt at a full-length novel—it has attracted favourable comment due to the vivid realisation of the three major characters: Roderick Hudson, superbly gifted but unstable and unreliable; Rowland Mallet, Roderick's limited but much more mature friend and patron; and Christina Light, one of James's most enchanting and maddening femmes fatales. The pair of Hudson and Mallet has been seen as representing the two sides of James's own nature: the wildly imaginative artist and the brooding conscientious mentor.

In The Portrait of a Lady (1881) James concluded the first phase of his career with a novel that remains his most popular piece of long fiction. The story is of a spirited young American woman, Isabel Archer, who "affronts her destiny" and finds it overwhelming. She inherits a large amount of money and subsequently becomes the victim of Machiavellian scheming by two American expatriates. The narrative is set mainly in Europe, especially in England and Italy. Generally regarded as the masterpiece of his early phase, The Portrait of a Lady is described as a psychological novel, exploring the minds of his characters, and almost a work of social science, exploring the differences between Europeans and Americans, the old and the new worlds.

The second period of James's career, which extends from the publication of The Portrait of a Lady through the end of the nineteenth century, features less popular novels including The Princess Casamassima, published serially in The Atlantic Monthly in 1885–1886, and The Bostonians, published serially in The Century Magazine during the same period. This period also featured James's celebrated Gothic novella, The Turn of the Screw.

The third period of James's career reached its most significant achievement in three novels published just around the start of the 20th century: The Wings of the Dove (1902), The Ambassadors (1903), and The Golden Bowl (1904). Critic F. O. Matthiessen called this "trilogy" James's major phase, and these novels have certainly received intense critical study. It was the second-written of the books, The Wings of the Dove (1902) that was the first published because it attracted no serialization. This novel tells the story of Milly Theale, an American heiress stricken with a serious disease, and her impact on the people around her. Some of these people befriend Milly with honourable motives, while others are more self-interested. James stated in his autobiographical books that Milly was based on Minny Temple, his beloved cousin who died at an early age of tuberculosis. He said that he attempted in the novel to wrap her memory in the "beauty and dignity of art".

Shorter narratives

James was particularly interested in what he called the "beautiful and blest nouvelle", or the longer form of short narrative. Still, he produced a number of very short stories in which he achieved notable compression of sometimes complex subjects. The following narratives are representative of James's achievement in the shorter forms of fiction.

- "A Tragedy of Error" (1864), short story
- "The Story of a Year" (1865), short story
- A Passionate Pilgrim (1871), novella
- Madame de Mauves (1874), novella
- Daisy Miller (1878), novella
- The Aspern Papers (1888), novella
- The Lesson of the Master (1888), novella
- The Pupil (1891), short story
- "The Figure in the Carpet" (1896), short story
- The Beast in the Jungle (1903), novella
- An International Episode (1878)
- Picture and Text
- Four Meetings (1885)
- A London Life, and Other Tales (1889)
- The Spoils of Poynton (1896)

- Embarrassments (1896)

- The Two Magics: The Turn of the Screw, Covering End (1898)

- A Little Tour of France (1900)

- The Sacred Fount (1901)

- Views and Reviews (1908)

- The Wings of the Dove, Volume I (1902)

- The Wings of the Dove, Volume II (1909)

- The Finer Grain (1910)

- The Outcry (1911)

- Lady Barbarina: The Siege of London, An International Episode and Other Tales (1922)

- The Birthplace (1922)

Plays

At several points in his career James wrote plays, beginning with one-act plays written for periodicals in 1869 and 1871 and a dramatisation of his popular novella Daisy Miller in 1882. From 1890 to 1892, having received a bequest that freed him from magazine publication, he made a strenuous effort to succeed on the London stage, writing a half-dozen plays of which only one, a dramatisation of his novel The American, was produced. This play was performed for several years by a touring repertory company and had a respectable run in London, but did not earn very much money for James. His other plays written at this time were not produced.

In 1893, however, he responded to a request from actor-manager George Alexander for a serious play for the opening of his renovated St. James's Theatre, and wrote a long drama, Guy Domville, which Alexander produced. There was a noisy uproar on the opening night, 5 January 1895, with hissing from the gallery when James took his bow after the final curtain, and the author was upset. The play received moderately good reviews and had a modest run of four weeks before being taken off to make way for Oscar Wilde's The Importance of Being Earnest, which Alexander thought would have better prospects for the coming season.

After the stresses and disappointment of these efforts James insisted that he would write no more for the theatre, but within weeks had agreed to write a curtain-raiser for Ellen Terry. This became the one-act "Summersoft", which he later rewrote into a short story, "Covering End", and then expanded into a full-length play, The High Bid, which had a brief run in London in 1907, when James made another concerted effort to write for the stage. He wrote three new plays, two of which were in production when the death of Edward VII on 6 May 1910 plunged London into mourning and theatres closed. Discouraged by failing health and the stresses of theatrical work, James did not renew his efforts in the theatre, but recycled his plays as successful novels. The Outcry was a best-seller in the United States when it was published in 1911. During the years 1890–1893 when he was most engaged with the theatre, James wrote a good deal of theatrical criticism and assisted Elizabeth Robins and others in translating and producing Henrik Ibsen for the first time in London.

Leon Edel argued in his psychoanalytic biography that James was traumatised by the opening night uproar that greeted Guy Domville, and that it plunged him into a prolonged depression. The successful later novels, in Edel's view, were the result of a kind of self-analysis, expressed in fiction, which partly freed him from his fears. Other biographers and scholars have not accepted this account, however; the more common view being that of F.O. Matthiessen, who wrote: "Instead of being crushed by the collapse of his hopes [for the theatre]... he felt a resurgence of new energy."

Non-fiction

Beyond his fiction, James was one of the more important literary critics in the history of the novel. In his classic essay The Art of Fiction (1884), he argued against rigid prescriptions on the novelist's choice of subject and method of treatment. He maintained that the widest possible freedom in content and approach would help ensure narrative fiction's continued vitality.

James wrote many valuable critical articles on other novelists; typical is his book-length study of Nathaniel Hawthorne, which has been the subject of critical debate. Richard Brodhead has suggested that the study was emblematic of James's struggle with Hawthorne's influence, and constituted an effort to place the elder writer "at a disadvantage." Gordon Fraser, meanwhile, has suggested that the study was part of a more commercial effort by James to introduce himself to British readers as Hawthorne's natural successor.

When James assembled the New York Edition of his fiction in his final years, he wrote a series of prefaces that subjected his own work to searching, occasionally harsh criticism.

At 22 James wrote The Noble School of Fiction for The Nation's first issue in 1865. He would write, in all, over 200 essays and book, art, and theatre reviews for the magazine.

For most of his life James harboured ambitions for success as a playwright. He converted his novel The American into a play that enjoyed modest returns in the early 1890s. In all he wrote about a dozen plays, most of which went unproduced. His costume drama Guy Domville failed disastrously on its opening night in 1895. James then largely abandoned his efforts to conquer the stage and returned to his fiction. In his Notebooks he maintained that his theatrical experiment benefited his novels and tales by helping him dramatise his characters' thoughts and emotions. James produced a small but valuable amount of theatrical criticism, including perceptive appreciations of Henrik Ibsen.

With his wide-ranging artistic interests, James occasionally wrote on the visual arts. Perhaps his most valuable contribution was his favourable assessment of fellow expatriate John Singer Sargent, a painter whose critical status has improved markedly in recent decades. James also wrote sometimes charming, sometimes brooding articles about various places he visited and lived in. His most famous books of travel writing include Italian Hours (an example of the charming approach) and The American Scene (most definitely on the brooding side).

James was one of the great letter-writers of any era. More than ten thousand of his personal letters are extant, and over three thousand have been published in a large number of collections. A complete edition of James's letters began publication in 2006, edited by Pierre Walker and Greg Zacharias. As of 2014, eight volumes have been published, covering the period from 1855 to 1880. James's correspondents included celebrated contemporaries like Robert Louis Stevenson, Edith Wharton and Joseph Conrad, along with many others in his wide circle of friends and acquaintances. The letters range from the "mere twaddle of graciousness" to serious discussions of artistic, social and personal issues.

Very late in life James began a series of autobiographical works: A Small Boy and Others, Notes of a Son and Brother, and the unfinished The Middle Years. These books portray the development of a classic observer who was passionately interested in artistic creation but was somewhat reticent about participating fully in the life around him.

Reception

Criticism, biographies and fictional treatments

James's work has remained steadily popular with the limited audience of educated readers to whom he spoke during his lifetime, and has remained firmly in the canon, but, after his death, some American critics, such as Van Wyck Brooks, expressed hostility towards James for his long expatriation and eventual naturalisation as a British subject. Other critics such as E. M. Forster complained about what they saw as James's squeamishness in the treatment of sex and other possibly controversial material, or dismissed his late style as difficult and obscure, relying heavily on extremely long sentences and excessively latinate language. Similarly Oscar Wilde criticised him for writing "fiction as if it were a painful duty". Vernon Parrington, composing a canon of American literature, condemned James for having cut himself off from America. Jorge Luis Borges wrote about him, "Despite the scruples and delicate complexities of James, his work suffers from a major defect: the absence of life." And Virginia Woolf, writing to Lytton Strachey, asked, "Please tell me what you find in Henry James. ... we have his works here, and

I read, and I can't find anything but faintly tinged rose water, urbane and sleek, but vulgar and pale as Walter Lamb. Is there really any sense in it?" The novelist W. Somerset Maugham wrote, "He did not know the English as an Englishman instinctively knows them and so his English characters never to my mind quite ring true," and argued "The great novelists, even in seclusion, have lived life passionately. Henry James was content to observe it from a window." Maugham nevertheless wrote, "The fact remains that those last novels of his, notwithstanding their unreality, make all other novels, except the very best, unreadable." Colm Tóibín observed that James "never really wrote about the English very well. His English characters don't work for me."

Despite these criticisms, James is now valued for his psychological and moral realism, his masterful creation of character, his low-key but playful humour, and his assured command of the language. In his 1983 book, The Novels of Henry James, Edward Wagenknecht offers an assessment that echoes Theodora Bosanquet's:

> "To be completely great," Henry James wrote in an early review, "a work of art must lift up the heart," and his own novels do this to an outstanding degree ... More than sixty years after his death, the great novelist who sometimes professed to have no opinions stands foursquare in the great Christian humanistic and democratic tradition. The men and women who, at the height of World War II, raided the secondhand shops for his out-of-print books knew what they were about. For no writer ever raised a braver banner to which all who love freedom might adhere.

William Dean Howells saw James as a representative of a new realist school of literary art which broke with the English romantic tradition epitomised by the works of Charles Dickens and William Makepeace Thackeray. Howells wrote that realism found "its chief exemplar in Mr. James... A novelist he is not, after the old fashion, or after any fashion but his own." F.R. Leavis championed Henry James as a novelist of "established pre-eminence" in The Great Tradition (1948), asserting that The Portrait of a Lady and The Bostonians were "the two most brilliant novels in the language." James is now prized as a master of point of view who moved literary fiction forward by insisting in showing, not telling, his stories to the reader. (Source: Wikipedia)

NOTABLE WORKS

NOVELS

Watch and Ward (1871)

Roderick Hudson (1875)

The American (1877)

The Europeans (1878)

Confidence (1879)

Washington Square (1880)

The Portrait of a Lady (1881)

The Bostonians (1886)

The Princess Casamassima (1886)

The Reverberator (1888)

The Tragic Muse (1890)

The Other House (1896)

The Spoils of Poynton (1897)

What Maisie Knew (1897)

The Awkward Age (1899)

The Sacred Fount (1901)

The Wings of the Dove (1902)

The Ambassadors (1903)

The Golden Bowl (1904)

The Whole Family (collaborative novel with eleven other authors, 1908)

The Outcry (1911)

The Ivory Tower (unfinished, published posthumously 1917)

The Sense of the Past (unfinished, published posthumously 1917)

SHORT STORIES AND NOVELLAS

A Tragedy of Error (1864)

The Story of a Year (1865)

A Landscape Painter (1866)

A Day of Days (1866)

My Friend Bingham (1867)

Poor Richard (1867)

The Story of a Masterpiece (1868)

A Most Extraordinary Case (1868)

A Problem (1868)

De Grey: A Romance (1868)

Osborne's Revenge (1868)

The Romance of Certain Old Clothes (1868)

A Light Man (1869)

Gabrielle de Bergerac (1869)

Travelling Companions (1870)

A Passionate Pilgrim (1871)

At Isella (1871)

Master Eustace (1871)

Guest's Confession (1872)

The Madonna of the Future (1873)

The Sweetheart of M. Briseux (1873)

The Last of the Valerii (1874)

Madame de Mauves (1874)

Adina (1874)

Professor Fargo (1874)

Eugene Pickering (1874)

Benvolio (1875)

Crawford's Consistency (1876)

The Ghostly Rental (1876)

Four Meetings (1877)

Rose-Agathe (1878, as Théodolinde)

Daisy Miller (1878)

Longstaff's Marriage (1878)

An International Episode (1878)

The Pension Beaurepas (1879)

A Diary of a Man of Fifty (1879)

A Bundle of Letters (1879)

The Point of View (1882)

The Siege of London (1883)

Impressions of a Cousin (1883)

Lady Barberina (1884)

Pandora (1884)

The Author of Beltraffio (1884)

Georgina's Reasons (1884)

A New England Winter (1884)

The Path of Duty (1884)

Mrs. Temperly (1887)

Louisa Pallant (1888)

The Aspern Papers (1888)

The Liar (1888)

The Modern Warning (1888, originally published as The Two Countries)

A London Life (1888)

The Patagonia (1888)

The Lesson of the Master (1888)

The Solution (1888)

The Pupil (1891)

Brooksmith (1891)

The Marriages (1891)

The Chaperon (1891)

Sir Edmund Orme (1891)

Nona Vincent (1892)

The Real Thing (1892)

The Private Life (1892)

Lord Beaupré (1892)

The Visits (1892)

Sir Dominick Ferrand (1892)

Greville Fane (1892)

Collaboration (1892)

Owen Wingrave (1892)

The Wheel of Time (1892)

The Middle Years (1893)

The Death of the Lion (1894)

The Coxon Fund (1894)

The Next Time (1895)

Glasses (1896)

The Altar of the Dead (1895)

The Figure in the Carpet (1896)

The Way It Came (1896, also published as The Friends of the Friends)

The Turn of the Screw (1898)

Covering End (1898)

In the Cage (1898)

John Delavoy (1898)

The Given Case (1898)

Europe (1899)

The Great Condition (1899)

The Real Right Thing (1899)

Paste (1899)

The Great Good Place (1900)

Maud-Evelyn (1900)

Miss Gunton of Poughkeepsie (1900)

The Tree of Knowledge (1900)

The Abasement of the Northmores (1900)

The Third Person (1900)

The Special Type (1900)

The Tone of Time (1900)

Broken Wings (1900)

The Two Faces (1900)

Mrs. Medwin (1901)

The Beldonald Holbein (1901)

The Story in It (1902)

Flickerbridge (1902)

The Birthplace (1903)

The Beast in the Jungle (1903)

The Papers (1903)

Fordham Castle (1904)

Julia Bride (1908)

The Jolly Corner (1908)

The Velvet Glove (1909)

Mora Montravers (1909)

Crapy Cornelia (1909)

The Bench of Desolation (1909)

A Round of Visits (1910)

OTHER

Transatlantic Sketches (1875)

French Poets and Novelists (1878)

Hawthorne (1879)

Portraits of Places (1883)

A Little Tour in France (1884)

Partial Portraits (1888)

Essays in London and Elsewhere (1893)

Picture and Text (1893)

Terminations (1893)

Theatricals (1894)

Theatricals: Second Series (1895)

Guy Domville (1895)

The Soft Side (1900)

William Wetmore Story and His Friends (1903)

The Better Sort (1903)

English Hours (1905)

The Question of our Speech; The Lesson of Balzac. Two Lectures (1905)

The American Scene (1907)

Views and Reviews (1908)

Italian Hours (1909)

A Small Boy and Others (1913)

Notes on Novelists (1914)

Notes of a Son and Brother (1914)

Within the Rim (1918)

Travelling Companions (1919)

Notebooks (various, published posthumously)

The Middle Years (unfinished, published posthumously 1917)

A Most Unholy Trade (1925, published posthumously)

The Art of the Novel : Critical Prefaces (1934)

CPSIA information can be obtained
at www.ICGtesting.com
Printed in the USA
LVHW050044031120
670492LV00020B/634

9 781662 717260